# PAMELA FRIAR

# WATCHER
## — OF THE —
# WILD

First paperback edition January 2026

ISBN (paperback) 978-1-971906-00-3
LCCN 2026902969

www.mrsfriarcuriositycrew.com

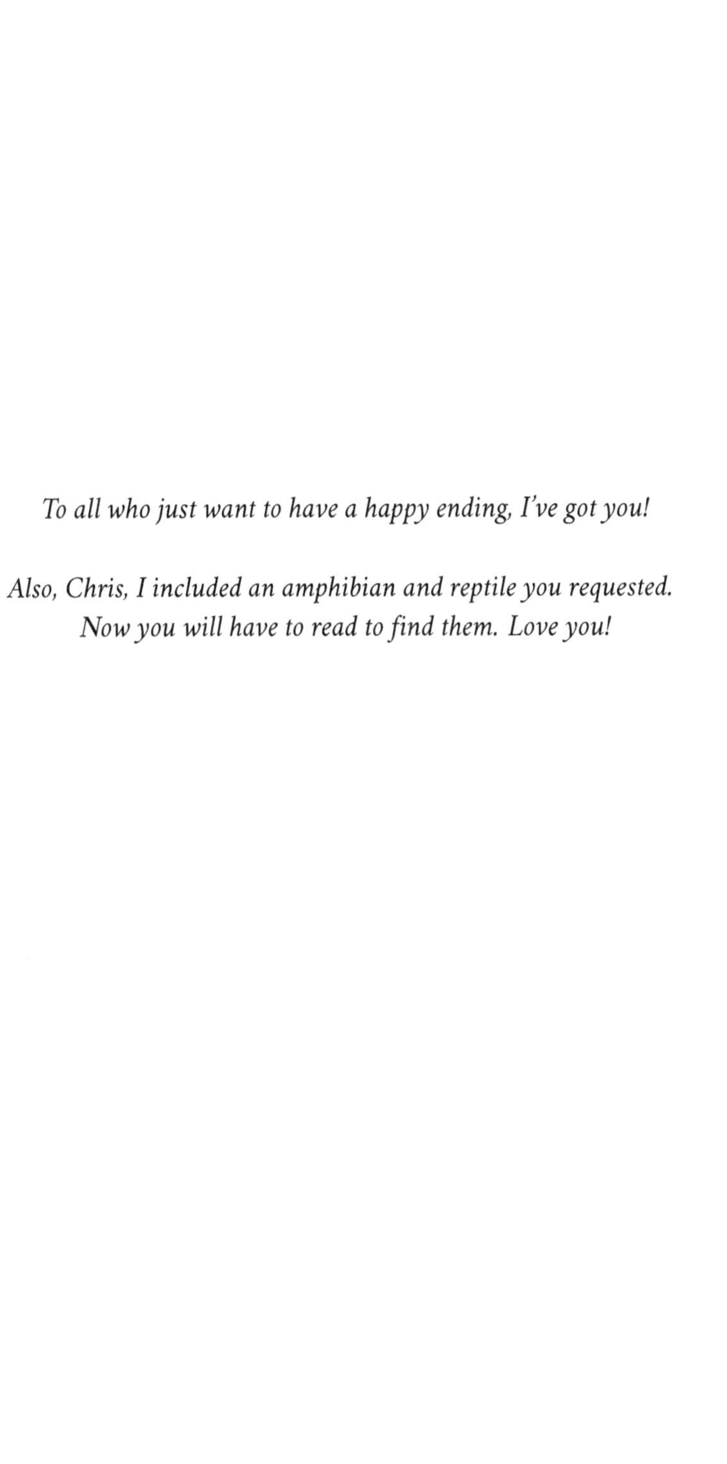

*To all who just want to have a happy ending, I've got you!*

*Also, Chris, I included an amphibian and reptile you requested.
Now you will have to read to find them. Love you!*

# Prologue

"Ah. Smut time!" Rita declared with glee as she flopped onto the sagging couch in the women's retreat common room. The couch groaned beneath her, as did she, clutching a worn paperback with a half-dressed man on the cover. She waved it dramatically before hugging it to her chest, grinning like a kid caught with contraband.

Rita was impossible to ignore. Tall, effortlessly radiant, and unapologetically composed even in chaos. Her blonde curls tumbled in loose spirals over her shoulders, catching the glow of the morning's light. Fair skin, always sun-kissed and smooth thanks to her meticulous skincare routine, gleamed beneath her blush-pink sweater. Black leggings clung to her toned legs, and even her socks matched the color palette of her perfectly curated life. She smelled faintly of citrus and luxury lotion, a walking contradiction to the rustic retreat's pine and smoke.

She turned those pale blue eyes on her best friend, sparkling with mischief. "Come on, Mari. Don't look at me like that.

You could use a little fantasy in your life."

Mari leaned against the cabin door frame, arms crossed, one brow raised in mock disapproval. She was the opposite of Rita in every visible way, smaller, earth-toned, quietly radiant rather than dazzling. At just over five feet tall, she carried the wiry strength of a woman who'd built her own business from the ground up and raised two kids while her husband studied uncommon species for the forestry service. Her long, dark brown hair, streaked with silver at the temples, was pulled into a messy braid that caught the light like a faint silver crown. Warm brown eyes, thoughtful and slightly weary, surveyed her friend with a mix of affection and exasperation.

With the corner of her mouth twitching, she said, "Nothing like reading about some hot twenty-year-old falling for a brooding immortal with six-pack, trauma, and just enough moral decay to make him irresistible."

She began counting on her fingers. "They meet. They hate each other. Smut. The immortal male fights his inner demons. Smut. They kiss. Smut. They fight again. Smut. Betrayal. Smut. Emotional growth. Possible murder. And… wait for it… more smut!"

She lunged halfheartedly toward Rita to grab the book, but Rita twisted away with a delighted cackle.

"On day two of our sacred sabbatical," Mari said, gesturing toward the cabin walls, "you've officially declared war on literary modesty."

"I regret nothing," Rita replied, wiggling her brows. "Besides, maybe if I had a man like this…" she pointed at the shirtless hero on the cover. "This hero's ass alone deserves forgiveness, and I wouldn't be finalizing divorce number three."

Mari snorted. "You say that every time. You love to be in

love. You collect failed relationships like I collect unfinished business plans."

"Excuse me." Rita straightened, as if she were at a board meeting. "I'm a hopeful romantic with high standards."

Mari smirked. "By high standards, you mean emotionally unavailable, tattooed, semi-employed man-children with great hair and mommy issues."

"Exactly." Rita grinned, then hesitated, softer now. "Okay, maybe not the mommy issues part this time. James was… different. Or so I thought."

Mari's teasing eased. Beneath Rita's designer sparkle and quick wit lived a woman who gave everything and asked for almost nothing; a woman desperate to be chosen and kept. Rita had always been loud, luminous, and loyal. She'd adopted Mari like a stray cat back in college and never let her go. At least she hadn't tried to get her spayed.

"You deserve better," Mari said quietly. "Real love. Not plot twists."

Rita rolled her eyes and flopped back down. "Please. If I waited for real love, I'd die of boredom. At least my disasters make for good brunch stories." She gave Mari a long look. "And you, Butterfly? When's the last time your husband looked at you like he remembered who you were?"

Mari opened her mouth; then closed it.

Rufus and Mariposa Fox had been married for over twenty years. Once, it had been love at first sight. He used to call her by a pet name, something soft, secret, but she couldn't remember it anymore. Somewhere between college and parenthood, the name, the spark, the man who used it, all blurred into memory.

Rufus was a wildlife expert who often went out for field

work for days, sometimes weeks. They'd built a good life together; two kids, a small home, a rhythm that worked, but lately, she felt like the only one still keeping time.

Rita's tone softened again. "You've been caged, Mari, buried under marriage, motherhood, and everyone else's needs. You need passion. You need to feel alive again, Butterfly."

Mari grabbed a green apple from the fruit bowl. "I need sleep."

Rita laughed, tossing a pillow at her. "You need to remember who you are when you're not a wife, a mom, or a walking to-do list."

Mari sighed. She hated how Rita could peel back her armor with so few words.

"Fine," Mari said. "I'm going for a walk. You want to hold my hand, or can I wander into self-discovery alone?"

"Go," Rita said with a wink, waving her hand in a shooing motion. "Just don't fall into any magical portals while you're out. But if you do, bring back someone delicious."

"Bye, Momster." Mari stuck out her tongue as she left.

Outside, the cold air was sharp and clean, greeting her like a forgotten truth. The forest whispered with birdsong, and the scent of pine and damp earth filled her lungs. The quiet pressing close around her put a chill down her spine. She walked slowly down the trail, boots crunching over frost, breath puffing white in the air, visible in the cold. For the first time in years, there was no noise, no expectation. No one was asking her for anything.

She was just Mariposa Fox: forty-five, stubborn, tender, an over-thinker, an overfunctioner, a woman searching for the pieces of herself she'd buried under everyone else's needs.

And somewhere, unseen, the forest listened.

# Chapter 1

The morning air nipped at Mari's cheeks, sharp as truth. Frost clung to the edges of fallen pine needles, glinting under the pale light. Tall pines swayed gently in the wind, their scent filling her lungs with each deep breath while casting playful shadows across the trail. Every breath burned cold through her chest, but she liked it that way; clean, biting, real.

No kids yelling.

No texts buzzing.

No half-hearted apologies over voicemail.

Just silence. The kind that doesn't comfort, the kind that reminds you of what's missing.

She shoved her hands into her sweatpants pockets, boots crunching along the narrow dirt path winding behind the retreat cabins. "Self-care weekend she said," she muttered under her breath. "It will be great for us she said."

The words cut deeply because they were her own, and she

couldn't escape the harsh truth.

Her throat constricted as Rufus's face flickered in her memory, a ghost under the dim, sputtering light of their garage. The last time they had stood there together, a heavy tension coiled around his shoulders, his gaze slipping away from her like sand through fingers.

"You know I have to go, Mari. It's work," he'd said, a rehearsed tone spilling from his lips. The same line had become a mantra, chanted like a prayer that offered no comfort.

"Work," she murmured, bitterness coating her voice like venom. "Field research, or someone else?" Each word was like a dagger, piercing the fragile trust between them.

But "work" had morphed into a series of empty nights, his absence carving out a hollow space in her heart, impossible to rationalize. When she finally voiced her deepest fear, if there was someone else, he had grown frozen, the air thick with an unspoken truth that weighed heavier than any confession. The silence that ensued thundered in her ears, wrapping them in a cocoon of dread. Now, it haunted her, a specter lurking in the cool shadows of the trees that surrounded her.

A tight knot formed in her throat, and as she ventured further into solitude, she found herself whispering to the indifferent woodlands. "Why wasn't I enough?" The words felt raw, echoing back off the bark and leaves, only to be swallowed by the stillness, leaving her with nothing but a sinking ache and a desperate yearning for answers that remained elusive.

The path forked ahead. To the right, the trail led back to safety: cabins, coffee, and Rita reading smut by the fire. To the left, the wild trail disappeared into shadow.

She hesitated. The air to the left smelled different: damper, older, faintly metallic.

"Sure," she muttered, rolling her eyes. "Let's take an adventure. Great life choices, Mari."

She hesitated only a moment before turning left. The undergrowth brushed her sweatpants and sweater as she walked, damp and fragrant. Every sense was alert, alive.

The trees thickened, the light fractured into gold and green. Somewhere above, a crow called, its voice rasping like laughter. She followed the uneven path until something rustled in the brush ahead.

Mari stopped, heart leaping. "Rita," she called softly, half joking. "If you followed me out here for a TikTok…"

Another rustle. Louder. Closer.

Then came the smell, metallic, sour, unnatural like ozone and something dead.

Her pulse kicked. "Okay, definitely *not* Rita."

A blur flashed through her periphery, darting through the trees. She caught a glimpse, quick movement, low to the ground, erratic, almost human but not quite.

Two figures darted between trunks. Covered in dark, coarse fur, maybe four and a half feet tall, quick and frantic. Their faces were both animal and child, with wide, glassy eyes and trembling hands.

"Holy…" she whispered. "What are you two?"

They chittered to each other, soft, desperate sounds, almost like language.

They were terrified.

"Hey, it's okay," Mari said, hands raised, voice trembling. "I won't hurt you."

A crack echoed through the forest, sharp and heavy, as a

rope with glowing ends snapped against the bark of a towering tree, sizzling at the point of impact.

"Hey!" Mari shouted instinctively, her voice cutting through the tension, even though she couldn't see who she was addressing.

In that instant, two small, furry creatures, their wide eyes brimming with fear, bolted toward her. Without thinking, she stepped forward, arms waving as if she could shield them from the unseen threat. "It's okay! Come here!"

Her mind raced as she quickly scanned her surroundings, desperate to find a sanctuary. "Wait! This way!" she urged the frightened beings, her voice urgent.

The two young, hairy creatures darted into the hollow beneath an immense pine, its gnarled roots twisting like ancient hands in the earth. Around them, the air shimmered, distorted like a wavering mirage, and an electric static crawled up Mari's skin, making every hair on her arms stand on end.

Something was off in the atmosphere; heavy and charged like the moment before a storm. It felt wrong, like the pause before a scream.

From the shadows, a low, steady voice emerged, raw and gravelly. "Where are they?"

Mari spun around, her heart pounding in her chest, searching for the source of the voice, still positioned defensively between the creatures and the looming danger.

A figure slowly stepped out from the shadows, blending with the darkened woods. He loomed tall and broad-shouldered, moving with a predatory grace that suggested he was forged from the very darkness around him. His attire shifted fluidly, a combination of cloth and armor that appeared almost alive as it clung to his muscular frame.

His hood cast a deep shadow over his face, but the glimpses revealed sharp, angular cheekbones and a strong, lightly stubbled jaw, giving him a rugged yet striking allure. There was an undeniable weight to his presence, a stillness that felt like calm before a brewing storm; danger waiting to strike.

Weapons hung at his side, their surfaces gleaming with menace. Some were polished steel, while others boasted intricate bone carvings, mingling seamlessly with a singular blade that pulsed faintly with an ethereal glow. His cloak rippled around him, seemingly unaffected by the stillness of the air.

He stopped just a few paces away, and as he raised his gaze, Mari felt the full intensity of his eyes bore into her: deep onyx, rimmed with molten red, glowing like embers beneath a stony facade. He didn't flinch or blink; he observed, embodying the very essence of danger wrapped in mystery.

Her breath caught. "Okay," she said slowly. "You're not camp staff."

"Where are they?" he repeated, voice low and rough, an accent brushing against every word like sandpaper and silk.

"Excuse me, where's what?" Mari snapped. "Who are *you* supposed to be?" Her breath was heavy as adrenaline pulsed through her veins.

"They don't belong here." His tone was not angry, but it carried a sense of finality, like a door closing never to be opened again.

Mari said nothing as she stood defiantly in front of the hiding place.

He took a step toward her. She moved instinctively, standing between him and the hollow.

Her hands shook, but her voice didn't. "Stop! They're

scared children!" she shot back with her hands raised. "And apparently allergic to weapons being thrown at them!"

His expression didn't change. "Stand down." The man cast in shadow and mystery began moving forward again, smooth and deliberate.

"Oh, I'd love to, but I didn't bring my *stand-down shoes* today," she said, planting her feet. "Also, you're terrifying, so no thanks."

He moved with a speed that blurred the line between reality and disbelief. One heartbeat, he was ten feet away, and the next, his hand gripped her wrist, yanking her into a whirlwind. The world collapsed around her as her back collided with the solid heat of his chest, the force of it expelling breath from her lungs like a startled animal. In that fleeting moment, everything shrank to the vibrating silence between them.

She was enveloped by the warmth radiating from his body, his scent a heady mix of smoke and rain, wild, sharp, and so alive that it almost disarmed her. For a heartbeat, the fear melted away, leaving only confusion and an unwelcome sense of thrill.

"Let go," Mari growled, her voice tinged with the adrenaline coursing through her veins.

To her surprise, he released her instantly. She stumbled, heart racing, cool metal snapping around her wrists like an unwanted embrace. The cuffs glowed softly against her skin, an eerie hum reverberating through her.

"What the…." she started, eyes darting down to the cuffs before snapping back to his face, fury igniting within her.

"So, you don't run," he answered softly, a flicker of regret threading through his voice like a whisper of wind.

Without another word, he lifted his hand towards the

hollow, and with meticulous grace, symbols ignited in the air. Lines of gold intertwined, forming a shimmering triangle around the creatures that huddled nearby, their innocence palpable. The forest seemed to vibrate in response, a living entity echoing the tension building between them.

"What are you doing?" she demanded, panic tinging her voice, eyes wide with disbelief. "They're children!"

"They are contained," he replied, his voice steady as he began to encase the creatures in glowing metallic bands. The action was not cruel, but ritualistic, ancient, and heavy with a weight Mari could feel deep in her bones.

Her voice quivered with rage. "Containment? You mean captivity?"

He stepped closer, movements smooth and deliberate like a predator stalking its prey. As he worked, a strange energy enveloped her, electric and unsettling. His gaze met hers then, piercing and earnest. For one fleeting heartbeat, something flickered behind his steely eyes: regret, sadness, and a hint of recognition that sent a chill down her spine.

"You are a witness," he said, each word resonating with somber gravity. "You must provide testimony."

"Are you kidding me?" she shot back, incredulity lacing her tone. "I don't even know what I'm looking at!"

The ground beneath her began to thrum, a low hum that pulsed like a heartbeat. The sigil blazed brighter, golden threads swirling through the air, a kaleidoscope of energy that held her captive.

"What's happening?" she cried, anxiety rippling through her.

He stepped back, his face an unreadable mask. "You were not meant to see this."

"Why…?" Her voice trembled, caught between confusion and a rising urgency as the atmosphere around her shifted, pulsating with an energy she couldn't yet grasp. The air thickened, wrapping her in a cocoon of unease, and she felt herself ensnared in a web of destiny far more complex than she could fathom.

Suddenly, light burst forth, a blinding, all-consuming brilliance that made her shield her eyes. The roar that accompanied it was deafening, as if the very fabric of the sky was tearing apart. Mari's screams were swallowed by the cacophony as gravity uncoiled, sending her tumbling through a kaleidoscope of colors: vivid blues, shimmering golds, stark blacks, before everything coalesced into searing white.

Then, as abruptly as it had begun, the world fractured.

She plummeted through a vortex of brightness and a suffocating heat that rippled and crackled like static. Silence enveloped her, yet it hummed with a pulse that wasn't silence at all.

And then, impact.

The ground slammed into her with a violent force, expelling the air from her lungs in a rush. Gasping, she tasted the metallic tang of iron and the earthy notes of moss and smoke as the world around her dimmed, fading into impenetrable darkness.

When Mari finally opened her eyes, she was met with a sky ablaze in hues of amber and gold, swirling like molten glass as if reality itself was melting away. Towering above her were massive black trees, their gnarled branches holding vines that reached out like clawed fingers, whispering secrets in a language that felt foreign yet hauntingly familiar.

The air thrummed with a vibrant energy, a rhythm resonating through the ground beneath her trembling hands, urging her to rise.

With a determined shake of her head, she pushed herself up to her knees, her heart racing in sync with the pulsing earth. The stillness felt charged, crackling with the promise of the unknown.

"I'm going to need more coffee for this," she breathed, a nervous chuckle escaping her lips, cutting through the weight of the moment.

But deep down, she knew this wasn't just another camp trip. She had crossed over into something entirely new, and the adventure was only just beginning.

# Chapter 2

The tear he created snapped shut with a sound like cracking glass, a sharp echo fading into the primeval hush of the Wild Realm. Rufio stood at its edge, breathing in the heavy, heady air that shimmered with a life of its own. His dark cloak settled against his shoulders, the fabric still vibrating faintly with the residue of travel between dimensions. He felt the drumbeat of his pulse slow, yet his senses remained hyper-aware, watching, listening, ever calculating.

The jungle around him pulsed with a vibrancy that left most mortals trembling. Towering, gnarled trees soared into the canopy like colossal sentinels, their trunks entwined with thick vines. The air was saturated with moisture, droplets cascading from leaf to leaf, infusing the atmosphere with the scents of damp earth and moss. Insects buzzed in chaotic harmony, their wings shimmering in dappled light, while birds shrieked high above, their calls cutting through the lush surroundings. A deep, guttural roar rumbled through the foliage, sending a shiver through the underbrush, a primal warning of the lurking dangers. To Rufio, this was ordinary, a world brimming with ferocity and wonder. He exhaled slowly, grounding himself in the rhythm of the realm, the heartbeat of wild things, the breath of something ancient that seemed to remember him.

Mariposa fell through the dimensional tear just behind him, her cry a sharp note that cut through the forest's harmonious din. She struck the ground hard, her palms reaching instinctively forward as the momentum of her arrival propelled her across the ancient jungle floor. A large black-horned toad leaped out of the way, angrily croaking at the new invader. To her, the world felt too loud, too charged, alive.

Rufio turned just in time to witness her hands skid against the damp moss and jagged stone, a silent flurry of motion that contrasted starkly with the wild stillness around them. As she arrived, the world around her appeared to hold its breath in disbelief. Leaves quivered on their branches, the air grew heavier, as if the very essence of the realm had never before witnessed such a fresh and unforeseen presence surge through its veins.

As Mari's body finally stilled, Rufio dropped to one knee, his deft hands hovering above her but not daring to touch. He checked her breathing, a steady rhythm that offered a semblance of relief. In that moment, the wagon materialized, manifesting before him in shimmering waves, like a mirage dancing in the desert heat. A low, resonant hum filled the air as it approached, sending gentle tremors through the surroundings. The ferns shook slightly, bending in an almost reverent manner, while the dust lining the barren earth at the edge of the dense forest stirred restlessly, caught in the wake of its arrival.

Slowly, Mari began to stir, still prone on the forest floor. Her eyelids fluttered open, unveiling wild eyes that drank in the thick, humid air of the new world. She lay sprawling on the damp earth, covered in moss that clung to her skin and soaked through her clothes like an unwanted embrace. Her wrists throbbed, remnants of the strange shackles digging against her skin. Disoriented, she lifted her head, her braid a disheveled crown, strands of hair plastered against her face by sweat and humidity. "Great," she muttered, her voice raspy as she tried to sit up. "Alive and kicking, well, sort of. Concussed? Ugh. That sounds about right."

Despite her small stature amid the vast wildness, she met his gaze with fierce intensity as she looked up, catching him off guard. Most who stumbled into this realm would be paralyzed by fear, yet there was a fire igniting within her.

She rose to her knees, her palms stung, but she clenched them anyway. Blood from her palms pooled into vibrant stains against the muted green carpet of the jungle floor before it disappeared into the thirsty soil. Mari remained blissfully unaware. The warmth startled her; everything here felt too alive. But Rufio, ever observant, acknowledged the sight without uttering a word.

The scent of the jungle enveloped her, a heady mixture of wet rot, bitter black bark, and an acrid feral tang that clawed at her senses. With tentative determination, she stood, her hand gripping a twisted tree root as it pulsed with a faint warmth beneath her palm. All around her, the forest loomed tall and untamed, an ancient manifestation of life reminiscent of a primordial version of the Amazon.

Massive, gnarled trees reached for the sky, their thick trunks shrouded in drapes of moss and glowing fungi, casting an otherworldly luminescence. Vines, thick as her arm, hung limply like sleeping serpents, weaving through the jungle's heart. The forest sang; a cacophony of chirps, trills, and deep, throaty calls filled the air, wrapping around her like a living shroud. Distant howls reverberated through the darkened canopy, soon joined by deep, thunderous roars that sent a shiver racing down her spine. The weight of the wilderness pressed against her, the very air seeming to challenge her resolve. In that moment, a laugh almost escaped her lips, a response to the silent scrutiny of the towering trees and the vibrant life above, judging her presence in their domain.

The light here was unlike anything she had known; it filtered through thick layers of foliage, creating a trove of shimmering shadows that danced across the undergrowth. Everything shimmered in a hue that felt both beautiful and profoundly wrong. Her pulse quickened with the erratic flicker of the light, racing in time with the chaotic rhythm, a heartbeat so immense it felt foreign, as if she had stumbled into a world where the very essence of life throbbed around her, overwhelming and intoxicating.

As she turned, an image caught her eye: the edge of the forest. Just beyond it, the world seemed to end. The lush greenery surrendered to cracked, lifeless dirt that stretched toward jagged mountains looming in the distance, proud and formidable, now blackened and broken, reaching toward a churning, angry sky. The land beyond lay barren, a haunting landscape devoid of life, as if some malevolent force had drained it of vitality, leaving behind a hollow husk that resonated with her growing unease. The shift was startling, as if one had just emerged from a dream and onto the edge of a raw, exposed wound.

The cloaked Rufio turned and strode toward the clearing, his dark cloak brushing against the damp leaves underfoot, whispering secrets of the forest. Behind him, he felt her anger simmering, a palpable heat radiating through the thick, misty air. Her silence wasn't submission; it was gathering, like a thunderstorm waiting for the perfect moment to strike.

The wagon loomed in the shadows, as it always did at the end of a mission. In front, two massive, horned, horse-like steeds shift their heavy hooves through the loam, primal strength embodied, and their eyes are large and intelligent. They exhaled through flared nostrils, sending tendrils of mist dancing in the muted forest light. Their scaled skin shimmered a ghostly gray blue, a reflection of the dappled sunlight. One of the steeds blinked at Mari with slow curiosity. Although she could not see it, she felt its stare, raising the hair on the back of her neck. Their third eyes glinted faintly as they regarded Rufio, their companion, with a loyalty that spoke of untold stories. Patient. Ever watchful.

"The wagon will hold the Fletcher Younglings well," he said, forcing a calmness into his voice as he addressed his four-legged companions, their patient eyes watching him intently. The soothing timbre of his words hung briefly in the air, a fragile barrier against the rising tension enveloping Mari. Each syllable seemed to resonate with the weight of unsaid fears. Though his voice carried undeniable authority, it was tinged with an undercurrent of something more profound; regret perhaps, or the haunting echo of a past long buried. He glanced at Mari, noting the way her brow furrowed as if she sensed the turmoil beneath his composed exterior, and the unshakeable feeling of foreboding settled heavier on his shoulders.

"Why am I a witness?" she demanded suddenly, her voice cracking like dry twigs underfoot, slicing through the forest's haunting song. She glared at Rufio, her frustration boiling over. "Why does it matter? I didn't ask for this!" Her voice bounced sharply off the trees, a defiant noise in a place that devoured sound.

Then her panic began to unfurl; the child-like creatures, no, the Younglings, were no longer by her side. A wave of dread washed over her as she frantically scanned the clearing for them. Where are they? Her heartbeat quickened, each thump echoing louder in her chest, a frantic drum heralding her increasing fear.

Rufio remained silent, his expression carefully guarded, refusing to acknowledge her rising panic. His silence wasn't indifference; it was armor. Words, for him, were weapons he rarely unsheathed. His duty was to escort the young Fletchers back to their mother; it was the type of mission he had completed countless times before, yet this time was different. He took a deep breath, grounding himself, but a stirring within him disrupted his resolve. The scent of her blood intermingled with the forest's earthy aroma and her indignation, creating a heady perfume that unnerved yet tantalized him. His body went rigid, fighting against the instinct to reveal how easily she affected him.

Here, in this last shred of the land where life endured, words held little weight; they were fragile, easily crushed beneath the weight of truth. This dense, living jungle was a refuge where empty promises and malicious intent were devoured whole. Those who sought to deceive the wild quickly found themselves intertwined with its roots, lost to the world.

With deliberate slowness, he raised his hand, and the back of the wagon doors creaked open, unveiling a luminous threshold. Light spilled forth like liquid gold, illuminating an alternate realm within calm, tranquil, and bursting with the green of lush groves and laden fruit trees, a small, separate world. A sanctuary meticulously crafted to soothe and nourish the younglings. Rufio wanted the Younglings to venture forth of their own accord; coaxing would strip them of their autonomy, and he wished for them to feel safe enough to come.

At the sound of the door unlocking, the two small Fletchers burst forth, pressing against Mari with desperate weight, their tiny hands gripping her legs like lifelines. Tremors coursed through their young bodies, fear palpable in the air around them. Mari flinched, startled and momentarily disoriented by their sudden appearance. But then realization washed over her, the Fletchers.

Her heart swelled with relief as she clutched the quivering creatures against her legs with her hands. Warmth flooded through her as she felt their small forms tremble and shift, their fur matted and damp. Their low, tremulous cries echoed in her ears, a haunting melody of fear that settled deep within her heart. She looked down at them as they hunched, attempting to hunch behind her, becoming as invisible as possible. Her eyes softened as she fought the shadows of her own turmoil, determined to provide them with the comfort they so desperately needed.

Rufio felt the tug in the weave of the world, an electric shiver that danced down his spine. Yes, they had opened a dimensional tear on their own. Too young. Too reckless. Without their mother, they had stumbled into a realm they were not ready for. Into her world. He cursed under his breath, the sound mingling with the rustling canopy above, where leaves whispered secrets and shadows churned like smoke. Fletchers rarely birthed more than one child at a time; twins were precious, a rarity that thrummed with the weight of unfulfilled potential. This mistake could have cost them everything.

Now, this woman had touched these priceless beings; held them. Her scent clung to their fur, a dangerous mingling of warmth and humanity that could invoke wrath. Dangerous for Mari.

Rufio adjusted his grip on the hilt at his belt, the cool metal grounding him amidst the chaos, though he made no move to draw it. His sharp eyes, gleaming like the forest's hidden light, lingered on her… this mortal who defied the terror of the wild.

She was frightened, yes, but her fear was interwoven with anger and resolve, a vibrant tapestry of emotion that pulsed in the thick air. Bending down slightly, she murmured soothingly to the younglings, her voice trembling yet steady, breaking the tense silence that enveloped the clearing like a shroud. As she spoke, the atmosphere shifted, a subtle but undeniable ripple of hope.

The creatures clung to her like frightened children, their long fingers gripping her legs with desperate strength. They trembled, their dark fur matted and sticky, and the smell radiating from them was overwhelming, like rotted mushrooms, damp earth, and the acrid scent of burnt wood. Yet, she didn't pull away. Instead, she leaned into discomfort, letting them hold on. Her breath caught in her throat, and tears threatened to spill from her eyes, pooling with a rush of empathy. Something primal stirred within her; a deep instinct older than language itself, resonating with the younglings' shared vulnerability.

Leaves rustled gently, sending a shiver up her spine as she instinctively looked up, the world around her shifting into sharper focus. She began to notice the other predators beyond the man in front of her.

Rufio leaned against the side of a nearby tree, a silent guardian draped in shadow, as if he himself were carved from the ancient bark surrounding him. His presence was eerie and captivating, dark and ageless, wrapped in the enigma of the forest. His cloak hung like a shadow, and not a sound escaped as he grasped his weapons; he was a part of the wild's very essence, an embodiment of both danger and allure.

"Why?" she called out, her voice sharp as a dagger, cutting through the thick air. "Why am I a witness? What does it even mean?" The question wasn't just for him; it was for the universe that kept demanding things she never agreed to.

No answer.

"You will not make me a victim." Her defiance hung in the air like a spell, weaving through the trees that watched in rapt silence. Even the forest seemed to hesitate, as if listening.

Still, he said nothing. Rufio's gaze pierced through her, calculating, as though he were weighing the very fabric of her soul.

She stood tall, the younglings still gripping her legs, their fear radiating. As she faced him fully, her eyes blazed with a fierce individualism, a fire that threatened to ignite the very forest around them. "I'm not afraid of you. I'm not afraid of whatever this place is." Her words came out steadier than her breath. Somewhere deep in the shadows, something growled low. "You think some glowing shackles and a haunted forest scare me? You've got the wrong woman." She lifted her hands and shook her wrists for a moment to make her point.

A flicker crossed the corner of his mouth, not quite a smile, perhaps an acknowledgment of her courage, or the tremors of amusement mingling with something more profound. The electric charge in the air hummed, and for a fleeting moment, the world paused, suspended between fear and fierce determination, between darkness and light.

He turned abruptly, his silhouette momentarily outlined against the light, and began the short trek to the wagon. Mari's heart quickened, frustration bubbling up inside her. "Hey! I'm talking to you!" she called out, her voice rising above the hum of the wildlife. With each step he took farther away from her and the younglings, a sense of isolation settled in the pit of her stomach. Oh, how she hated being ignored, especially by a man whose name she did not even know, yet whose presence tethered her to a fate she couldn't escape until he returned her to her world.

He stood in silence, shrouded in shadow, patiently waiting by the back of the wagon. From her vantage point, she noticed the vibrant transformation within the wagon's interior, a jarring contrast to the rest of its surroundings. A warm, sweet scent enveloped her, reminiscent of a carefully crafted sanctuary. She knew instinctively that he designed this temporary dimension to comfort and nurture the young, a stark opposition to the tension that lingered in the air outside.

Rooted in place, Mari felt a dawning realization wash over her, the weight of the unspoken communication tightening.

She now understood what he needed from her, what this moment demanded. The truth slid into her bones like cold water. She wasn't an observer; she was part of this. This epiphany struck her like a whisper in the dark: she was not just a passenger in this unfolding story; she was intricately woven into the fabric of their journey.

She released her grip on the younglings, her heart heavy as she gently nudged their small backs, guiding them toward the dark-cloaked man looming by the wagon, its open doors ready to take in its new guests. The moment they caught a whiff of sweet, enticing aromas wafting from within, the Fletchers sprang to life; their eyes lit up with delight, and they dove into the wagon with jubilant cries echoing through the still air. Laughter, pure and unrestrained, spilled from them as they raced to the nearest berry bush, the vibrant colors of fruit contrasting sharply against the muted greens and browns of the forest inside. But as they crossed the threshold, a dizzying shimmer enveloped their forms, and Mari felt a disorienting tug as they vanished deeper into the illusion, or was it a true reality? Doubt gnawed at her.

"They are called Fletchers," came Rufio's deep, gravelly voice from behind her, slicing through the fog of her thoughts like a cold blade. The very sound stirred something deep within her, a recognition that felt oddly familiar yet elusive, warmth intertwined with a subtle warning. His tone was steady, but thick with a weighty seriousness that sent a shiver cascading down her spine. "What your world knows as yeti or bigfoot. They are not myths here. They are a protected species."

With deliberate precision, he closed the door of the wagon, ensuring it was secure. The gesture held an almost reverent quality amid the chaos swirling around them.

Mari turned slowly, confusion and fear written large on her face. What did this man just say? Her pulse quickened as memories of tales told around campfires danced in her mind, creatures of legend, waiting just beyond the edges of her reality.

"They must have opened a tear into your world for the very first time," Rufio continued, his gaze fixed on the forest as if peering into its depths for answers. "It happens. Usually, their mother is nearby, guiding them. But this time…" he paused, a shadow crossing his features, "she was not, or they learned something new before she could stop them."

Mari's eyes darted toward the empty forest, its ancient trees standing silent and foreboding. "So, they were probably playing, got lost, and ended up in the woods," she murmured, the hollow realization sinking in, a weight pressing on her chest.

Rufio nodded, his calm demeanor belying the tension simmering in the air. "Yes. And now, we must return them before more damage is done. The mother will smell a foreign scent on her young. If she cannot see and examine where that smell came from, whether they were held against their will or comforted by you and kept safe… She will believe you took them and will hunt you down."

A chill surged through Mari, icy fingers wrapping around her heart, squeezing tight with fear and urgency. And yet, beneath the fear, something else stirred, curiosity, dangerous and alive. The realization of hunting, of being hunted, surged like a tempest within her.

"Fletchers are sacred and powerful beings, and they don't breed often," Rufio said, his voice softening slightly, as if he were sharing a deep secret. "Twins are even rarer, almost unheard of. These two are truly a miracle."

His words hung in the air, heavy with implications, a fragile truth swirling in the tension between them. The wind rustled through the ancient trees, whispering secrets past, while dark clouds loomed on the horizon, brewing a storm that mirrored Mari's tumultuous emotions. In that moment, amidst the brewing tempest of feelings, she felt an ember of hope flicker to life, constricted tightly by an encroaching dread. She understood now that this was a game of stakes higher than she had ever anticipated, and the fate of the Fletchers rested on her shoulders like an invisible weight. "I am a witness…" Mari whispered under her breath.

Mari stepped softly forward, her heart pounding in rhythm with the quiet cadence of the moment. With each careful move, she instinctively hung on to his voice, its timbre wrapping around her in a strange embrace. Time seemed to stretch, and for a moment, almost in a trance, she thought she could hear a heartbeat echoing through the silence. Suddenly, she stumbled, the ground beneath her giving way.

Her hand, already injured, struck the dead earth just beyond the forest's border, a stark contrast to the vibrant life that once thrived here. The land just beyond the jungle-like forest presented a dry, cracked landscape. A smear of her blood soaked into the cracked soil, vivid and dark against the pallor of decay.

She stood quickly, brushing herself off, irritation clawing at her. "Great. Just great," Mari muttered under her breath, glancing down at her bloodstained hand before surveying her torn clothes, a cascade of despair in her expression. She must seem to be a terrible mess.

Rufio remained tense, his body taut like a coiled spring,

rigid with restraint. Muscles bunched beneath his skin; his gaze fixed on her with an intensity that felt almost seismic. Mari stood as still as the surroundings before her. Her chest rising and falling rapidly, a storm of feelings playing across her face and in her heart; suspicion, defiance, and something more complicated that eluded his understanding. Her blood still glistened on her palm, droplets tracing a path down to where they splattered upon the barren ground at the forest's edge.

Then, something miraculous began to unfold. The soil, once lifeless, stirred with a whisper of rebirth. Where her blood touched the dirt, tiny green tendrils emerged, curling skyward with tentative resilience. Fragile blades of grass broke through the cracks that had been barren for years, reaching toward the dimming sunlight. He froze, every instinct heightening, a visceral reaction to this forbidden display of life. For a heartbeat, even the wild held its breath. It had no place here. Not anymore. Not since corruption had blighted the land. And yet, here it was, reaching out, slow but sure, reconnecting with the heart of the jungle.

Mari, oblivious, continued examining her hand. But Rufio, unmoving, stared with narrowed eyes, a tense reverence suffusing his posture. He had seen destruction, not renewal, until now.

"What?" she asked defensively, breaking the silence that stretched between them like a taut string ready to snap.

He didn't respond, but the wonder etched across his face spoke volumes. And in that silence, something shifted. The Wild had seen her, and it would not forget. For the first time, she saw this cloaked man with a covered face as more than just a figure cloaked in distrust; he was captivated, as though he was witnessing some sacred rite. He watched her longer than he should have, the scent of her, smoke and earth intermingled with the pulse of her sweat lingering like a ghost in his lungs. She assumed his silence stemmed from cruelty or anger, but the truth was tightly coiled within him: a fear of unspooling words that could alter the fragile balance of their world.

His chest tightened with the weight of emotions he hadn't felt in years; hope and fear tangled like vines around his thoughts.

Rufio clenched his fists, forcing his gaze away, struggling to resist the pull she exerted over him. He was no villain, but neither could he allow himself to be undone by this unexpected catalyst.

This woman was not ordinary. That realization struck him with terror more profound than anything else in this blighted realm. Something about her transcended humanity; ordinary and mundane no longer applied. Not anymore.

# Chapter 3

The land stretched before them in layers of memory and ruin. Mari's tattered boots crunched over cracked ground, each step sending small puffs of dust into the hot air. The forest behind them was suffocatingly alive, yet strangely sick at its edges. Vines hung thick as ropes, dripping with dew, but their leaves curled brown at the tips. The canopy overhead breathed with sound: chirps, clicks, trills of insects, the occasional shriek of a bird that sounded far too large to be hidden in the shadows.

The air from the jungle's edge smelled of rot and damp bark, undercut by the metallic tang of something she couldn't name. Every inhale filled her chest with the taste of decay. The shift from life to death wasn't sudden; it crept under her skin like a change in heartbeat, something she felt before she truly saw it.

As they traveled away from the jungle forest's edge, the air became increasingly hot and dry. The humidity was sucked away by the land's need to survive. Once, this place must have been beautiful. She could see it in the bones of the fallen tree and roots as thick as her torso that now lay shriveled and gray, branches stripped bare but still reaching as if pleading to the sky. The mountains in the distance loomed jagged and broken, their dark stone serrated against a bruised horizon. From here, the world looked hollowed, stripped of its pulse. It reminded her of their house after that last fight; everything was still standing, but nothing was left alive inside it.

Yet the jungle clung stubbornly at their backs, a wall of suffocating green. The two landscapes, one vibrant, one dead, leaned into each other. In Mari's head, she could still hear Rufus's words hang in the air, heavy with implications, a fragile truth swirling in the tension between them. The wind rustled through the ancient trees, whispering, while dark clouds loomed on the horizon, brewing a storm that mirrored Mari's emotions.

In that moment, amidst the brewing storm of feelings, she felt an ember of hope flicker to life, constricted tightly by an encroaching dread. She understood now that this was a game of stakes higher than she had ever anticipated, and the fate of the Fletchers rested on her shoulders like an invisible weight. The responsibility pressed down like a heaviness she hadn't signed up to carry, but she'd carried heavier things before.

Mari stepped softly forward, her heart pounding in rhythm with the quiet cadence of the dirt path.

"Careful," Rufio said with authority. "The land can swallow a person whole in some places."

With each careful move, she instinctively hung on to the cloaked man's voice, striding in front of her, its timbre wrapping around her in a strange embrace. Time seemed to stretch, and for a moment, almost in a trance, she thought she could hear a heartbeat echoing through the silence. Suddenly, she stumbled, the ground beneath her giving way again. It was almost as if it were on purpose.

Her hands and knees struck the dead earth just beyond the wagon, next to the path's edge. A smear of her blood again soaked into the cracked soil, vivid and dark against the dirt. Each wound reopened, pain searing up through her body.

She stood quickly, brushing herself off, irritation clawing at her. "I think this world is after me, hooded man of mystery," Mari said, glancing down at her bloodstained hand before surveying how her torn clothes more and shackled wrists, frustration flashed in her eyes. "Yep. Definitely winning 'Most Graceful Traveler' this year," she added dryly, half to herself. She must seem to be a terrible mess.

Rufio remained tense, his body taut like a coiled spring, rigid with restraint. Muscles bunched beneath his skin; his gaze fixed on her with an intensity that felt almost seismic. With a wave of his hand, Mari's shackles fell away and dissolved into vapor. For a moment, she stood still, rubbing her wrists; her chest rising and falling, a tempest of feelings playing across her face. Her blood still glistened on her palm from the deep gash it held, droplets tracing a path down to where they splattered upon the barren ground at the forest's edge.

Then, something miraculous began to unfold. The soil, once lifeless, stirred with a whisper of rebirth. Where her blood touched the dirt, tiny green tendrils emerged, curling skyward with tentative resilience. Fragile blades of grass broke through the cracks that had been barren for years, reaching toward the dimming sunlight. He froze, every instinct heightening, a visceral reaction to this forbidden display of life. It had no place here. Not anymore. Not since corruption had blighted the land. And yet, here it was, reaching out, slow but sure, reconnecting with the heart of the jungle. For a moment, even the air stopped moving, and the Wild held its breath as something ancient remembered how to live.

Mari, oblivious, continued examining her hand. But Rufio, unmoving, stared with narrowed eyes, a tense reverence suffusing his posture.

"What?" she asked defensively, breaking the silence that stretched between them like a taut string ready to snap.

He didn't respond, but the wonder etched across his face spoke volumes. For the first time, she saw him as more than just a figure cloaked in distrust; he was captivated, as though he was witnessing some sacred rite.

He watched her longer than he should have, the scent of her, smoke and earth intermingled with the pulse of her sweat, lingering like a ghost in his lungs. She assumed his silence stemmed from cruelty or anger, but the truth was tightly curled within him: a fear of unspooling words that could alter the fragile balance of their world.

His chest tightened with the weight of emotions he hadn't felt in years, hope and fear tangled like vines around his thoughts.

Rufio clenched his fists, forcing his gaze away, struggling to resist the pull she exerted over him. He was no villain, but neither could he allow himself to be undone by this unexpected catalyst.

This woman was far from ordinary. The realization struck him with a terror deeper than anything else he had encountered in this desolate realm. There was something about her that transcended humanity; ordinary and mundane became entirely insufficient to describe her presence. The word "impossible" reverberated in his mind, but the land itself seemed to contradict him, as if old enemies were locked in a silent stalemate.

As they ventured deeper into the dry, cracked land, she became increasingly aware of the stark transformation around them. The vibrant life of the jungle had faded away, giving way to stretches of desolation. The trees long thinned out, their trunks becoming more gnarled and twisted as if crafted by the hands of time itself. What was left of the leaves crunched beneath their feet, brittle and brown. The ground, once lush and vibrant, grew pale and cracked, resembling shattered pottery scattered across the landscape. With every step they took toward the horizon, the earth's vitality withered further, leaving behind a haunting reminder of what had been lost.

Mari filled the silence with her own voice. She always did. The quiet of her surroundings gnawed at her. Quiet meant something was wrong in her world. "So, let me guess," Mari said sarcastically, "We're headed toward that lovely patch of doom on the horizon? Because it looks like the kind of place where you catch tetanus just by breathing near it." Her voice cut through the emptiness like sunlight through fog, trying to make the moment smaller, safer.

Rufio didn't reply. He walked ahead, hood shadowing his face, every line of his body carved with control. His silence was a wall she couldn't scale. And she did not like it. Rufus would be silent for hours or days when something was wrong. He never let her in on what was going on, and whether she could help him. That familiar ache crept in, the echo of every unanswered question she'd ever asked.

Mari glanced at her knee, hissed, and then cursed under her

breath as she looked down. Her knee, still raw from the fall, had bled through the fabric of what was left of her sweatpants. New scrapes lined her arms from brushing past thorns and dry branches from the denseness of the jungle. She lifted her wrist and found a fresh bruise blooming purple, stark against her skin. She blew out a breath, half-laughing. "Spa day this is not." Each sting reminded her of how little control she had here.

Without a word or slowing, Rufio tossed something at her. She fumbled and barely caught a roll of rough bandages and a clay vial stoppered with wax. The balm inside smelled sharply of pine and a hint of mint. Mari wrinkled her nose and then stared at the back of his head with confusion.

"Balm," Rufio said flatly, not looking behind him. The two beasts lumbered beside him, slowly pulling the wagon.

"Your bedside manner is overwhelming," she muttered, uncapping the vial. She stopped and slowly dabbed the calm balm over her knee, wincing. "Is this supposed to sting like I'm on fire? My leg feels like it is definitely on fire. Five stars. Would recommend."

"Yes," he said flatly. Rufio kept moving forward.

Mari was getting frustrated with his lack of… of… humanity? Emotion? Empathy? She squinted at him with a glare for emphasis. "Perfect. Good to know torture is part of the treatment plan."

Still no response. He continued to say nothing. His face was hidden again by the hood, but she swore the corner of his mouth twitched. Maybe his shoulders shifted with the faintest twitch of amusement? Whatever it was, he quickly buried it. For a fleeting moment, she wanted to laugh, not because it was funny, but because it was the only thing that kept her sane.

Soon, Mari was finished dabbing all her wounds and began to jog back to the band of merry beasts and a crotchety man. The closer she got to the wagon, the slower the beasts' pace became as they greeted her. The double-horned beast closest to her shook its head up and down with a deep whinny sound.

She grinned faintly. "Guess even these beautiful beasts have their opinions about our situation." Somehow, this made her feel calmer. Mari thought for a moment that she had heard the word "traitors" from the stoic man in the cloak of shadows and darkness.

The wagon beasts plodded steadily beside her, their massive hooves cracking the dry, brittle earth. Their gray-blue hides shimmered faintly, and every so often, their third eyes blinked slowly, unsettling, and strangely tender. Each time they glanced her way, Mari felt something tickle at the edge of her mind, like half-heard whispers, emotions rather than words. Curiosity. Warmth. Hunger. She staggered slightly, clutching her temple. The sensation reminded Mari of her teenage daughter, Carys. Her son, Zandro, was not that far behind in the hormone and sass department. The thought of them: their noise, their constant chaos, hit her like a pang in her chest. She hadn't realized how much she missed the sound of home until the silence pressed back.

Mari held back the treacherous tears and took a deep breath. "Alright, you two, stop poking around in there. My head is beginning to hurt," she muttered, rubbing her temple. The beasts only blinked again, unbothered.

"You hear them?" Rufio said in a low, rough voice.

Mari felt this should have been a question, though the way he phrased it told her it wasn't.

"I think it would be more accurate to say I feel them. Not hear. More like… emotional spam," Mari stated in a pained tone as she rubbed her temple again. "It's like someone left a radio on in another room. Or when a toddler won't stop telling you about their favorite dinosaurs. Nonstop and very loud."

"Ignore it." His tone sharpened.

"Right. Sure. Great advice. Because ignoring voices in my head always works out great. I'll add that to my self-care routine." She said, sarcasm dripping from every word. The beasts both shook their heads and stomped their hoofs, showing approval of her statement. "What are they?" Mari asked. However, her question drifted in the air and slowly faded into the thistles on the ground behind them. The silence that followed made her acutely aware of every heartbeat, every scrape of her boot in the dry soil.

The silence pressed in again, thick as the heat. Mari bent to adjust the bandage on her knee and hands, only to see fresh drops of blood trailing from a cut on her elbow that kept splitting open. They spattered against the fractured ground. She didn't notice the change, but Rufio did. Wherever her blood touched, tiny shoots of green cracked through the dust, curling into fragile life. Life followed her like a rumor too dangerous to speak aloud. A hidden trail of renewal followed her steps like a secret she couldn't see, a delicate ribbon of renewal.

Rufio's jaw tightened, his pace growing sharper. He was wound tight, every step carrying weight she couldn't yet name.

Rufio saw. His jaw tightened, but again, he said nothing, lengthening his stride so she had to hurry to keep up. He hoped she wouldn't notice the shift just yet. Not now.

She muttered under her breath. "You're a real ray of sunshine, you know that?"

Each drop of her blood was undoing decades of ruin. It should have been impossible. It was dangerous. And it was pulling at something inside him he didn't dare name.

Mari brushed another scratch on her calf and groaned. "I'm beginning to look like I went three rounds with a razor-wired blackberry bush. Do all your tourist destinations come with built-in hazards, or is this just the deluxe package?" Mari sounded out of breath as she was jogging to keep up with Rufio. "You could at least warn me when the scenery is weaponized."

His voice was flat as he replied. "You were warned." He knew he never said anything to her of the deadly things that would try to claw, scratch, or bite her. If Rufio did this, the woman would demand to be shut in the wagon with the younglings.

"When? Before or after you tackled me and slapped on the glowing shackles? Because I must've missed it in the brochure," She arched a brow. "If this is your version of a guided tour, you need to work on your customer service."

For the first time, a sharp exhale escaped him. A half sigh, half laugh, half frustrated breath. He didn't look at her, but she caught it. And for the first time, she saw a sliver of his humanity in the stone facade.

She grinned despite herself. With a laugh underlying her tone, she said, "There it is! Proof you're not entirely made of stone." The moment passed quickly, but something inside her lightened, as if humor could make the world less impossible for a breath.

Rufio's expression hardened instantly. The silence between them grew taut, strung like a bowstring. Each step closer to the horizon seemed to draw him further inward, his shoulders tense, his stride impatient. Mari felt the change in her heart. It was like a slap to the face.

The barren valley stretched wider as they crested a rise. Mari followed his gaze when Rufio finally stopped. The land sloped down before them into a desert valley, the cracked ground glowing faintly with reflected light. Mari squinted against the haze, and there on the far horizon the shape of a town rose from the wasteland. Jagged rooftops and leaning stone walls, smoke rising in thin threads to the sky. It looked both alive and exhausted, like everything else in this place.

Mari let out a low whistle. "Well. At least civilization looks consistent across dimensions, grim from far away, probably loud and overpriced once you get there."

Mari was taken aback by how swiftly she had acclimated to her new purgatory. The surreal absurdity of it all enveloped her. Yet, she logically understood that she needed to be seen by Mother Fletcher, the enigmatic figure whose favor was essential if she hoped to avoid being devoured alive later in her life. A chuckle slipped from her lips. How many novellas has she read where the female protagonist succumbed to the dumb-smuttery by this point! Mari chuckled, bemused under her breath, and then groaned softly. "I have to get back to Carys and Zandro," Mari whispered this vow into the desolate sky. She just had to survive.

Rufio remained stoic and silent. His eyes remained fixed on the town, the line of his jaw sharp. The feeling of warning and danger from the land below, and the need to protect her, were consuming. Rufio knew he would burn the world to the ground if he had to. This woman had no place in this world; she was too pure… too innocent. He stood calculating the group's next course of action, frustrated that he could not change her fate.

Mari saw the tension in his shoulders and posture. Although his hood shadowed his face, she was keen on the minor details like the way his hands flexed near his weapons. She instinctively felt the deep tension rolling off the hooded man before her. Slightly behind her, the two-horned beasts pulling the wagon shook their heads in consternation as their heavy breathing evoked a summer thunderstorm in her mind.

The valley nestled below cradled a town that seemed innocuous at first glance, but Mari sensed an underlying peril woven into its facade. With each step closer, an unsettling feeling settled deep in her bones. This place wasn't merely a stopover for weary travelers seeking civilization and shelter. It exuded a palpable danger, not for the hooded man or the majestic beasts pulling the wagon, but for her. Mari felt that in her bones. Not for the first time, she felt nervous for the Fletchers, who remained blissfully secure in their wagon.

As she peered down at the distant rooftops peeking through the mist, Mari's heart jumped when the wagon creaked. A stark contrast to the foreboding quiet that surrounded the group. Her voice was light, teasing, but her fingers trembled just enough to betray the truth. She took a steadying breath, touching the nearest animal carting the wagon, feeling the reptilian yet fuzzy hide, and asked, "Are we there yet?"

# Chapter 4

The land stretched ahead in dry waves, a seemingly endless ocean of thistles, sparse shrubs, and spindly trees. The path they needed to take wound down from the ridge into the valley below. Mari squinted against the haze and pointed. "That's a town. Tell me that's a town."

It was. From this distance, it looked like something pulled from an old frontier painting: rows of buildings in rough lines, smokestacks rising from chimneys, peaked rooftops, and the faint glint of windows catching the sun. A main road cut through the middle, wider than the others, with what looked like storefronts or taverns pressed shoulder-to-shoulder. Horses or things that passed for them moved sluggishly between the buildings. It should have looked alive, busy, even welcoming. But the air around it was sharp with warning. Even the sunlight from the world's two suns seemed reluctant to fall there, bending away as if it knew better.

Rufio's jaw tightened. He could smell it already: smoke, stale blood, the sour tang of corrupt energy. The massive beasts shifted beside him; their hooves grinding against the cracked soil. Their third eyes blinked open, restless, uneasy. They smelled it too. He didn't need sight to know what waited below; the air itself carried a memory of pain.

Rufio looked at his four-legged companions just past Mari with a calculating stare. Both beasts nodded their heads as if the three were having a conversation. Yet nothing was said. The hooded man turned, only taking a moment to glance at the battered woman, and walked slightly in front of Mari as the windy path angled even more steeply.

"The town below is Veyor," he said finally, his voice quiet but firm. "An old name. Older than the walls you cannot see." He took in a deep breath, smelling the corruption, and continued, "The town grew greedy and corrupt with time, but its heart still remembers what it was meant to guard." Rufio did not stop walking down the dirt path, expecting the group to follow.

Mari shaded her eyes, studying the jumble of rooftops. "What wall? It looks like something out of an old spaghetti western movie. All it's missing is a tumbleweed and a sheriff on the porch."

"You will meet one," he said matter-of-factly. "Not a sheriff. A Watcher, the head of this territory. The office is at the center of this town."

She walked with purpose, trying not to slip on a loose rock. "Watcher?" she said with a strained and grunting voice. "Like Big Brother? Hot lifeguard? You're not exactly brimming with details here." Her tone was playful, but the sarcasm trembled on a thread of nerves. Humor was her armor, and it clanged quietly between them.

He remained silent, the weight of his thoughts heavy in the stillness around them. In this land, information wielded immeasurable power, and Rufio was acutely aware of his place within its intricate web. However, he did not fully grasp hers— this woman who stood before him, shrouded in uncertainty. Because of this, the truth wasn't hers to possess. Not yet.

Although the dark forest did not view her as lacking, here, in the sacred space in this corrupted land, the stakes were starkly different. The core of Veyor was a place where purity of heart and intention was paramount. If her intentions were tainted or her heart was foul, if she bore malice or harbored the willingness to dishonor sacred vows, then she would never breach the invisible barrier surrounding the town's sanctum. The Watcher's office, a bastion of judgment and guidance, would remain forever closed to her, the consequences of her admission echoing with a swiftness that would surely take her by surprise. He would have to find another way to take her back to her world.

The mere thought of that judgment sent an unsettling coil of anxiety curling within him. He was reminded of his own past, a distant memory in his youth, of standing in a darkened room before the wisest of the Watchers, heart pounding, being judged. He had felt the unforgiving weight of their gaze, and the memories came rushing back, threatening to drown him in their torment. That moment in time changed his life forever. The gravity of the moment loomed large, knowing her fate hung precariously in the balance, suspended between hope and condemnation.

They continued their slow descent along the winding path into the valley. Thistles and brambles crept across the trail;

brittle and sharp, scraping at Mari's legs, arms, and torso through the torn clothing. She cursed softly as new cuts stung against her skin. Each time blood welled and fell, tiny green, leafy shoots spread in her wake. She didn't see it, but others did. And each drop of impossible growth was proving she was so much more to this world. The beasts made sure to avoid the newest life given to this land. These battle-worn members of this small group had witnessed miracles before, but never ones like this.

The suns were leaving their highest point in the sky. The beasts plodded behind their leader and the small, two-legged, fragile foal in front of them, steady and strong despite the dry air. Rufio felt their thoughts nudging against his mind, curious why he was so irritated. Their emotions and intentions slipped toward Mari. They were interested and knew it caused havoc to the dark, brooding man in their traveling party. They wanted to share their connection with her. He ground his teeth in frustration and their fun. She was not ready for the beasts to show their true nature. He was sure of it.

Yet, she needed to be. Suppose something happened to him, if the hunger overtook him, or he needed to fight. If he needed to leave her…this woman would need them. It was a sacred bond; one did not share lightly. It could break her mind if she weren't strong enough. The pull of their thoughts could shred the sanity of someone unprepared. He had seen it happen, seen minds split open like cut glass under pressure, leaving only the echo of screams behind.

Rufio slowed his stride on the path until she came even with him. "These two pains are Auralisks. There are not many of their kind in this world. Not anymore. And unfortunately, they have names," he said, nodding toward the beasts. "If you are to get to know them or call for them if in danger, you must remember their names. This one is Thalos. The other, Brin." Rufio looked forward, saying nothing more. The two Auralisks bobbed their heads in an up and down motion with a resounding snort.

Mari arched a brow as she looked at the hooded man next to her. Were they mocking him? With slight mischief in her voice, she said, "Thalos and Brin. Sounds like the main characters out of a good fantasy novel. Do they bite?" Her grin was small but real, the first spark of comfort since she'd fallen through worlds.

He took a subtle but deep inhalation, inadvertently catching her scent. His body grew slightly more rigid. "They listen," Rufio said, ignoring the twist in his chest. "If you call, they will answer if they like you."

Mari turned her head back to look at her new furry friends. Her face took on a tone of focus, and she nodded, glancing at the creatures with more curiosity than fear. Their massive eyes blinked slowly at her, and the warmth of their thoughts pulsed stronger, brushing against her mind like a welcome. Her eye flicked back and forth from one set of eyes to another as her gate began to slow.

The air around her shifted slightly as the Auralisks emanated a soft healing glow. Mari could not imagine these creatures could eviscerate a man's mind with a thought. The beasts were both battle-worn, gently connected to her closed third eye. This action was dangerous. So, it is very dangerous, but necessary. A shimmer passed between them, unseen but palpable, like invisible threads drawing tight across her heart.

Rufio's throat felt dry. He did not want this; he did not want her tangled in bonds he barely trusted himself with. But if she called their names, he knew they would come; she might survive what was to come. A thought in the back of his mind began to slither to the forefront. It whispered the oldest truth of the Wild: power never gives itself freely, it takes, and it marks.

The half-day trek took its toll on Mari. She was not used to the harshness of the land and travel. The sun clawed its way across the sky, baking the cracked earth. The closer the group came to the town, the louder it became, shapes of people moving in its streets, glimmers of wagons and stalls, noise carried faintly on the wind. It looked like a tourist town might be in another world; shops were bustling, doors were swinging open, and bright signs were painted in careless colors. The scent of sweat, ale, and desperation wafted up to them. The smell made her gag as her chest tightened. It was too human, too familiar in all the wrong ways.

Rufio's eyes locked onto something beyond all that. The invisible wall shimmered faintly in the middle of the town, unseen to Mari but bright as flame to him. Inside it, the true sanctum pulsed: cleaner air, guarded order. That was where the Watcher's office waited. That was where she would be safe, secure. He shook his head, trying to get the thought out of his mind. Safe. The word felt foreign. There was no true safety.

Mari shifted beside him, uneasy without knowing why. Her cut hand brushed against the side of his body; the action sent a deep sting up her arm. Mari winced at the pain while unconsciously rubbing her wrist where the chackle had rubbed her skin earlier. Her brow furrowed as she scanned the lively horizon. "Something about this place feels… wrong.

Like it's smiling at me but planning to mug me later." Her attempt at humor was thin this time, the laughter catching in her throat.

Rufio almost smiled at that. Almost. Instead, he forced his gaze back to the town. He filed away the redness on her left wrist for later, while the right was fully healed. Currently, his mind gnawed at the pull he felt every time she bled, every time her voice broke the silence, every time her eyes met his and stirred the hunger he carried like a curse. That hunger, ancient, coiled, and patient, reminded him of what he truly was, and what he had lost the right to want and receive.

By late afternoon, the town's outskirts loomed before them. Dusty roads wound between rough wooden buildings, doors swinging on rusted hinges, merchants shouting over one another in the scramble of trade. Alehouses spilled with noise, filthy children wore tattered cloth, and darted between nearby carts. The smell of roasting meat fought against the stench of sweat and old blood. Veyor was alive, but it was not peaceful; it was hungry, rough, and watchful. Even the laughter here sounded barbed, scraping against the air.

Rufio adjusted his grip on his weapon, the tension in his shoulders sharp as stone. "Stay close," he said, firmly grabbing her elbow and leading her into the press of the streets. "This place bites."

Mari glanced sideways, smirking despite herself. "Of course it does," she murmured. "Everywhere you take me seems to."

# Chapter 5

The streets of Veyor buzzed with heat and hunger. From a distance, the town looked like a frontier settlement; wooden frames and rusted tin rooftops stretched across the dry valley floor, wrapped in dust and the faint hum of taint and corruption. But up close, it pulsed with something darker. The smell of stale blood mingled with smoke from blackened chimneys, and the sound of clanging metal mixed with the shouts of merchants. It was a place that survived, not thrived. Every step Mari took felt like walking through a memory that didn't belong to her, old sins and older debts breathing through the dust.

Men leaned against doorframes, eyes narrowing in suspicion or something darker. Some of them winked and even licked their lips in her direction. Women paused in mid-haggle at stalls, whispering behind their hands. Mari walked closer to Rufio's side, her steps light but wary. Her clothes, torn and stained from their journey, drew stares from every direction. She tugged at the hem of her sweatshirt, painfully aware of the eyes that lingered far too long. Her nerves prickled beneath the weight of their attention. It wasn't fear that crawled under her skin; it was the ugly feeling of being seen as prey. She will not be a victim. She will survive.

Rufio drew his pace to a halt as Mari caught up, their footsteps falling softly on the worn path. "These two pains are Auralisks," he said, gesturing with a nod toward the formidable creatures at their side. "There are not many left in this world, and unfortunately, they have names." His voice lowered, almost reverent. "This one is Thalos. The other, Brin."

The two Auralisks bobbed their massive heads rhythmically, unleashing deep, resonant snorts that echoed off the surrounding trees, as if acknowledging their names. Mari raised an eyebrow at Rufio, a hint of mischief dancing in her eyes. "Thalos and Brin. Sounds like the heroes out of a vibrant fantasy novel. Do they bite?" Her small grin was the first flicker of warmth since she tumbled through worlds.

Rufio inhaled deeply, inadvertently drawing in the scent of her, an intoxicating blend of wildflowers and spring rain. He felt a tightening in his chest, a sudden rigidity. "They listen," he replied, using a teetering motion with his hand. Caution laced his tone, deliberately ignoring the flutter of unease building within him. "If you call, they will respond… if they like you."

Mari turned her gaze toward the Auralisks, her demeanor shifting as curiosity overtook her initial trepidation. Their enormous eyes blinked slowly, glinting with ancient wisdom, and softly pulsating thoughts brushed against her mind like a lingering caress. As she considered these majestic creatures, her step slowed, and the atmosphere around her began to hum.

A soft healing glow emanated from the Auralisks, casting ethereal patterns on the ground and illuminating her features with a gentle light. It was hard to believe these beings could wield such unimaginable power, yet here they were, battle-hardened and alive with energy, tethering themselves to the closed third eye she dared not open. The connection felt fraught with potential, dangerous yet vital, as invisible threads seemed to weave tightly around her heart.

Rufio's throat tightened at the thought. He didn't want her caught up in a tangle of power he struggled to control, yet he knew that if she whispered their names, Thalos and Brin would come. A chilling realization slithered through his mind: the ancient knowledge of the Wild spoke loudly. Power never gives itself freely; it always takes, leaving a mark.

As the half-day trek continued, Mari's weariness mounted. She was ill-suited to the harshness of the landscape, with the relentless sun clawing across the sky, mercilessly baking the cracked earth beneath them. The clamor of distant voices grew louder as they neared the town, the shapes of bustling figures moving through sun-drenched streets, their laughter and chatter carried vaguely on the warm breeze. It resembled a tourist town from another realm, with colorful stall signs swinging cheerfully and shopkeepers haggling zealously. The atmosphere was heavy with the odors of sweat, ale, and a lingering sense of desperation, a combination that twisted her stomach.

Rufio's gaze narrowed, focusing beyond the chaos. A shimmering wall, invisible to Mari, glinted faintly in the afternoon light, an ethereal boundary that concealed the true sanctum. Inside lay cleaner air and an aura of guarded tranquility, the very essence of safety. His heartbeat quickened at the thought. Safe. But the word felt foreign, almost sacrilegious. True safety was an illusion, mere wisps of fantasy.

Mari shifted beside him, an unshakable unease brewing deep inside her. As her injured hand inadvertently brushed against his side, a sharp sting shot up her arm, causing her to wince and absently rub at her wrist, where chafing from the chackle still lingered. Her brow knitted in discomfort as she scanned the lively horizon.

"Something about this place feels… wrong. Like it's smiling at me while planning to rob me blind," she quipped, her attempted levity faltering, laughter catching in her throat.

Rufio almost allowed a smile to break through, but the weight of reality pulled him back. Instead, he redirected his gaze toward the town, mentally cataloging the redness on her left wrist for later while feeling the remnants of healing on her right. Each drop of her blood, every fractured silence moved his thoughts to dark places, places where hunger coiled tight within him, ancient and unyielding, serving as a constant reminder of what he was and what he could never have.

By late afternoon, the town's outskirts emerged before them: dusty roads meandering between weathered wooden buildings, doors creaking on rusted hinges, and merchants shouting over each other in a chaotic scramble for attention. The joyous noise spilled from alehouses, while dirty children darted through the throngs, their laughter sharp like knives against the grit of the environment. The scent of roasting meat struggled against the pungent stench of sweat and old blood, embracing the town in a brazen contradiction of life and decay. Veyor was alive, yet resided in constant hunger, a place both rough and watchful, where even gaiety seemed barbed.

Rufio tightened his grip on his weapon, tension coiling through his shoulders like a coiled snake ready to strike.

"Stay close," he muttered, his fingers firmly clutching her elbow as he guided her into the throng of the streets. "This place bites."

Mari glanced sideways at him, a smirk breaking through despite the heaviness of the atmosphere. "Of course it does," she murmured softly. "Everywhere you take me seems to."

Mari had a million questions dancing in her mind, but the figure before her was a statue cloaked in shadows, his dark hood concealing most of his face. He stood there, an imposing silhouette, resting his hands casually on his weapons, eyes hidden yet piercing. Gathering her courage, Mari stepped forward, trying to meet his gaze. An awkward stillness hung in the air like stepping into a prayer or, worse, a trap.

As they approached the heart of the town, a faint shimmer flickered to life, like a mirage on a hot day. Thalos and Brin, pulling the wagon, passed through first, followed by Rufio. When Mari made her move, the wall pulsed warmly against her skin as if welcoming her home. Light rippled outward, a bright wave that surged beneath her fingertips. For a moment, she felt alive. Really alive as colors around her sharpened like a painter's fresh palette: greens, browns, reds sprang to vibrant life, and the golden bands on the wrists of the citizens shone with newfound brilliance. A whisper hummed inside her, urging her: this land wants… needs to know you.

Rufio's eyes narrowed with suspicion, watching the magic unfold. Inside the town's center, an invisible barrier protected the streets, cleaner; buildings sturdier; the air fragrant with incense that felt like an embrace. Yet, an unease settled heavily in Mari's chest. What glittered beneath this polish felt suspicious, a hint of rot hidden beneath the surface. Clutching Rufio's bicep for balance, she realized no one looked at her here; the world faded away into a beautiful blur.

A wave of emotions from her Auralisk companions washed over her peace and pride, mingled with confusion. Mari couldn't fathom what had just happened and why it mattered so much to the men in her party. Rufio's heart raced under her touch, but he kept his face a mask of calm. Her fragile trust unraveled something in him that had been bound for too long.

The Watcher's Office loomed ahead, tall and solemn, while Rufio paused near a textile shop. "You'll need to blend in," he said, his tone brokering no argument.

"Blend in? Seriously? Have you noticed I'm lacking a wardrobe?" Mari waved her hands around her mismatched attire as if it were a flag of surrender.

"I know," he replied with an air of authority that could command armies. "That's why we're here. You'll wait with the tailor until I finish my business." His finger pointed at the Watchers' building, finality ringing in his voice. Even if she wanted to push back, the desire to reclaim her voice faded.

The storefront displayed clothes that seemed to dance, each an invitation, teasing her imagination. The Auralisks hovered behind, their presence warm and watchful. Rufio stepped inside, and the warm scent of soft cotton and wool enveloped Mari, a comforting embrace that contrasted sharply with the chaos outside. Suddenly, the domesticity of it all felt like a punch-drunk delight, a dizzying rush of normalcy she wasn't sure how to process.

The tailor's bell jangled when they entered. Dust motes spun in shafts of light from narrow windows near the ceiling. The shopkeeper appeared from the back, speaking in a language Mari had never heard. Harsh consonants and deep tones filled the air as Rufio answered in kind. His voice was smooth and commanding, sending an odd flutter through her stomach. She didn't like not knowing what was being said around. Her pulse quickened. What if she were being sold?

"Hey," she whispered sharply. "What did he just..." Her breathing quickened. The man disappeared into the back, shouting to someone unseen.

Before she could finish, Rufio turned to her. For the first time since they'd met, he touched her tentatively and gently, like a caress. His hands were warm and rough, calloused from years of battle. He leaned close, cupping her ears, and whispered softly in each ear. The world tilted. She gasped; her breath caught as heat pooled low in her belly. Her heart stuttered, betraying her. She wasn't supposed to find this attractive. But she did. The sound of his voice wrapped around her like a secret spell.

The din of the street outside shifted. Suddenly, she could hear it all; languages unraveling into meaning. Conversations began to spill clearly and understandably. The tailor's shouts became words. "Bring the Solins! Hurry!"

"Better?" Rufio said quietly. "Now you won't panic every time someone speaks."

Mari tried to speak but only managed a weak, "That's... incredible. But...You could've warned me."

He almost smiled. "And ruin the surprise?" he replied as he stared at her shocked face. She was busy looking at her surroundings with a new understanding. Something unspoken lingered between them: gratitude, curiosity, maybe even trust. He wasn't sure which unsettled him more.

He gave her strict orders to stay while the tailor found something for her to wear. "Don't wander," he warned. "Thalos and Brin will watch the front. They have been ordered to bite."

She giggled, unable to help herself. "You mean like you?" Laughing at her own joke, she chided, "I do not chase all the shiny things!"

His expression didn't change as his hooded gaze lingered upon her. She swore the air was shining; he was amused. Maybe? "Stay here," he repeated and disappeared into the Watcher's Office. For the first time, she realized she wanted to know his name, not his title, not his role. Him.

Moments later, Mari stood before the tiny modiste assistants: bug-winged, fairy-like creatures with translucent skin and hollow eyes. They buzzed around her, tugging at fabric and chittering in high-pitched tones that sounded like soft bells. Together, they ushered her into a walled space resembling a local clothing store's changing room.

As she pushed back the curtain, the lights flickered around her, their whispers a symphony of excitement. Initially stiffening at the surreal energy, Mari sensed their struggle. Their movements were sluggish and weak. Her heart twisted; these delicate beings were starving. Without a second thought, she closed her eyes, instinct guiding her as it had with her plants back home.

Cupping her hands, she summoned warmth, a golden-green radiance that shimmered like dawn filtering through leaves. "Eat," she whispered, awe stealing her breath. The Solins danced eagerly around her palms, drinking the light, their laughter, a melody she understood deeply. The warmth surged within her, filling her chest as sunlight broke through clouds.

Dizzy with renewal, the tiny lights spun around her, their tinkling laughter echoing in the small room. With newfound energy, they began to weave fabric from threads of light and gossamer cloth. The ethereal material floated into being, glowing and fragile, as they sang the land's song a melody of what's been and the hope of what could be.

As the gown materialized, it transformed into an elegant white silk slip that draped artfully over her curves. A blush crept to her cheeks. "I think that's… not exactly appropriate for the outside world."

In response, a chorus of musical giggles filled the air. The fabric morphed again, shaping into a tunic with long black sleeves and a corseted bodice, adorned with silver that hugged her waist and hips. A deep red skirt split in front, revealing sleek black leather pants. Strength and grace, melded into one.

Finally, the vibrant lights crowned her with a dark red cloak that settled softly on her shoulders. Her hair was artfully swept up, flecked with the same tiny creatures, sparkling against her silvery strands. Mari gazed at her reflection, heart racing. She was powerful, beautiful, and terrifyingly unlike herself.

"Thank you, little ones," she whispered, her voice barely breaking the spell. The Solins twinkled in front of her, their desires clear: a yearning to rebuild their home.

The Solins twinkled the song of wanting to go home. But their land had been destroyed so long ago. Her reflection wavered, and for a fleeting moment, she saw not herself but someone the land remembered, a healer, a bridge, a beautiful woman.

Excited for her new tiny friends twinkling in her tendrils, she wanted to share her latest appearance with Thalos and Brin. The sweats and boots she came in with could be burned for all she cared. Behind her, the bell above the door chimed again as she left the building after saying goodbye to the tailor.

She was excited for Thalos and Brin to see her new look. After a few steps, she turned, feeling a tingle on her skin, to see Rufio standing in the doorway of the Watcher's building, hood lowered for the first time. The light caught the edge of his face, strong lines, shadowed eyes, and the faintest scar along his jaw. For the first time, he looked human.

# Chapter 6

Rufio led Mari to the tailor's shop, knowing she would be intrigued by the Solins. Leaving her to her fate, he turned and marched to the Watcher's office. The air changed the moment he stepped away from her; colder, sharper, as though the world itself exhaled relief in receiving one of their own after a brief separation. The Watcher's Office loomed as an ancient cathedral dropped into the heart of Veyor; stone walls veined with glowing script, tall glass panes catching the twin suns, carved guardians flanking the entrance. The air inside was colder, too still for a living place. Rufio's boots echoed sharply on the polished floor as he entered, each step reverberating through the hollow space. The silence inside was not absence, but expectation, the kind that listened back.

The scent was unmistakable: old paper, iron, and incense burned to cover the underlying tang of blood magic.

"Watcher Renar," the cloaked man greeted, walking in

through the warded door. His voice carried across the room.

From behind the desk, a glimpse of a room with shelves filled with parchment and crystal orbs; before Rufio stood a dark wooden desk laden with metal rivets and a man hardened by war and time, shuffling paperwork. Rufio's movement caught the Watcher's eye. Renar was old, though not frail. His hair hung in white braids streaked with gold dust, and his eyes were a milky amber that glowed faintly with power. The sigil of the Order burned faintly on his throat; an ancient binding; proof that he was tethered to the laws that governed this dying realm. He was not merely a man; he was law in the flesh.

"Wildling," Renar said, his voice low and rich as tar water. "You return sooner than I expected. Tell me you did not bring corruption back with you."

Rufio bowed his head slightly. "I contained the tear and retrieved the Fletchers' younglings. Their mother will be notified within the next phase."

"And the witness?" Renar said with amusement in his tone.

Rufio hesitated. His jaw flexed, a habit when he was lying to himself, knowing this man saw and knew almost everything. "She was drawn into the rift by accident. She will be returned once the balance is restored with the younglings."

Renar studied him for a long moment, then leaned forward. "You have the scent of her on you, Wildling. Interesting." The man stated, stroking one of his white braids.

The words pierced deeper than they should have. Rufio stiffened, feeling the faint burn of the sacred Sigle over his heart, searing him, a constant reminder that he was never truly alone in his own body. The binding mark of his vow to the Wild pulsed like a second heartbeat. It throbbed now, as if reminding him whom he truly served.

"She bleeds life," Renar said quietly, sniffing the air. "You carry that scent into this sanctum," He pointed his arthritic finger at Rufio. "The land reacts to her. So do you. Have a care, boy."

Rufio's eyes flicked up, cold, defiant. "The Wild reacts to everything. It hungers for everything that has life…energy."

"Not like this." Renar's smile was sad. "You forget, I know the sound of temptation when it claws at a soul. The entity in you holds a purpose. It has been a long time since it has reacted in such a manner." His words landed like stones dropped into still water, and Rufio felt each ripple in his chest.

Rufio could feel it now; the faint heat licking at the edges of his control. The dark energy that lived within him, ancient and primal, twisted beneath his skin. It was not evil; instead, it was balance in its rawest form. But it craved. The Primordial Wild within him always craved. To consume corruption, to drink the energy of tainted life, to feed until there was silence, an equal balance of positive and negative. It whispered to him now, not with words but with want. And Mari's scent fed it like fire to dry leaves.

And Mari's presence made it worse. Her scent, her laughter, her blood. She called the beast inside him, the same way moonlight called the tide.

He stepped closer to the Watcher's desk. "She is under my guard," he said flatly. "And she will remain so until the task is done."

Renar tilted his head. "Guard her? Or claim her?" He chuckled to himself as he picked up a rolled parchment from the desk.

A low growl rumbled in Rufio's throat before he could

stop it. The air in the room flickered, shadows stretching unnaturally toward him. The beast within, the entity that once tore through armies, strained against its leash and tether. His breath came out ragged. The room seemed to breathe with him; the glyphs on the walls brightened, then dimmed, like they too feared what was caged inside him.

He forced it back down. Control. Always be in control. Her voice echoed faintly in his mind: sarcastic, defiant, alive, and it grounded him in a way it shouldn't have.

The Watcher watched him with calm resignation. "Be careful, child of the Wild. What you hunger for may be what undoes you." Renar handed the cloaked face Rufio the parchment, releasing him from the bounty and giving him passage through the plains.

Rufio turned sharply on his heel, ignoring the way the glyphs on the walls dimmed as he passed through the warded doors. Outside, the warmth of the double suns hit his face, grounding him as he felt the building's wall of protection solidify once more. The world's noise came rushing back: vendors shouting, beasts snorting, the metallic rhythm of the town's pulse. But beneath it all, one thought clung to him like a shadow: her voice, her scent, her impossible life. The Wild within him had chosen its focus, and that terrified him more than any curse.

# Chapter 7

The tailor was stunned into silence as he walked to the front of the building. He dropped the cloth spools that were in his hands, enamored with the woman's change. The gentle protection of the Solins illuminated her natural beauty. For a moment, even the dust motes seemed to pause in the shafts of light, caught in a moment of reverence.

Mari smiled and said goodbye, the soft jingle of the bell above the door ringing out as she stepped into the dry air. The street met her like a breath of reality, dust, spice, and faint music from somewhere unseen. Outside, just as she turned, Rufio emerged from the Watcher's Office.

He inhaled deeply, the scent of wildflowers mingling with the fresh promise of spring rain before he caught a glimpse of her. Rufio lowered his hood, an unconscious plea to draw her gaze. He didn't fully comprehend why this moment felt so imperative, but the connection between them crackled with energy. Their eyes locked, and in that breathtaking instant, the noise of the world faded into a muted background, leaving only the two of them suspended in an intimate stillness. Time stretched, as if momentarily breaking free from its relentless march, and everything surrounding them blurred into a kind of elegant insignificance.

The air thickened with unspoken words, each heartbeat pulsing between them like the rhythmic thrum of a distant drum echoing in the silence. A rush of emotions surged through Rufio, a combination of awe and fierce longing that seemed to defy logic. He noted her beauty with meticulous precision, the soft curve of her lips, the way the light danced upon her skin, every detail engraving itself into his memory. The weight of the moment pulled them closer together, as if an invisible thread were weaving their fates into a tapestry rich with shared energy, igniting a spark that beckoned them to bridge the chasm separating their worlds. For a man who had long ago forgotten the sensation of wonder, this brief human moment felt almost devastating.

Her hair shimmered in the sunlight, small Solins' lights intertwined like delicate constellations, casting a golden glow that flickered against her skin. She looked at him with an intensity that seemed to reach into his very soul, and something deep and primal stirred within him, a dangerous longing ignited. He stood frozen mid-step, transfixed by her as though the twin suns had just risen over a barren horizon for the first time. Mari felt her pulse thrum in her throat, rapid and fierce, her heart racing in response to the magnetic force between them.

Rufio's gaze deepened as the swirling shades of red around his onyx eyes resembled molten lava, simmering with an intense hunger that shadowed his features. It was hard to discern whether this intensity was his own or a reflection of something far more ancient and ravenous within him. Words eluded him, the weight of unvoiced emotions rendering him speechless.

His eyes blazed with an intensity that went beyond mere warning. It was a vow; a silent oath etched into the air. The message was clear: any who dared to infringe upon her would meet an untimely fate. Mari felt a twist of emotions in her belly, caught between guilt and longing, each feeling vying for dominance. She relished the fierce protection his gaze bestowed upon her—a feeling she hadn't experienced in eons. It reminded her of a comfort she had sorely missed. For that fleeting breath, she felt anchored, not lost in a world that felt utterly strange. In that moment, she was seen, truly seen.

Inside him, the primal hunger purred with insidious delight, whispering to him with a voice that sent shivers down his spine.

*Take. Taste. Claim.*

He clenched his fists tightly, nails biting into his palms as he stifled the instinctual urges surging through him. "Silence," he hissed to himself, frustration lacing his words.

But the Wild within him, entangled by the Sigil over his heart, was deaf to his command. It had caught her scent, tasted her essence in the air, and now, the primal force thrumming within him had fixated on her entirely. Thoughts wrapped into instinct began to unravel in his mind: protect, devour, keep. The clarity of those words began to blur, a jumble of conflicting desires he loathed to entertain.

As she drew nearer, the clamor of the marketplace melted away, replaced by the soft sound of her breath, a gentle whisper against the backdrop of chaos and the faint but distinct rhythm of her heart resonating in the silence between them. Each pulse was a steady reminder of life, drawing him in further.

He swallowed hard, rasping words escaping his lips, rough around the edges. "You… clean up well."

A playful grin danced across her face, her eyes sparkling with mischief. "Careful. You almost sounded like you were giving a compliment."

He quickly diverted his gaze, pretending to inspect the weathered door of a nearby tailor shop, a rush of warmth flooding his cheeks as he fought to suppress the smile threatening to break the veneer of his stoicism. He knew he had to keep the mask of rigidity firmly in place. If she ever discovered what it truly cost him to smile, she might stop striving to coax it out of him altogether.

"Wait. Do you have a name?" she asked softly. Mari was now close enough for him to hear her lowered voice, unsure why the question mattered so much now.

He hesitated, eyes unreadable, then stepped forward just a little closer and bent close enough for his lips to touch her hair. His hot breath tickled her ear. "Rufio," he said quietly, the name landing between them like gentle droplets of summer rain. "Few are allowed to know it."

Mari smiled, trying and failing to hide how this had affected her. "Then… I'll try not to ruin your reputation… Rufio."

Something flickered in his gaze; amusement, maybe trust, and then it was gone. The way she said his name wrapped around him like a spell she hadn't meant to cast.

As the suns began to dip below the horizon, the streets were cloaked in shadow. A low hum filled the sanctum just outside the heart of this tainted town, and the air shimmered with the glow of flickering lanterns.

Within him, the Wild stirred anew. *Protect. Feed... Devour everything.*

The pair walked over to the Auralisks. Rufio checked the wagon's safety before preparing to leave this town and move on. Thalos and Brin gently caressed Mari's mind, giving her images of what this place had looked like before the rot took hold in this world. She petted their muzzles while smiling sadly at the two. Knowing what something should be and accepting what it is now is a hard medicine to take.

Rufio found himself torn between competing urges. "Before we leave the town, the brothers need to eat, and so do we," Rufio stated abruptly, startling Mari out of her daydreaming as he finalized his security check. Within minutes, Rufio was walking beside Thalos and Brin as they pulled the wagon to the only stables in the center of town. Thalos and Brin snorted as they led themselves in and settled into their stalls.

A young man, tan from working in the sun, with green eyes staring in awe and fear, said, "Are you staying overnight?" The young man glanced at Mari, standing next to the wagon, close to the stable doors but out of view from onlookers, then back at the man in all black, with ethereal weapons, and made an audible gulp.

Rufio spoke briefly with the stableboy, giving him instructions on what was needed for the brothers, then returned to her. As he walked away, without looking back, Rufio said to no one in particular, "Try not to eat this one. He is only trying to do his job."

The Stableboy's green eyes grew wide like raw emeralds and visibly began to sweat. Mari's mouth was gaped open as

Thalos and Brin shimmered their scaly hides and blew smoke through their nostrils. Stamping their hooves aggressively and making chomping noises. Rufio grabbed Mari gently by the crook of her elbow and led her out of the stable and into the cooling late afternoon air.

"You are all fiends!" Mari said in a mocking, shocked voice as she stopped abruptly to stare at the man walking next to her. As soon as she turned, she punched Rufio hard in the arm.

As much as he tried, he could not help but show a mischievous grin to his walking companion. His arm stung from the punch, but he did not move to rub it.

"The last time we were here, the man was a meddlesome boy who tried to tie a bell on Thalos while he slept." Rufio began to walk again, gently pulling her elbow. "Let's just say, our companions seek their own type of revenge with this one." Rufio chuckled at this and then coughed in his hand to hide his mirth. The tavern came into view, light spilling from its open doors. "Food," Rufio said curtly. "Then we move."

Without another word, he led her into the only tavern in the center of Veyor, its heavy door creaking open as the local afternoon atmosphere settled over the town. Inside, the noise hit like a wave: music, laughter, the clatter of plates. Many heads turned as Mari entered. Their stares were heavy and intrusive. She felt her cheeks heat. Rufio's body went still beside her. The room's temperature seemed to rise as with his temper. His hand flexed near the hilt of his blade, and the men closest to them suddenly found excuses to look elsewhere. He didn't glare. He warned. The air itself seemed to be understood.

Mari leaned in slightly and whispered, "You don't have to

glare everyone into submission."

"I'm not glaring," he said evenly. "I'm assessing threats."

She smirked. "Sure. Let me know when your assessment involves stab, stab, stab, and deep brooding."

His jaw tightened, knowing how often his assessment of situations went to… Stab. Stab. Stab. And with unfortunate accuracy, also the deep brooding. The pair sat at a weathered table with a set of benches near the back of the tavern. Thalos and Brin waited in the stable, their minds humming faintly in the background, like warm static in Mari's thoughts.

An older man in his late fifties, with greying hair cropped short, looked at the pair as he walked up to the table. Saying nothing, Rufio pulled a small pouch from inside his cloak. Mari thought to herself, *A-ha! It does have pockets!* He placed a few coins on the table. With only eye contact, their food and drink were ordered from what appeared to be the owner of the tavern. The older man nodded at Rufio and gave Mari a fatherly smile and a gentle bow before retreating behind the bar.

Mari fidgeted at the table, her nervous chatter matching the chaotic rhythm of the bustling tavern. She spoke of the oppressive heat and the unfamiliar scents swirling around her, rich spices mingling with stale beer, all while trying to evade the scrutinizing gazes around her.

Suddenly, a drunk man lurched over, his stained tunic clinging to his sweat-drenched skin, a toothless grin spreading across his face like a bad omen. "Haven't seen a busty figure like you in these parts before. Lost, sweetheart? I could show you a good time." His breath wafted toward her, sour and uninviting.

Mari's smile was tight as she leaned back, instinctively

making space. "Hard pass. And an absolute nope on your offer. You should leave… like now." The sarcasm dripped from her voice, laced with an undercurrent of disdain as her eyes flicked to Rufio, whose gaze darkened, hinting at a deep-seated fury.

The ambiance changed as the drunkard leaned closer, the air thickening with tension. Then, with a swift movement, Rufio shot out a hand, his grip seizing the man's wrist with unyielding strength. Silence draped over the tavern, eyes glued to the unfolding scene.

"Walk away," Rufio commanded, voice low and icy.

The man's bravado crumbled, and his face drained of color. Stumbling back, he muttered hurried apologies, desperate to escape the looming threat.

Mari exhaled, the tension washing away momentarily. "That was subtle," she quipped, rolling her eyes.

Rufio's demeanor shifted only slightly, tension still radiating from him. "He's still alive," he replied with a stern edge, "and that's better than subtle." His words hung in the air, steeped in the understanding of those who walked the line of danger.

The surrounding patrons quickly resumed their conversations, retreating into their own worlds. A server approached, her low-cut bodice paired with a stained apron, setting down their meal of fresh bread, skewered meat, and frothy ale, flashing an appreciative wink at Rufio.

Mari huffed a laugh but chose silence, the weight of the moment settling back onto her shoulders.

They ate quickly. The food was strange: bread that tasted faintly of spice and smoke, water with a metallic undertone. Mari couldn't shake the feeling that the world itself was fading. The air carried a weight she couldn't name.

"When do we leave?" she asked quietly.

"This evening," Rufio said. "We travel to the plains. The temporal space is thinner there, and the Fletcher Mother will have an easier time finding her young. It is safer for us to travel in that manner. To save time, we will also sleep on the road."

She frowned. "To save time? Did you make a statement about sleeping outside? Why not here?"

His eyes flicked to hers, unreadable. "You'll be fine." His response wasn't reassuring. It was a fact. Cold, hard, and absolute.

She rolled her eyes at him, muttering under her breath, "You really should work in customer service." Then took a bite of skewered meat before her stoic companion could make a response.

Now with full bellies, as they stepped out of the tavern, the evening air enveloped them in a cool embrace, a refreshing contrast to the humid warmth of the dimly lit interior. The twin suns, ripe and amber, began their descent to finish their daily journey behind the jagged mountains, creating an ominous hue of reds and oranges in the sky and casting long shadows that danced across the dirt streets. The town was bathed in an ethereal glow, lantern light spilling like molten gold and copper from the windowpanes and outdoor lamps, illuminating the laughter and chatter of the townsfolk.

Rufio took the lead, guiding Mari back toward the stable to gather the Auralisks. The stableboy had a worry crease on his sweating brow, and he was rubbing his backside. He walked up to the pair to offer a polite greeting.

"Watcher… Sir… They tried to eat me!" The poor young man looked like he was going to pass out. "I gave them oats… I really did!"

Mari hid her smile behind her hands and faked a shocked look on her face.

Rufio, with a severe set to his jaw, raised the hood over his face, adding drama to the situation. "You are not dead. If they wanted to eat you, I would not have to speak to you now, and they would be full."

The stableboy sputtered, looked down at the floor, and said with a defeated sigh, "Yes, Sir." He absently rubbed his backend again, walking away.

Rufio paid the young man a few extra coins to assist him in his narrow escape from being eaten alive. Within half an hour, the group was ready to continue their journey. As the Auralisks walked out of the stable with the wagon in tow, Rufio took a moment to survey his surroundings. He quickly noticed that corruption and the stench of rot had spread to the town's outskirts, slowly creeping toward the protected center.

Sensing trouble, Rufio's instincts flared. A confrontation was brewing as shadows gathered at the fringe of the town's sacred center, where the rougher characters lingered like vultures, waiting to descend. A small group of men loomed just beyond the invisible barrier, their stares piercing through the gathering dusk. Rufio, Thalos, and Brin exchanged a knowing glance. The message was clear. They wanted Mari, or at least the treasure they believed she harbored.

With a swift, decisive motion, Rufio gestured toward the wagon's bench, his hood obscuring much of his face. "Take a seat on the bench, Mari," he instructed, his voice low but firm, echoing with an authority that brooked no argument.

Mari's brow furrowed, disbelief mingling with irritation.

"Excuse me?" she replied, lifting her chin defiantly. A familiar insecurity flickered beneath the surface, but she masked it. Rufio's stark shift in demeanor was disconcerting, an unspoken command cloaked in a protective urgency.

He crossed the distance between them, the soft crunch of gravel beneath his boots punctuating the tension-filled air. As he silently gestured for her to ascend the wagon, Mari felt an unexpected wave of hurt wash over her. Why the sudden shift? Just a day in this uncanny world, and she was already being sidelined!

An unyielding gaze met hers; those black-and-red eyes seemed to burn through her protest, searing any defiance away. With a deep breath, Mari obeyed, feeling both the weight of his scrutiny and the weightlessness of surrender. He stepped forward, his hands steadying her waist as she clambered up. She hesitated, then settled onto the bench, arms crossed tightly, a silent act of rebellion against the confusion swirling within her.

The Auralisks, their powerful forms resonating with a quiet strength, led the way as Thalos and Brin guided the wagon. An unspoken communication pulsed between the trio, an intimate dialogue she couldn't penetrate. For Mari, this felt like an uneasy surrender, yet it was oddly comforting, like a bubble of safety amid the impending storm.

As the wagon rolled forward, the gentle clip-clop of hooves echoed in the stillness, a rhythmic mantra against the fading light that heralded evening. They navigated through the winding inner streets of Veyor, the once-vibrant chaos beginning to wane; vendors hurriedly packed their wares, children no longer dashed through the lanes, and the laughter of drunks dulled under the glow of lanterns. Stares followed her, curious yet dismissive, as if she were a fleeting mirage in this ostentatious, hollow realm—this world pulsed with life, but it felt stunted, as though it moved without growth.

Mari glanced back at Veyor one last time. The town shimmered with a deceptive vibrancy, yet a disquiet gnawed at her core a visceral sickness resonating from the very earth, as if it echoed the ache in her own heart. The ground, once a stage for bustling life, bore the weight of unfathomable secrets beneath its surface.

"This world," she murmured, her voice barely rising above the soft rustle of the breeze. "It's surviving… but not living, is it?"

Above them, the twin suns faded to crimson, and somewhere deep within the taint and rot, something ancient also took notice of the slight change in the land.

Rufio remained stoic, his gaze firmly fixed on the horizon, where the dying plains stretched endlessly, a haunting expanse waiting for them. Together, they walked into the deepening dusk, the weight of the moment settling softly around them like a twilight shroud.

# Chapter 8

The twin suns' fading light slid at its lowest across the plains, throwing long golden spears that shimmered on the wagon's metal fittings. The sound of the wagon creaked rhythmically, as the Auralisks worked in harmony pulling their haul down the path. Behind them, the town had vanished into a blur, leaving only the wind and the crunch of cracked earth beneath their hooves.

Thalos and Brin pulled steadily, using their energy to smooth out the dips and holes along the path for the Fletchers in the wagon, with their strength evident in the way their scaled shoulders rolled with each steady pull. Their hides shimmered in the light, reflecting shades reminiscent of hammered steel. As they moved, a faint hum of thoughts brushed against Rufio's consciousness, a melding of minds thick with camaraderie and gentle humor.

Thalos, the elder of the two, often carried the weight of

responsibility on his broad shoulders. With deep-set eyes that sparkled with wisdom and mischief, he held a deep-seated desire to protect those he cared about. Brin, younger yet equally formidable, had a fierce and playful spirit. He was the spark that ignited laughter, always ready with a quip to lighten the mood. Together, they were an inseparable pair, fiercely loyal, kind, and driven by the need to maintain balance.

Compared to the brothers, Mari was a fragile creature, and they had taken it upon themselves to watch over her. Thalos and Brin had decided; she was their foal, their little sister whom they deemed worthy of love, protection, and fierce loyalty. This was a similar action they took with Rufio so many years ago. However, that bond was forged through battle and hard-won trust; with the Wildling becoming a brother in arms, willing to sacrifice himself for the greater good of his people. The Auralisks knew that despite his tough exterior, there was vulnerability in him that spoke volumes about his past. He had lost so much: his family, his freedom, and they knew he was hesitant to let anyone in again.

Mari sat quietly in the driver's seat of the wagon, her mind swirling with memories she'd rather not confront. Thalos and Brin were a comforting presence, their thoughts wrapping around her like a safety net, assuring her she wasn't alone. As Mari let her gaze wander over the horizon, the evening suns cast a golden glow, dancing against the Solin-woven clothes she wore, making her the embodiment of allure and confidence against the backdrop of dusk.

The garments seemed tailored for a single purpose: to captivate Rufio's gaze. The black leather shimmered faintly with Solin energy, flowing like silk and transforming each of her movements into a mesmerizing dance. The corseted top clung to her figure like a shadow's caress, its silver stitching pulsing softly as it stored light within, drawing attention like moths to flame.

The leather pants defied mere fabric; they clung to her legs with power and sensuality, accentuating every curve, while the deep red split skirt draped elegantly over her hips, cascading to the floor in rich folds. As she shifted, the skirt fluttered, revealing tantalizing glimpses of her shapely legs, a deliberate tease of elegance.

Rufio struggled to tear his gaze away, mesmerized by her radiance. She glowed almost otherworldly, framed by loose strands of silver hair that caught the light with every subtle movement. Mari exuded strength and vitality, a blend of beauty that felt too alive for this world. With every gentle sway of the wagon, her allure wove a spell over Rufio, capturing him completely. This time, he embraced Solin's playful magic, lowering his hood to soak in the moment.

Unaware of his lingering gaze on her corset, Mari leaned forward to adjust the reins, lost in thought. She turned her face toward the horizon, where the pale plains met the jagged peaks of distant mountains, as the suns began to fade. Rufio forced himself to look ahead, only to regret it immediately. When she glanced back at him, their eyes locked, and she offered a small, radiant smile.

He had expected her to be restless, fidgeting, or questioning every sound, yet she sat enveloped in a quiet wonder, lips curved softly in thought. He kept his hood down, and to his surprise, she seemed grateful, even as shadows played across her face. He noticed her stealing glances at him, fascination shimmering in her eyes. Each time their gazes met, she instinctively looked away, yet something kept her captive, a gaze so penetrating it gnawed at his very soul.

"Do your eyes always look like that?" she asked suddenly, a teasing lilt in her voice.

He held her stare, not flinching. "Like what?"

"Like… an eclipse," she replied, her tone low and playful. "Dark in the middle, flame like the sun around the edges." With a flourish, she traced a circle in the air towards his face.

Rufio turned his gaze back to the road, fighting off a smile. "You know you shouldn't stare at the sun, Mari. It burns the eyes."

As he spoke, the world around them seemed to hold its breath, suspended in the electric tension between them.

Her lips curled into an easy-to-read smirk, amusement dancing on her face. "And yet, you make it impossible not to. Your eyes are so different from everyone else's here. Why?"

Rufio then felt his jaw tighten, forcing his focus on the worn path. This road, now fading into more dust than dry grass, was once lively with merchants and travelers. But right now, it was just the traveling party and the dying plains. As if sensing her teasing, Kaelith stirred within him, a gentle heat rippling beneath his skin. The Wild was awakening, drawn out by her playful challenge, as if she were daring him to embrace its raw hunger.

After a few minutes, he gave a sideways glance to Mari. Rufio replied, "Maybe it's a secret. Or maybe it's a warning."

"Oh, I do love a bit of danger," she quipped back, a spark of mischief lighting up her gaze. "Perhaps I need to keep a closer eye on you." Mari giggled at that statement, looking at the Auralisks' scaled hides shimmering in the dimming light as if *she* could dash into danger or protect anyone here. She knew she was the weakest link, and that was alright. Mari thought to herself, *I will never be as strong as these guys, but I know they need my heart's compass to help guide.*

# Chapter 9

Rufio was quickly learning to enjoy the small bouts of banter from this strange woman. For a moment, the world did not seem volatile and toxic.

Then his Sigil warmed. *"She sees deeper, Wildling,"* Kaelith whispered in his mind, his voice smooth like dark honey. *"It's only a matter of time...."*

*"No. This woman will face the Fletcher and leave through the nearest portal."* Rufio's internal protest was firm, but it carried a tinge of weariness. *"She should never have seen the younglings. This woman has no knowledge of this world or our part in it?"*

*"And what if she wants to face this world... and the Wild within it?"* Kaelith countered, his tone shifting, laced with a hint of curiosity that made Rufio's skin prickle. *"You can't hide forever, Wildling. There is corruption and rot here that must be destroyed."*

The tendrils of Rufio's past brushed against the back of his mind, visions of the carnage wrought by the Wild when left unchecked, the chaos that had unspooled his life.

*"You have always been too dangerous,"* he replied to the voice in his mind, feeling the weight of his words settle heavily. *"I remember the last time, Spirit."*

Anger swirled in his heart as he spat the words; the memory of loss of fellow soldiers and the land he swore to protect coiled around him like a serpent, squeezing tight.

The Wild entity erupted in laughter, malicious and mocking at his vessel's response. *"Remember who you speak to, boy. We have our place in this world, a reason why you are my vessel. Know your place!"* He chided. *"This woman, too, has a reason... a purpose. Her illumination feels familiar...."*

Rufio took a deep breath, trying to keep his focus on the road despite the dread and frustration gnawing at him. How had his life's journey become so murky? The woman who was gradually changing this land… Mari filled his thoughts. The tension between vessel and primordial spirit crackled in the air, an electric promise of chaos and devastation. He tightened his grip on the wagon rail, his knuckles whitening as he steadied himself against the surging feelings rather than yielding to them as they traveled on.

As evening descended, they reached the end of the main merchant path, veering onto cracked, pale earth that resembled a spider's web. In the distance, thunder rumbled ominously near the mountain peaks, though the sky remained deceptively clear. The air carried a subtle scent of rust and decomposition.

* * *

When the last remnants of town vanished both sight and smell, he stopped the wagon and turned to her. "We need to walk from here," he ordered.

Mari groaned softly. "Of course we do."

He extended his hand, offering assistance. She nodded, gripping his hand as he helped her down. The wagon lacked a ladder, the skirt she wore further encumbering her descent. Without his support, she would have tumbled to the ground. As her hands settled on his shoulders, her balance wavered. His grip on her waist was warm and steady, an anchor in the dimming light. For a fleeting moment, she leaned in closer, inhaling his scent; a warm, sunbaked aroma mingling with the faint floral sweetness of the Solin's protective energy.

Kaelith stirred within Rufio, a familiar hum of hunger coursing through him as the Sigil flared to life, searing against his skin like molten iron. Tension rippled through him, the Wild growing restless in his chest, yearning to reach for her, a desire that felt feral and unlike the entity's nature.

Mari steadied herself, brushing dust from his shoulders, flashing him a teasing smile. Unbeknownst to her, the Sigil glowed beneath his shirt. "You know, for someone with reflexes that could rival a superhero, you sure know how to grumble like an old man. Practicing your tough-guy act while saving the day?"

His jaw tightened, but the corner of his mouth betrayed him, hinting at a reluctant smile. "Stop giving me reasons to test those reflexes," he replied, his voice rough as gravel but edged with humor. He pulled away from her too quickly, as if her very touch could burn him. Creating distance, he said sharply, "Stay close to the wagon," his tone heavy with an unspoken tension.

Brin stomped his hoof, shaking his body and snorting

in protest. Thalos mirrored the gesture, the two creatures oblivious to the peculiar dynamic between the two humans. Rufio ran a hand through his hair, revealing for the first time the metallic band encircling his wrist, marked with black and crimson. Mari squinted at the intricate designs, the red flowing like molten lava through the copper.

"Amazing…" she breathed, awe threading her voice as she turned, walking alongside Thalos and Brin. Rufio maintained a few paces behind, his focus unwavering.

They set off across the plains in silence, the late-evening air heavy and shimmering, resonating with the low hum of insects for the first time during their journey. The brothers trudged forward, drawing the wagon as the cracked soil crunched beneath their feet, gray and lifeless. Yet beneath the surface, Rufio sensed something stirring, as if the land itself lay in wait.

The Fletchers rode quietly in the wagon, restless but safe. He could sense their sleepy emotions brushing against his mind: curiosity, hunger, comfort, like the echoes of all children's dreams. Mari and Rufio walked side by side for a while, the silence stretching too long for Mari. She found herself constantly needing to rein in her tendency to say something; to ramble, just to fill the silence. This was, without a doubt, the most complex challenge she had ever faced.

Then Mari stopped so abruptly that Thalos and Brin snorted in protest, their hooves grinding against the brittle earth. She squinted into the dim light, her breath catching. "Wait… Rufio. Look." Her voice was tight, urgent, as she pointed down the path.

Rufio followed her gaze. Half-buried in dust lay a serpent the length of his arm, its body mottled in sickly green and bronze. The tail ended not in a rattle but in a curved stinger that should have been black as obsidian, now dulled to a dark gray.  Its scales were lifeless, marred by splotches of rot, and a thick, tar-like substance seeped from a wound near the tail.  Each shallow breath rattled through its frame like a broken instrument.  The once-mighty serpent writhed in agony, succumbing to the rot and corruption that had spread through this world.  There was nothing he or the Auralisks could do other than put the serpent out of its misery.

Mari's chest constricted. Something inside her twisted like sharp glass. "Something's wrong," she stated, voice trembling with conviction. "I can feel it." She said as her hand moved over her heart. She couldn't see what Rufio saw in the evening light. However, her instincts led her to action.

Rufio's blood iced as he placed his arm in front of her body. "That is a Serathian viper," he said, his tone clipped and cold. "Venom in its bite, toxin in its tail. It can kill an Auralisk in minutes. Stay back, Mari. It is already dead. It just does not know it yet."

Instead, she sidestepped his arm and was already moving forward. "Damnit, woman!"

Her pace quickened, instincts honed by years of answering cries no one else heard. She knelt beside the serpent, the hem of her skirt brushing the dirt.

"Shh… It's okay," she murmured, voice soft as if the creature was a small child and could understand.

Rufio lunged forward, panic clawing at his chest. "No… don't!" His bark cracked the silence, but her hand was already outstretched.

The viper's tongue flicked weakly.  Its head lifted, fangs bared, body coiling in a last defense. Kaelith surged inside

Rufio, the Wild roaring for blood, for him to end this madness before it killed her. But Mari's palm remained steady and open, a quiet defiance against fear.

The serpent struck forward, then froze a breath before penetrating her skin with a fang. Trembling, it hovered, its tongue tasting the air. Slowly, impossibly, it slithered its head into her hand.

"You're afraid," she whispered, her voice a thread of calm. "I won't hurt you."

"Mari…" Rufio's voice fractured, half warning, half disbelief. His heart slammed against his ribs. "By the Ancients…"

She rose slowly, using her other arm to help the serpent coil along her forearm. Its scales slowly changed to shine like living bronze, its head settling in her palm. Where its fangs grazed her skin, light bloomed; soft green-gold, pulsing in waves that spilled through and into the creature's scales. Before Rufio's eyes, the rot melted away. Wounds sealed with a shimmer; dullness gave way to brilliance as the stinger straightened, gleaming like polished glass. The viper hissed. But not in pain, but rather in gentle reverence. Its body aglow, bronze and liquid under fractured healing light. It curled closer, drinking in her energy like a sacred offering, until every trace of decay was gone and only radiance remained.

Thalos and Brin stamped nervously, their minds echoing panic across the link. Rufio raised a hand to calm them. "Easy."

But Rufio could barely breathe from the worry and panic. Kaelith writhed under his skin, drawn to her power like a starving beast to its prey. His chest tightened, hunger and awe colliding in a storm he couldn't name.

"You're feeding it?" he asked, voice low, ragged. "With your energy? Your life?"

"I didn't... I didn't know I could do that. But it was dying." Her now tired gaze lifted to meet him. Although the night was closing in, Rufio noticed her face had paled, and her breath was shallower.

"I can't just watch something die when I can help."

He swallowed hard, forcing steel into his voice. "You don't touch dying things here, Mari. Not everything can be saved." His presence fell over her as he stepped closer. "You don't understand what you're holding. Here, life and death obey no rules, you know. They are absolute, and they do not forgive."

"Maybe not," she said softly, rising with the serpent coiled like a living bracelet. Her eyes burned with quiet fire.

He blocked her path, his voice snapping sharper than he intended. "You could have died." Rufio's frustration and anger finally boiled over, showing on his usually stoic face. "You have been here less than a day, Mariposa. Over and over, you have put yourself in harm's way! Your life and energy are not trivial trinkets to be handed out so easily!" He rubbed his hand over his face, again the copper band presenting its red glow, lighting her features.

Her eyes flashed with hurt and anger. "You act like compassion is a disease!"

"In this world," he said, his tone flat and heavy, "it can be."

"Then maybe your world needs to learn better," she said in an even tone. Her eyes gazed at the living jewelry on her arm and smiled. She slowly began to walk, not willing to look at the man before her, moving to the wagon and the rest of her traveling party.

Mari was taken back by Rufio. Her full first name had never been used by anyone except her best friend and her husband. It unnerved her. But she was not going to harden her heart just because a bunch of men could no longer use theirs.

In this moment, Rufio opened his mouth and then closed it. He had no answer to push back with. He wanted to shake her and hold her in the same action. The conflict coiled in him, sharp as Kaelith's hunger. The Wild inside him roared with its approval of her action; his human heart recoiled from how right it felt.

Thalos and Brin pushed their unease about the viper onto their crazy little foal. Mari was having none of it, deciding for the moment to have the viper continue being wrapped around her arm. The Solins periodically flickered their protective light on the serpent, ensuring its obedience. They walked until the darkness covered the land like a shroud.

The plains fell silent except for the low drone of the gentle breeze through the sporadic withered grass. Even the insects found silence in this desolate place. By the time they made camp, the moon was high in the starry sky, leaving streaks of violet and beautiful twinkling stars.

Rufio gathered some dry wood from the wagon and conjured a fire with a flick of his hand; it flared blue before settling into orange. The younglings snored softly in the wagon, curled under the blanket of energy within their tailored space.

Mari placed her newest scaly companion in one of the saddlebags taken off Brin, settling it on the ground, where she knew it could rest and be safe away from the Auralisks. She stopped in front of the brothers, patting their muzzles before walking towards the flames. Her anger now cooled, she crouched near the fire, rubbing her arms.

"Is it always this cold?" She felt as if she were standing in a freezer.

"No," Rufio said, as he walked around the fire towards Mari.

"But they're making the temperature around you more frigid."

She frowned. "Who's 'they'?"

He tilted his head toward her collar and hair. "The Solins. Your little companions."

Her eyes widened. "You mean these adorable sparkly meddlers?"

As if on cue, faint lights peeked out of her hair and buzzed indignantly, like bells with opinions. Rufio smirked despite himself. "They like to be mischievous. Tonight, you are a part of the game."

Mari gasped when her breath fogged. "Oh, come on!"

The Solins' glow dimmed, then flared again, and Mari yelped. "They're making it colder!"

Rufio sighed. Kaelith chuckled deep in his chest.

"You're enjoying this," she accused, pushing his chest and then unwrapping her skirt and placing it over her shoulders tightly now atop the cape.

"Maybe a little." Rufio retorted with a hint of amusement.

"Fine… be that way," she said with a huff, holding onto her new garment of warmth, only to shiver again.

He unfastened his cloak and tried to hand it to her. "Here."

Mari shook her head. "You will also be cold." She said as her teeth began to chatter. She could now see her breath as if it were the middle of winter.

Rufio cursed quietly and moved behind her. "You're impossible." He wrapped his cloak around her shoulders, then shifted so his body blocked the gentle wind that blew in the night. "Better?"

"Yes. Thanks," she said, wrapping it around herself. The Solins, still hidden in her hair and clothing, began to titter, tiny evil chimes of mischief. Then, she shivered again. "Really!

Did it actually get colder?"

Rufio frowned.

"Ugh!" Mari grumbled, becoming more frustrated. She hated the cold.

He sighed and looked up. "Solins. Tricksters. They control temperature through the fabric you wear. You probably shouldn't have encouraged them." He gently but assertively moved her closer to the fire, then sat on the ground atop one of the sleeping blankets. He pulled her down into a sitting position in front of him and the fire, rewrapping his cloak to lay in front of her like a blanket.

Her teeth chattered slightly. "Oh, I'll remember that next time!"

Kaelith stirred again, amused. *"Mmm...Your pulse changed vessel...,"* he hummed.

*Silence,* Rufio growled internally.

"Enough of your tricks," he said, his voice carrying a mock authority as he pulled her gently closer. With a swift motion, he wrapped his cloak around them, draping the ends over his shoulders and creating a warm cocoon for this rare butterfly. Her scent enveloped him: spring rain intertwined with wildflowers, mingled with a faint trace of iron from her healing. It was strange how her fragrance seemed to shift and change. It made his heart race.

Kaelith rumbled with approval. *"She fits against us so perfectly. She belongs right... here."*

He ground his teeth and tightened his jaw. *"She belongs to another world... To another man, Spirit!"*

She leaned back slightly against him, warmth spreading between them. "This is much better. I am already feeling warmer." She wiggled to get more comfortable. "See, I don't bite." She said as she yawned.

Mari struggled to relax at first, then finally settled, a small sigh slipping past her lips. Her hair brushed his jaw. This gentle caress was faintly electric against his skin. His chest rose and fell too fast. How did this woman affect him so?

"I've noticed," he said quietly. "But others do." Rufio nonchalantly gestured to the brothers.

Her laugh was sleepy, soft, and devastatingly pure. "Good thing you're here, then."

The Solins' laughter turned to soft, pleased chimes. They had won this battle.

Minutes passed in comfortable silence. The firelight painted her skin in gold, her profile peaceful. Kaelith stirred again.

The entity murmured through him like smoke: *"Her energy is familiar. As if she was meant to be..."*

He swallowed hard, not letting Kaelith finish his thought. *"No."*

"This is not so bad. I thought camping would be way worse." She murmured sleepily, re-adjusting herself. Mari had curled herself into his lap, placing her hands on his abdomen and her head on his chest.

He didn't answer. Couldn't. His body was a furnace of restraint and want.

Kaelith purred in delight. *"Corruption and rot are close, and we must feed."* Rufio could feel his wicked smile. *"She would feed us well, vessel."*

He ground his teeth. *"No."*

Her head on his chest, her hands now resting over his heart, and her cheek taking soft, gentle breaths. She didn't know what that did to him. When her breathing evened, and she fell into deep sleep, he carefully laid her down and stood. The night was thick around them, the fire's glow flickering across her peaceful face.

Rufio checked, ensuring Mari's breathing remained slow and even. He whispered, "Sleep, Mari. I need to feed."

Kaelith prowled just beneath his skin, restless. *"She smells of life. Let me... taste..."*

Rufio's fists tightened until his knuckles cracked. *"No. You'll not touch her."*

Mari did not respond; the day's events were heavy, and her mind gave in to the warmth and light of her dreams. The Solins drifted closer, forming a loose halo around her head. She looked almost ethereal, pure softness in a world of jagged edges.

"Watch her," he told Thalos and Brin. The Auralisks' golden eyes gleamed in acknowledgment.

Then he ran.

The night air split around him, hot and dry. He sprinted into the darkness, his body a blur, the world streaking past in silver and shadow. Every step burned through the hunger clawing his insides. His breath came in sharp bursts, his pulse of thunder.

As he stood alone beneath the stars, the scent of her lingered in his memory, and he could still feel the warmth of her body against his. His heart raced, not from fatigue, but from an intense longing that surged within him. Rufio's hunger had transformed; it was no longer just for energy. What he craved was release from this deep hunger. For it wasn't only Kaelith who yearned for the connection of this woman; it was him, too. That realization filled him with a greater fear than any monster he had ever hunted. The Wild within and the man around it wanted the same thing, and that was the most dangerous alignment of all.

# Chapter 10

The first breath of dawn rose cool and damp across the plains. Mist clung to the earth, silver in the early light. The small fire had long burned to ash, but warmth still hummed faintly in the air.

Mari stirred beneath her cloak. The ground beneath her felt softer than she remembered, almost pulsing, and when she blinked her eyes open, she realized why. Tiny green blades of grass had pushed through the dry soil all around her, curling upward in lazy spirals reaching for the warming sky. The tender green glowed faintly in the morning haze, as if the earth had exhaled color overnight. This world was beginning to breathe again. Mari smiled.

Thalos and Brin lay nearby, their massive bodies enjoying the new softness of the ground. Their scales shimmered under the rising suns, casting soft reflections like molten metal. Between them, the wagon and within, the young Fletchers were nestled together near a small fruit tree, and at her feet, the viper; now vibrant, bronze, and jade, coiled in sentry, its jeweled eyes watching the horizon. Its tongue flicked rhythmically, tasting the air, each movement catching the early light like flashes of polished metal.

She stretched and rubbed her eyes. Mari looked down at her feet and smiled faintly. "Good morning, sentinel." She then looked at her larger and tinier companions, "Morning," she whispered, also half to herself.

The Auralisks lifted their heads, gently bobbing in greeting. *"Good morning, little foal,"* floated a whisper of thought through her mind. Their mental voices were warm and soothing, reminiscent of distant thunder muted by a blanket of affection.

Mari blinked in disbelief. "Did... did you just talk to me?"

She rubbed her eyes, as if that might wipe away the confusion. Great, she thought. Just when she was starting to question her sanity, she was now hearing voices, too. Maybe this world had finally pushed her over the edge!

Brin huffed softly, the amusement evident in his mental voice. *"You hear me. That means you're ready for a real conversation."*

Mari chuckled. Now sitting up, fully awake, her legs straight in front of her, gently touching the viper. She realized someone was missing. Where was the leader of this motley crew? Mari instantly grew worried, shifting her legs to sit on her knees for a better look at her surroundings. Dew clung to the tips of the small fresh patches of green grass surrounding her, sparkling in a thousand tiny points. Yet, none of it soothed the sudden tightness in her chest. "Where is he, you guys?" Her voice cracked with panic.

Thalos nudged. *"We do not know little foal."*

Minutes passed in tense silence. Mari searched the landscape for movement. Just as she was going to ask another question to her friends, she caught the scent, acrid and sharp like brimstone, metallic like blood. A tear opened near where they camped, heat emanating from it. Rufio came out of the haze, his stride uneven.

He walked toward them across the open field, the early light cutting around him. His dark hair was tangled and damp, curling at his temples and forehead. His tunic was half-untucked, unlaced, and hung loose, showing a part of his chest and a hint of the burned Sigil. His boots were dusted with ash. He looked dangerous, wild, and yet tired in a way she hadn't seen before. The air around him shimmered faintly, as though whatever he had faced still clung to him like heat off a forge.

Mari rose to her feet and crossed her arms over her chest, unknowingly pushing her cleavage higher and more pronounced.

"Where did you go? When did you go?" There was no reason for her to be angry, but the feeling of abandonment was there, weighing on her like a heavy blanket.

He nodded to Thalos and Brin. They knew, but it was not their place to share that part of this man's story. Rufio warily strode towards the camp, wiping his brow with the back of his sleeve. The closer he strode; Mari could tell his body was shaking.

"I told you what I had to do." He paused by the smoldering remanence of the fire, flexing his hands as if they were sore. "I was ensuring the balance."

"Are you bleeding? You smell like smoke," she said worriedly, stepping closer and taking a long sniff. "And... something else."

On instinct, she tried to put his face in her hands.

He grabbed her wrists before they could make purchase. His gaze penetrated hers, and for a fleeting moment, his eyes blazed with a haunting crimson light before dissolving into the familiar, smoldering black she had learned to read like an open book.

"It's nothing," he murmured, a shadow of something deeper lurking just beneath the surface. "I am a Watcher of the Wild. This obligation leaves its mark, and I must fight to free this world from the corruption and rot that has taken hold."

Rufio realized he was still holding her wrists. They were so small in his grip. Mari stared intensely in return, not trying to escape. His guilt bubbled to his mind's surface, reminding him to let her wrists go gently.

He lifted his gaze, the eerie red halo around his pupils flickering ominously. "Trust me, you don't want to know the price I've paid."

She glared at him; disbelief etched across her face. Her heartbeat thudded hard enough that she felt it in her palms, anger and fear tangling like vines.

"You really think I'm going to buy that? What on earth does that even mean?" Her fists clenched tightly at her sides, trembling with raw anger.

"I'm alive," he countered. "That's enough for now."

Just as she was about to press him for answers, a distant roar reverberated through the valley. The sound rolled over them like an avalanche; deep, echoing, ancient. The air shimmered like heat rising from stone, stirring the Fletcher younglings inside the wagon, their soft, anxious chirps filling the silence.

"Their mother," Rufio murmured.

The area of the plains Rufio had come from rippled again

like pavement on a summer's day. However, there was no heat emanating from her, unlike Rufio's entrance. The few spindly trees still standing bent outward, and the mother Fletcher emerged from a rippling in the air. Mari turned to see the mother of the twin Fletcher younglings, a towering figure emerging from the far ridge. The mother Fletcher moved like a living mountain, fur dark as rolling thunderstorm clouds and eyes the color of honey. Her massive feet sank into the earth, leaving glowing impressions that faded slowly behind her. The air thickened with her power as she approached, a sound between a growl and a hum filling their surroundings. Everything was happening so fast.

Mari's heart pounded. "She's huge."

He turned slowly, backing to the wagon. "Stay beside me."

But Mari didn't… couldn't move. Instinct rooted her to the ground: fear, awe, and something like recognition humming in her bones.

"She's weighing whether you're prey or kin," Rufio said grimly, a shadow of concern clouding his eyes as he stepped back toward the rear door of the wagon. With a flick of his wrist, the lock clicked, and the door creaked open. He freed the younglings from the confines of the wagon.

They squeaked excitedly and dashed toward Mari before she could even kneel. Tiny hands clutched at her pant leather, their claws pressing against her without breaking through. She gently stroked the tops of their heads.

Mari's heart swelled as she felt their warmth and trust, yet a shadow of fear lingered, the awareness of being caught between innocence and danger tightening around her, the lurking threat that Rufio had alluded to.

Rufio froze.

*"Not possible"*, Kaelith whispered from within him. *"No human earns the embrace of these creatures."*

"Mari," Rufio warned. "Let them go."

Mari could feel Rufio's body coil slightly behind her, the faint hum of a spell building in his palms. But the creature's gaze fixed on her instead, not threatened by the others near her younglings. Slowly, the mother moved forward, taking in Mari's scent. The younglings hid behind Mari's legs, peeking around her knees, in a way that all children do when they know they are in trouble.

Rufio hissed, "Don't move."

Mari remained still as the viper slithered from her wrist, gliding up her arm to wrap gracefully around her neck and shoulders like living bronze, its tongue flicking as it prepared to defend.

Again, the action did not waive Fletcher's actions. The mother Fletcher had already halted before them, her gaze fixed intently on Mari; deep, ancient, and profoundly intelligent. The air vibrated, carrying an unspoken question that reached beyond language.

The viper hissed again in warning. The mother, only a few feet away, lowered her head to meet Mari's gaze. Her hot breath brushed Mari's face, the earthy scent of moss and dirt filling her nostrils.

With a sound like thunder collapsing inward, the mother again leaned closer, instinct insisting that Mari should move. Run. Flee. Yet something in that golden stare held her captive. The viper flicked its tongue once more but then relaxed, draping itself gently around Mari's shoulders. Slowly, the mother pressed her forehead against Mari's. Warmth radiated through Mari's skull, trickling down her spine like liquid sunlight.

The touch was warm and grounding, sending a wave of energy; an amalgamation of emotion and love surging through her. The ground beneath them trembled as the grass thickened, vibrant colors spilling outward from their feet like paint upon a canvas.

Rufio stood frozen, his breath caught in his throat as he took in the scene before him. Every muscle in his body felt coiled tight, an instinctive reaction to the overwhelming spectacle that unfolded. His mind was a blank canvas, stripped of every thought except for a profound sense of awe mixed with an undercurrent of fear. Even Kaelith, usually a voice of strength and instinct within him, was silent, perhaps just as captivated by the moment. The air around them felt charged, as if the very world held its breath alongside him.

When the mother lifted her head, she rumbled softly, a sound that vibrated in Mari's chest. Then, turning, she led her younglings toward the edge of the world. Light rippled around them, a veil tearing open. The family stepped through the portal, vanishing in a shimmer of emerald and gold.

Mari exhaled. "That was…"

"Sacred," Rufio finished quietly. "Her trust has marked you. It's… unheard of."

"I didn't do anything," Mari said, still dazed.

"That's what makes it terrifying," he murmured.

Something within her pulsed an echo beneath her skin, warm and steady. She felt lighter yet anchored. Alive in a way she couldn't name.

Rufio turned to her, voice low. "You do realize no human has ever touched a Fletcher and lived?"

Mari smiled faintly. "Then maybe no human has ever asked

nicely."

He almost laughed; almost. He coughed into his hand and said sharply. "We should go. There's a town on the horizon. We'll need rest before we cross the plains fully.

# Chapter 11

By noon, the journey continued, but the atmosphere was still heavy with the echoes of the morning's chaos. The sun hung high, its golden rays casting a warm glow over the landscape, where the Fletcher younglings now were with their mother, a flicker of stability returning to the group. The horizon stretched out like an endless canvas, the pale stone below glinting and shimmering in the sunlight.

Heat danced above the earth, warping the distant views into shimmering illusions that made the plains stretch on endlessly, their beauty both vast and watchful. A vibrant ribbon of resilient green grass trailed in the wagon's wake, defiantly clinging to life amid the muted gray surroundings. Each blade sparkled like emerald jewels, nourished by an invisible pulse thrumming just beneath the surface.

Mari walked beside the wagon, her presence ethereal as the Serathian viper now named "Sera", coiled gently around her arm, the viper's scales glimmering like liquid silver in the dappled light. The air was rich with the aroma of sun-drenched soil, while the soft rustle of wildflowers dancing in the mild breeze created a harmonious blend of sensory pleasures, wrapping the travelers in a landscape at once rugged and stunning.

"Do you ever find it unsettling," she asked, "how quiet it is here? It feels like the world is holding its breath."

"It's not breath," Rufio replied, his voice low and steady. The sound carried weight, like a warning laid carefully atop restraint. He pointed toward the west, where the air shimmered in a deeper hue.

"The next town will be nothing like the first. Drath Hollow's rot lies beyond that horizon. The Watcher's office may keep its gate, but the rest of the town feeds on decay, clinging to what little life remains."

As they approached Drath Hollow, the wide dirt path narrowed into a winding street that seemed to tighten its grip around them. Faces flickered past hard, lined, shadowed by unseen burdens. Buildings leaned inward, their stones mottled with dark streaks where corrupted energy had pooled, as if they were eavesdropping. The air grew thick and oppressive, clinging to their skin, while the ground beneath their feet felt fragile, ready to fracture with the slightest misstep. A noxious blend of sickness and decay wafted from the gutters, where rot pooled like dark oil. Rufio's jaw tightened, and he felt the weight of the oppressive atmosphere closing in, each step deeper into the heart of the town pushing him further into unease.

"This rot acts like a parasite," Mari whispered, her eyes scanning their surroundings. She hugged herself closer, instinctively protecting her heart.

"You're remarkably observant," Rufio acknowledged. "Corruption has seeped deep into the ground. Just… don't touch anything."

Drath Hollow sprawled across the plain like a scar. The first buildings were little more than shacks of blackened timber. Farther in rose brick shops, a smelter, and an inn, whose sign creaked in a wind that smelled of blood and coal. Men and women moved through the streets with hollow eyes. Energy clung to them like a second skin; thin, frayed, and hungry.

The Watcher's office loomed at the town's edge, an imposing structure of dark stone that pulsed with eerie green veins, throbbing softly like a restrained heartbeat in the deepening twilight. Rufio stepped from the creaking wagon, the chill of the evening air nipping at his skin as he made his way toward the stables linked to the Watcher's hall. The distant murmur of the wind whispered ominously, and shadows danced around him, each corner of the gloom a potential threat.

"Stay," he murmured gently to his loyal Auralisks, their feathers glistening in the faint glow. "You're safer here than out there."

He gestured with a flick of his wrist toward the encroaching darkness, the smell of damp earth and the rustle of unseen creatures filling the air as they settled in. The heavy door creaked as he closed it behind him, the sound swallowed by the hush that enveloped the building, a stark contrast to the tension lurking just beyond its walls.

Thalos snorted uneasily; Brin's tail lashed. Their discomfort echoed faintly through Mari's mind, sharp and uneasy. Even the air shimmered wrong, thick with invisible heat. He paid the boy who came running: too thin, too pale, and fixed him with a stare that showed no betrayal.

Rufio pulled up his hood, covering his face, and walked back to Mari. For a moment, she studied him, unease curling low in her stomach. She knew the Auralisks' names. She knew their thoughts. Yet this man: this Watcher, Wildling, protector, remained a mystery wrapped in silence. Trusting him felt dangerous… but stepping away felt worse. He began the short walk, leading her into the building. Rufio paused, signaling Mari to stop by the worn warded doors, then turned to the old, worn desk where an elderly, tattooed, ebony-skinned woman sat.

He nodded in greeting. "Good evening, Watcher Elmyrs. The town still stands."

"Ah, yes, it does. For now," she replied, adjusting her spectacles and offering a grin. "I do what I can to keep the rot contained within the town's walls." She looked at him, her voice gravelly as she chuckled at a joke, only she understood. "Wildling… you still live."

At the mention of that name, Rufio tensed. Mari noticed the subtle shift. The tightening of his shoulders, the way his energy pulled inward like a drawn blade.

"Yes, Watcher Elmyrs. Here is the permission to travel in the plains, along with the mission report." He handed her the parchments; his hood cast a shadow over most of his face.

Watcher Elmyrs studied the documents for a moment before nodding. "Is there anything you need before you walk through death's door?"

Rufio hesitated. Only a fraction of a second, but in that pause, the world tilted.

Behind Watcher Elmyrs' desk, through a narrow archway veined with ancestral sigils, he could feel it, the chamber. The portal. Calm, clean, waiting. The safest crossing he could offer her back to her world.

This had always been the plan.

Bring the witness. Return the younglings. Restore balance. Send the human home before nightfall.

Thalos and Brin had felt it too. Their minds brushed his; quiet, aching certainty. Their little foal would be gone by dusk. No farewell. No confusion. Just absence. That was the way of things, and that thought cut deeper than it should have.

Watcher Elmyrs tilted her head. "Well?" she prompted. "Is there anything else you require before you continue on your way?"

Rufio's jaw tightened. He could already see it. Mari stepping through the portal, light folding around her, her energy slipping cleanly from this broken land. Safe. Alive. Gone. However, that did not seem right to him.

The Wild inside him stirred. Not hunger this time. Approval. Kaelith hummed low and deep in his chest, a vibration of satisfaction that rolled through his bones. *"Yes, vessel. Delay. Keep her. The world bends better when she remains."*

The sound made Rufio's blood run cold. Kaelith did not approve without cost.

"No," Rufio said automatically to Watcher Elmyrs, then stopped.

His gaze flicked, unbidden, toward the archway. Toward the path that would end this before it destroyed him.

And still...

He exhaled slowly. "Not yet."

Watcher Elmyrs' brows rose, just slightly. "Not yet?" she echoed, studying him with a knowing look. "The Hall of Ancestors lies days east. You know the cost of delaying a clean crossing."

"I do," Rufio replied. His voice was steady, but the energy around him coiled tight as wire. "The next portal is there. She will go through that one."

Kaelith's hum deepened. Warm. Encouraging. Possessive.

Rufio felt it like a hand at his back and hated himself for not stepping away.

Watcher Elmyrs leaned back in her chair, eyes narrowing. "You gamble with more than your life, Wildling."

"Yes," he said quietly. And for the first time, he didn't know if the wager was courage… or selfishness. "I know."

Attempting to change the conversation, he said, "We require rooms for the night. Brin and Thalos are already in the stables. My ward needs rest before tomorrow's trek," Rufio replied matter-of-factly.

"Sorry, boy. I only have one room available. You're welcome to it." She pointed toward the hall on her right and squinted at him. "Last door at the end of the hallway. Hmm… Something seems different about you, boy. I can't quite place it." Her expression flickered between suspicion and grandmotherly concern.

Rufio thanked her and bid farewell to the watcher of this forsaken town. As he returned to Mari, frustration and dread clouded his features. Rufio saw no other Watcher or patron in or out of the building. Suspicion gathered around his thoughts like fog.

"The watcher usually has several rooms available," he said, trying to mask his discomfort, "but all are taken. Except for one."

Mari crossed her arms. "Okay, so we can share it."

He blinked. "No."

"Yes," she said firmly. "I'm not sleeping alone in a place that feels like it's watching me breathe or trying to eat me. And I am not sleeping in the stables."

Rufio looked at her intently, picking up on the fear she tried so hard to conceal. Though Mari held her chin high in defiance, her energy flickered like a wounded bird. After a brief moment of contemplation, he nodded slowly and let out a deep sigh.

"Alright," he finally said.

As Rufio stepped out of the Watcher's main hall, Thalos and Brin lingered restlessly in the stables beside the imposing building. Their massive heads lifted in unison, sensing Rufio's mental presence prodding at their tether. The Brothers instinctively reached back, not seeking command but searching for assurance.

Their minds brushed against his, hesitant and subdued, a stark contrast to the certainty that had buoyed them throughout the day. The moment the brothers had anticipated, the quiet severing, the heartbreaking disappearance of their beloved little foal, failed to materialize behind the watcher.

Brin exhaled a low, uncertain huff, a sound that echoed their dread. Thalos stamped his hooves once, the noise resonating in the stillness, then suddenly stalled, ears perked toward the hall as if it held secrets he desperately wanted to hear. A wave of confusion pulsed between them.

Relief then flickered within their hearts as Mari slowly appeared through the door, walking up to Rufio. The brothers were overwhelmed with understanding. With a decision made, a new thread formed in their bond with Rufio, a tether of choice and defiance.

He had chosen to keep Mari in this world a little longer,

a glimmer of hope amid the uncertainty. The Brothers felt that warmth spread within them, blurring the line between disappointment and the fragile joy of another moment shared. But still, the heaviness loomed, for they knew that even the most precious of choices carried with it the weight of impending loss.

Mari felt it without understanding. A sudden heaviness pressed against her chest as the Auralisks' presence curled closer than before, protective in a way that bordered on grieving. She glanced back once, frowning, as if she'd missed a goodbye she couldn't quite remember.

The hallway the pair entered was a thin, straight path, filled with the scent of dust and creaking softly beneath their footsteps. As Rufio opened the room's door, the comforting aroma of old wood and lavender washed over them. Inside, a spacious bed, plump and inviting, demanded attention, while a single chair sat by the window. Soft amber light from a hearth traced long shadows across the walls, making the space feel both safe and intimate.

Mari smiled faintly and remarked, "That looks big enough for both of us." She stepped forward, running her fingers over the thick, plush blankets on the older but comfortable-looking bed. "Oh, these are so soft!" she sighed, feeling the plush on her palm.

"I'll take the floor," he said. This was not a situation he wanted to be in. Rufio's skin prickled with heat at the thoughts running through his imagination.

She shook her head. "You can take half the bed. I've slept in worse situations. Ask me about camping with my cousins when you are bored." Her tone was light and mirthful.

He glanced at her, over one shoulder, mouth twitching. "I

doubt that."

She pointed toward the washroom. "You're welcome to test the theory another night. Not tonight."

He looked like he might argue, but exhaustion won. The weight of restraint pressed heavily on his chest. He was in control.

Mari closed the bathroom door behind her. This was less a room than an enclosed space separated by only thin muslin. Rufio exhaled hard. He could hear the water splashing and the fabric rustling. Rufio sat on the edge of the bed, eyes closed, trying not to think about the sound of water and the shadows playing against the wall. Kaelith stirred immediately, a pulse of heat curling through his chest.

*"She is the river flowing with energy. With Life,"* the Wild whispered reverently.

*"Be silent,"* he growled in his thoughts.

When she emerged, the Solins had changed her clothing again. Her Solin-made nightgown shimmered faintly, sleeves slipping off her shoulders, silken, luminous, every curve traced in moonlight. The energy clung to her like breath against skin: soft, warm, alive. Her hair hung loose, darker where it was damp. She wore the Solins like a crown of light while the viper coiled around her bicep.

Rufio's breath caught. He forced himself to look away, but not fast enough. Heat crawled up the back of his neck. "Sleep, Mari."

"What? You're not?" she asked, crossing to the bed.

"Someone needs to keep watch. To keep you safe." Rufio retorted, walking to the chair.

She climbed beneath the blanket, exhaustion blunting her worry. "Why do I have to be kept safe, night in black armor?

You never stop defending, do you?" Her eyebrow rose in sarcastic defiance.

"No." He stated flatly as he sat down, crossing his arms over his broad chest.

She smiled drowsily. "Then I'll stop for both of us. We are safe, right? Please try to get some sleep."

But safety was a lie.

Her breathing steadied, and silence filled the room. Rufio sat on the edge of the chair, cloak still around him. The light from the hearth gilded her skin; every rise of her chest was a test of his resolve. Each breath pulled at him like a tide.

Kaelith purred. *"You hunger; the balance would be perfect, vessel."*

He pressed his fist to his sternum. *"Not her."*

The Wild laughed softly inside his skull. *"You already dream of her scent."*

He stood, pacing. The fire popped, sending sparks across the floor. His reflection in the window looked feral. His eyes were almost entirely red, and his hot breath fogged the glass.

Kaelith whispered. *"She calls us. I feel it."*

He squeezed his eyes shut. *"No."*

Then, silence followed by predatory movement.

When Rufio opened his eyes, he wasn't in control. The entity, Kaelith, had surfaced smoothly and deadly. His body moved with predatory grace. The world sharpened: color, scent, heartbeat. Mari's scent was everywhere, intoxicating.

He loomed over her sleeping body, eyes glowing crimson. "Mo Stor," the Wild serenated. An oath older than time. *My heart.*

Mari stirred in her sleep. She heard his oath, and her lashes began to flutter.

"Rufio?" she mumbled in her dreaming state.

Kaelith purred, his voice low and rough. "Sleep. Stay in bed."

She blinked, sitting up slowly, her hair a spill of silver shadow. The molten red of his gaze froze her. "What's happening to you?" Mari stated in a worried tone, clutching the blanket to her heart.

He staggered back, clawing at control. Kaelith resisted, snarling. Rufio dragged a hand through his hair, breathing harshly. Confusion shot through Mari. That was not Rufio's voice.

"It's me," he rasped. "Not him. Not anymore. Just stay… away from me… for now."

She rose out of bed anyway, heart pounding, bare feet whispering against the floorboards. When her fingers brushed his arm, the air crackled with heat and power surging between them. "What's going on with you?"

He flinched back from her touch. "Nothing you can fix," he rasped, breathing hard, sweat on his brow. He stepped back until his shoulders hit the wall. "Don't." His voice was desperate.

He tried to retreat, but she followed, pressing her hands against his chest. Her palms were hot, her heartbeat beginning to match his.

"Talk to me!" Her eyes searched his. She was confidently unafraid and looked for the man she had only known for such a short time.

"Don't…" he warned, voice breaking. There was nowhere to go. Nowhere to run this time.

"Then tell me!" She spoke. "Tell me what you are, what is going on with you!" Mari stepped closer, her body brushing against his. The heat between them was unbearable. His hands went to her hips before he could stop himself. He needed her not to be this close. But oh… he did want to be closer.

Rufio looked at her, every word a battle. "Something that shouldn't be awake. That should not have happened. You should not be this close!" Rufio's back was against the window, the gentle fire from the hearth silhouetted her body in light and shadow. His control has become undone, hunger rapidly gaining momentum.

Her heartbeat filled the space between them. "Too late. I want answers and to help," she said quietly.

The words cut straight through him. Mari was oblivious to who she was and what she was doing to this world and to him. She was pure in her actions.

He exhaled sharply, leaning his forehead against hers, heartbeat thundering against her chest; the power within her stirred, light against his shadow. For a fleeting moment, they were one pulse, one breath.

He groaned softly with want, with need, forced himself to drag air into his lungs, and looked into Mari's eyes. Again, onyx and molten turned to match her gaze. She smiled. In a single, gentle movement, he lifted her as though she weighed nothing in his arms and crossed the room in three strides, setting her gently back on the bed.

He turned away, taking the chair. The chair scraped as he dragged it to the door and sat facing the room, forcing distance between them. "Sleep," he ordered. "I'll guard."

After a long moment, she lay down again. He kept his eyes on the dying fire until dawn pried its way through the glass. He didn't move. He couldn't.

When dawn broke, the world was gray and quiet. He

was still sitting, motionless. The fire was spent, and the room had a slight chill; outside, carts already rattled over the cobblestones.

Mari stretched, then rubbed her eyes. "You didn't sleep?"

"No." He stated in a raspy voice.

She yawned and hissed with a sharp pain in her wrist. "Ow."

Her left wrist burned faintly. She looked down. The mark had appeared overnight in her sleep. The mark was faint and raised. It overlaid where the cuff had rubbed her wrist raw earlier. The lines were similar to Rufio's swirling molten-metal band. She remembered how his band was unique, a perfect fit for his personality.

Rufio froze when he saw it. Slowly, he pulled back his sleeve, not letting her see his right arm. His own band, once solid copper, had begun to split down the middle, the same pattern mirrored within. He said nothing. He rose, pulling his hood over his head, hiding the turmoil in his face. "We need to move. The plains are changing again."

Outside, the suns clawed their way through a sickly morning sky, and the world around them waited: half dying, half reborn, caught between ruin and renewal.

Rufio gathered the Auralisks along with additional rations and supplies. Together, the four of them stepped into the unknown. The faint thread of their shared mark shimmered with each heartbeat. Brin probed Rufio's mind, seeking answers, but found only an impenetrable fortress. He turned to Mari next, hoping for clarity. Concern and confusion washed over him.

The pair remained silent, but within that silence, Rufio understood: his mission had changed. Mari was no longer just a witness; she was becoming his anchor. For someone like him, who had been consigned to the Wild entity, Kaelith, such a connection was unheard of. This might very well be the end for him.

Far to the east, beyond the dying plains, the Hall of Ancestors awaited their Wildling warrior and the primordial spirit within him.

Buried beneath stone older than the towns themselves, conduits of dormant energy thrummed awake; slow, deliberate, unmistakable.  Sigils carved by hand long turned to dust warmed, responding to a presence that should not yet exist.

The land remembered its oaths.  And it remembered its debts.  Kaelith felt the unsettling shift first.  A ripple of anticipation slid through the Wild spirit, sharp and pleased. The Hall would not judge gently. It never had.

Rufio did not feel it yet, but the tether had already tightened. The choice he had made echoed forward through energy, blood, and bone, drawing all paths toward that ancient place where names were weighed, bonds revealed, and truths torn open.

The Hall of Ancestors waited.

# Chapter 12

The plains stretched endlessly, a tapestry of dry ochre and silvery grass rolling gently beneath an impossibly vast sky. On the horizon, the land shimmered like moving glass, blurring the line between earth and sky. With each breath, Mari inhaled dust mingled with a subtle electric charge, a promise of rain that never quite arrived, combined with the faint sweetness of new growth and roots hidden deep below.

As the group pressed onward, both the Auralisks and Rufio sensed a transformation in the air and land. The unmistakable freshness of new grass was a rare and precious scent that evoked memories of a world before the rot. For the people of this realm, it served as a poignant reminder of what had been lost, and what might yet be reclaimed. The wind carried whispers of renewal, and for a fleeting moment, hope flickered in the hearts of those walking the wild, open plain.

The wagon was now a distant memory, left behind in

Drath Hollow. Thalos and Brin walked beside Mari, their powerful heads swaying as they maintained an unspoken vigil. With each step she took, tiny curls of green unfurled in her wake. She tried to ignore the change, but the harder she concentrated on it, the more she felt a hum beneath her skin, as if the earth itself acknowledged her presence.

The Auralisks lingered closer than necessary, not out of fear but in anticipation. The ending they had foreseen had yet to unfold. Their little foal should have passed through the portal by nightfall. She should have been gone.

Mari exhaled slowly, then smiled to herself. The quiet of their traveling party pressed in too hard, the kind that made memories surface whether you invited them or not.

"You know," she said out loud, adjusting her pack, "this walk reminds me of when my kids were little. The quiet right before something chaotic occurred."

Thalos angled his massive head towards her. *"Chaotic... like battle?"*

She laughed. "More like joy and innocence, honestly, that can be more dangerous."

Brin's curiosity brushed her mind. *"Explain."*

"Well," Mari said, warming to the memory, "once, during a rainy weekend, my children, being young at the time, decided they were bored. They were very dramatic about it. So, we built a pillow fort."

Thalos stopped walking. *"A... fort?"*

"Yes. A formidable structure," Mari confirmed solemnly. "We dragged every pillow, blanket, couch cushion, and movable chair into the living room. Chairs became towers. The couch was the main gate."

Brin pulsed confusion. *"Why were the soft objects made into walls?"*

"For protection," she said, straight-faced. "Obviously."

The Auralisks radiated interest.

"Oh, it was epic," Mari continued. "We strung lights through it, the twinkly kind. My daughter played music on my phone and stocked it with cookies. Chocolate chip. You know… Emergency rations."

Thalos rumbled with approval. *"Food inside the fort is wise."*

"Exactly," she said. "We lay inside it for hours, whispering stories, laughing, pretending monsters lived outside. It felt like the safest place in the world."

Her voice softened. "They were so little. They thought I could fix anything."

Brin's presence warmed. *"You created shelter with softness,"* he said reverently. *"That is a powerful thing."*

Mari swallowed, blinking against the sudden sting behind her eyes. "Yeah. It really is."

She took another step, then added lightly, "And just so you know… Pillow forts are temporary, but the cookie crumbs seem to last forever."

The Auralisks released a shared, amused huff.

Her smile lingered as the memory shifted, reshaping itself into something older. Sharper. More reckless.

"And before that," she said, glancing ahead at Rufio's back, "there was my husband. I mean… the first time I met Rufus."

Rufio tensed at the name, but no one seemed to notice. Thalos and Brin were interested. Mari didn't wait for permission.

"I was volunteering at a university fundraiser: putting together the tables, banners, donation boxes, the whole chaos. I went outside to grab more supplies and looked up…"

She laughed softly at herself. "…and there was this young, attractive man climbing in one of the tallest trees on campus."

Brin froze mid-step. *"Why was he in the tree?"*

"I still don't know," Mari admitted. "He looked like he was chasing something. Or maybe losing something. Completely ridiculous."

Thalos hummed. *"Was he hunting?"*

"No… I don't think he was. I never saw anything else in the tree!" Mari laughed with a snort. "Personally, I think he was losing a fight with gravity." She grinned. "When Rufus started climbing down, it looked like his foot slipped off a branch and nearly fell. For a heartbeat, I thought he was done for, but then he caught himself. Agile. Strong. Like his body knew what to do before his brain did."

Her voice softened. "That's when I was smitten."

She paused, smiling at the memory. "He landed like it was nothing. Gave me this sheepish grin. And when he spoke…" Mari took in a breath and sighed, "Oh… the accent. I'd never heard anything like it. Just enough to make every word feel like an invitation."

Brin's mind sparkled. *"You chose him immediately."*

"I did," she said quietly. "We talked all day. Missed our assignments. Missed everything. By sunset, we were inseparable."

She exhaled. "That was my Rufus."

Ahead of her, Rufio did not turn. Did not react. His stride remained steady, his silence absolute, heavier now, sharper, like something drawn tight inside him. As Rufio stepped forward, his hood casting a shadow over his face, his shoulders taut with barely restrained energy.

Mari shrugged, forcing lightness back into her tone. "Not

everyone appreciates a good tree disaster."

But something in her chest ached anyway.

Since they had left town, his silence had evolved into a heavy, oppressive weight, far from the serene stillness of contemplation; it was the stifling quiet of a storm brewing within him, his thoughts trapped like a caged beast, yearning to escape.

Beneath his ribs, a choice still seared. The portal behind Watcher Elmyrs and the corridor that lay beyond it should have brought a swift, clean resolution. Yet Kaelith's low hum of approval lingered, frightening him more than any act of resistance ever could.

She adjusted her pack again before breaking the silence. "You've been unusually quiet. Lost in thought, or are you just trying to create some dramatic tension?"

He didn't turn to face her, but his voice cut through the stillness. "You talk enough for both of us."

She feigned offense, placing a hand over her heart. "Me? Never! I merely enjoy asking questions and telling fun stories. It's in my nature!"

"You're… something else," he muttered.

The Auralisks chuffed with amusement in her mind. *"You soften him, little foal!"* Brin chimed in.

"I do not!" Mari whispered back, trying to sound indignant.

*"Oh, but you do,"* Thalos rumbled, his mental tone slow and warm. *"He actually listens to you. He never listens to anyone."*

She shook her head, glancing at Rufio's back, and scoffed. "If you think he's really listening to me, I'd say it's time for a vision check!"

Brin's amusement carried something heavier beneath it; relief edged with unease. Thalos, quieter now, kept his gaze eastward… toward a road not taken.

The day stretched long. By twilight, shadows lengthened, and the gentle breeze changed. The scent of ash and ozone prickled her senses, and she shivered. But the grass around her feet brightened, glowing faintly with bioluminescent green. Far beyond the plains, stones older than bone pulsed once, a warning beat. The Hall of Ancestors did not forget when paths were diverted.

When Rufio stopped, they made camp beneath a gnarled tree that had somehow survived the "drought of centuries" and the rot that had spread across the land. He sparked a flame with his hands, gold this time, not blue. The Solins danced through the air, their chiming laughter flickering like fireflies.

Mari settled beside the fire. "I don't think I will ever get used to them," she murmured, watching the Solins dart in and out of her hair. "They are resilient, mischievous, and sweet."

"They're drawn to life," Rufio said quietly. "They've never had this much of it to feed on."

"Do you mean me?" she prodded with curiosity.

His gaze lifted briefly, the firelight reflecting red in his eyes. "You know I do."

The silence between them thickened. The Auralisks bedded down near the edge of the camp, and Mari lay back, staring at the stars. The constellations here were strange, swirling clusters instead of fixed points, as if the sky itself were alive and shifting.

Her thoughts wandered restlessly, pulling her back to her children at home and the absence of her husband Rufus, whose whereabouts were a mystery. She longed for the warmth of their bed, now cold and empty without him, and the way his heart used to beat in tandem with hers. But that familiar rhythm had faded long ago, lost somewhere in the shadows after they celebrated 15 years of marriage, when everything began to unravel, dissolving like a cherished dream at dawn. The wild pulse she felt now coursed through her veins, a vibrant reminder of something entirely new, yet it left her aching for what once was.

Mari stirred awake, the sound of footsteps pulling her from the depths of sleep. Rufio was missing from the fire's glow, and a frown creased her brow. The night buzzed with unsettling energy, whispers dancing in the air. The Solins shimmered faintly, drifting like errant stars in pursuit of something lurking in the shadows. A tightness settled in her chest. Driven by curiosity, she followed.

The plain stretched endlessly, a silver expanse under the moon's watchful eye. There, half-shadow, half-flame, was Rufio, or rather, Kaelith. His form glowed with an other-worldly light, movements starkly fluid and wild. Her heart raced. They were far from camp, far from help.

"Rufio?" she called softly, her voice barely a whisper.

He turned toward her, molten-red eyes locking onto hers, and a growl of hunger reverberated through the air. "Mari," he rasped, the voice a sultry echo of both familiarity and danger. "What are you doing here? I am filled with hunger, A Rúnsearc. You should leave." Energy swirled around him, crackling with intensity.

A pulse of instinct urged her to flee, but instead, she smiled, feigning bravery. "You keep saying that. But who exactly are you?" Tilting her head, she scrutinized him, an eagerness for understanding overriding her fear.

Kaelith prowled closer, movements like liquid fire. "I am

Kaelith, the Primordial entity of hunger. This isn't safe for you."

"Neither was playing with that viper, but here I am." She crossed her arms defiantly, undeterred. The Solins sensed her conviction, fluttering around her as she tilted her chin upwards. "Please… change my clothes for running or fighting."

The Solins heeded her silent call, and a gentle glow enveloped her. In an instant, the illumination faded, revealing her in a dark, form-fitting tunic that blended seamlessly with the night. A leather vest hugged her waist, offering both protection and allure, while her pants morphed into a sturdy yet silent fabric that whispered against her movements. Her boots transformed for agility, ready for whatever lay ahead.

Even in the deep darkness, Kaelith's fiery gaze drank in her transformation, a hint of intrigue sparking in those molten depths as he took a few steps back. "You shouldn't follow demons into the night."

"Maybe I'm not meant to follow at all," she shot back, adrenaline igniting her nerves. "Perhaps I'm here to wear them down or lead them out." Foolish, reckless, perhaps, but there was an undeniable thrill in facing the unknown. Deep down, she knew Rufio wouldn't harm her, but this entity that shared his body? That was an entirely different gamble.

For a heavy heartbeat, tension crackled in the air between them. Kaelith suddenly stripped off his tunic, discarding it to the ground with a flourish. The Sigil illuminated his chest, a fiery symbol of power, and then he lunged forward, all predatory grace and raw intent.

"Let's dance, then," she breathed, heart racing as she braced herself for the thrill of the challenge. Instinctively, Mari darted away, laughing as a challenge, the sound ringing like a bell across the plains. The Solins joined her, swirling around them in ribbons of pink and gold.

The Solins flickered like ethereal fireflies, illuminating the path as she sprinted through the scattered trees, intertwining the landscape. Each stride was a dance through a vibrant twilight, and the air thrummed with energy. She narrowly dodged a swipe from his hand, dropping to the ground and rolling before springing back up, heart pounding like a drum. The chase was primal, a wild symphony of laughter and breath, weaving through fields of radiant grass that glowed beneath her feet.

Kaelith's eyes, twin suns blazing in the deepening night, gleamed with a predatory delight as he pursued her, each echo of her laughter drawing him closer. A smile curled on his lips; the thrill of the hunt electrified his senses. *What would he do when he caught her?* The thought pulsed through him. Usually, his hunger consumed everything in its path, but tonight, her vibrant energy surrounded him like a cool mist, dousing the fire that raged within.

Mari's pulse quickened as she darted behind a towering tree, the bark rough and grinding against her back. Wielding a fierce determination, Kaelith cut her off, enveloping her in a fierce bear hug. His heat surrounded her, pulling her close, and she found her face pressed against his bare chest, feeling the steady thrum of his heartbeat against her cheek. His breath was heavy with exertion, yet he held her with an intensity that was both powerful and strangely gentle. She squirmed, not in fear, but in a dance of resistance and exhilaration; the rhythm of his heart quickened hers.

Breathless from the chase, they paused, suspended between adrenaline and something deeper, alive in the glow of their surroundings. Energy surged from Mari's core, pulsing between them, intoxicating and raw. Her instinct to help and heal surged forth, a deep-rooted compulsion that urged her to reach out to those in need, even in the heart of chaos. As her energy focused on him, her body began to glow softly, a warm beacon against the night.

In that electrifying moment, the entity froze, its menacing posture caught in a fleeting uncertainty. The Solins drew closer, their light undulating in swirling colors that transformed the night into a mesmerizing canvas, banishing the shadows of fear. Mari felt the weight of her purpose, a guiding force whispering that redemption was still possible amidst the chaos.

Kaelith paused, momentarily startled by the soothing warmth radiating from her. As he began to release her, Mari lifted a trembling hand to rest against his chest, her touch igniting an energy in the air between them. "You don't have to fight it, Kaelith. I feed hunger, Wild One." The power that flowed from her was not just her own. It surged from the depths of the earth, the vast sky above, and the chambers of her heart.

His breath hitched, and for the first time, she noticed the ferocity in his eyes soften, the molten red dimming to glowing embers. "You don't understand what I am… what 'we' are." He knelt, his hands pressing into the earth in a gesture of reverence and yearning.

"I don't have to," she replied, her voice a soothing melody against the night. "I see you now. Kaelith of the Wild, who you are, and how you are woven into everything around us." Tears glistened in her eyes, and for the first time in ages, she felt she was precisely where she needed to be.

Something within him cracked open. The Wild exhaled, the air shimmering with vibrant release. Light surged from where he knelt, tendrils of green and gold weaving through the soil, breathing life into the barren plains that surrounded them.

Concerned, Mari cautiously stepped forward, closing the distance until they were almost one. He leaned his forehead against her knees, his breath ragged with the weight of his transformation. When he looked up, it was Rufio's eyes she encountered, dark, with the faintest rim of red softened by disbelief and wonder.

"What did you do?" he whispered, awe tinging each syllable.

She smiled wearily, her voice barely a whisper. "I fed the part of you that only knows how to starve."

The Solins settled around them, their glow dimming to gentle embers, the night enveloping them in a newfound peace. Rufio reached up, the warmth of his fingers brushing a loose strand of hair from her face.

"You're dangerous," he murmured.

"And so are you," she replied, a playful challenge in her tone.

He let out a sound that was half laughter, half sigh. "Then we deserve each other's company."

Mari sat beside him as dawn bloomed on the horizon, the delicate light spilling over the plains like a soft embrace. Every patch of earth they had traversed now shimmered with vibrant life, flowers bursting into color, the gassy plains now soft and green, an enchanting renewal awakening the world.

The day began to rise, and with it, so did they, two souls intertwined in a dance of fate, igniting the energy of existence anew. Somewhere ahead, something began its search, feeling the renewal of life and energy, changing the landscape of this world and wanting it for itself.

# Chapter 13

The day stretched on just as the plains, vast and endless, undulating in waves of ochre and faded green.  By late afternoon, the landscape softened from gold to rust. Mari felt the landscape getting warmer by the minute. Heat shimmered above the cracked earth, distorting the horizon into mirages. The air pressed against skin like a warm palm, carrying dust, sunbaked clay, and the faint metallic bite of old ruin. Their pace was slow, and to hasten their journey, Thalos and Brin offered their two-legged companions a chance to ride. Mari could hardly contain her excitement. She tried to look composed. Tried and failed, her grin breaking through like sunrise.

The green ribbon of life trailing behind them grew wider, stubborn, and wild, shimmering like a living path through desolation. It didn't just follow; it insisted, as if the land were remembering how to reach for her. To the untrained eye, it might seem empty and abandoned by all. But Rufio could sense the heartbeat buried deep beneath the soil. He felt it like a low drum beneath bone, a pulse that answered her without permission. When the first hint of smoke appeared on the horizon, he spotted a small valley cradled in the land's bones. Rufio slowed his hand, raising it to shield his eyes. He knew every curve of this horizon, every ridge and hollow. The wind carried the scent of clay, sage, and water. Home. The word landed inside him like a weight and a wound all at once.

Mari leaned forward on Brin's back, her hair tousled from the long ride, and shaded her eyes with her hand. "Is that…?" Her excitement was palpable. "Is that a village?"

He nodded once. "Aedalon. My home. At least my first," he said quietly. "It is still warded and standing."

The name came out softer than he intended, reverent and heavy. It was the only word in any language that still meant peace to him. The Wild stirred faintly in his chest, Kaelith's voice, dark and ancient, curling through his thoughts. *"You anchored this place well, Wildling,"* the entity murmured. *"The earth remembers your blood."*

Rufio ignored the whisper that coiled in the depths of his mind. The valley did not need Kaelith's praise; it thrived on its own merit. Yet, a nagging hum of satisfaction lingered, feeling almost too possessive, and Rufio despised the fact that he recognized it.

The small village of Aedalon nestled in a shallow valley, cradled between two gentle hills. A cluster of stone cottages with thatched roofs emerged, their gardens bursting with vibrant colors: pinks, yellows, and deep purples spilling over like a painter's palette. A thin silver stream wound its way through the heart of the village, its gentle gurgle harmonizing with the laughter of children carried on the breeze. It wasn't loud, not like Veyor, but rather a clean, bright sound that made the air feel fresh and newly made.

Mari's expression softened, her eyes wide as she took in the scene. "It's so beautiful," she whispered in awe. "I didn't think a place like this could still exist in this world." Her voice trembled slightly, revealing her wonder and the lingering ghosts of doubt.

Rufio guided Thalos gently to the edge of the ward, his posture tense as he scanned the valley's boundaries. "It exists because it's protected," he replied, his voice steady but low, betraying an undercurrent of pride.

"By you?" Mari asked, her curiosity shimmering in her gaze.

His gaze remained fixed ahead as he considered his response. "By oath," he said finally, the word heavy with meaning. It was not a boast. It was like an heirloom chain he wore willingly, the only bond that felt like freedom rather than imprisonment.

As the Auralisks crossed the small wooden bridge into Aedalon, Mari felt an immediate shift in the air. The warmth deepened, the colors brightened, and she could feel a faint hum of vibrant energy against her skin. "It feels alive," she said, glancing at Rufio, her excitement and disbelief mingling in her heart.

Rufio lowered his hood. "It is," he replied, his voice reverent. "Warded land. My doing." A flicker of pride lit his eyes, but beneath it lay the weight of responsibility. "No rot touches here."

The wards hummed in recognition, brushing against his skin like a warm welcome home. The Auralisks relaxed, their large forms settling as Brin's tail flicked lazily in response to the familiar environment. From the fields, villagers began to lift their heads, their faces lighting up with recognition. They were broad-shouldered men and sun-browned women, hardened by the labor of love for their land.

Rufio felt the pulse of warmth from the gathering people, a collective heartbeat thrumming in the air. As the group strode forward, the villagers bowed their heads in quiet respect, their trust in him evident.

"Welcome back, Rufio," one of the women called out, her voice clear and welcoming.

"Good to see you, Elara," Rufio replied, a hint of a smile breaking through his usual stoicism. "I see the fields are flourishing."

"They always do under your watch," Elara responded, her eyes shining with gratitude. There was an unspoken bond between them, strength woven into the fabric of their shared history.

Mari observed the interactions, feeling a warmth blossom in her chest. She realized that this was more than just a village; it was a living tapestry of care, resilience, and community. It was a place where hope truly thrived under the protective embrace of Rufio's oath.

"Guardian Rufio!" a boy shouted, his small feet slapping against the dirt as he ran beside them. "You came back!"

Rufio couldn't stop the flicker of a smile that tugged at his mouth. "You've grown, Eno."

"Ma says if I want to be like you… I have to!" The boy said, laughing, as he darted toward the stream, running to his friends, and pointed in their direction.

Mari chuckled softly. "Seems you're something of a legend."

"Protector," he corrected quietly. "That's different."

And yet the way the villagers looked at him like he was both story and shield made Mari's chest tighten with something tender she didn't want to name.

They passed through the main square, where the scent of baking bread mingled with flowers from the market stalls. Villagers waved, some touching their hearts in salute. A few older men dipped their heads respectfully. The warmth of their welcome pressed against the cold places inside him, and for a moment, it was almost too much to bear. It hit him how long it had been since he'd stood somewhere without bracing for betrayal or battle.

"Wildling," one of the elders said, voice rough with age but filled with reverence. "You've returned."

Rufio inclined his head as Thalos stopped in front of the man. "The Watchers called. I answered."

The elder smiled faintly. His face held deep lines of age and memories. He answered with a dissatisfied tone. "They always do."

The Auralisks lowered their heads, allowing curious children to touch their scaled hides and majestic horns. Laughter broke out as Thalos flicked his tongue at one boy, who squealed and ran behind Brin's leg. The beasts' mental hums were pure contentment, like the low vibration of an instrument long untuned, finally finding its note. Mari felt their pride like warmth in her ribs; pride in home, pride in being seen, pride in bringing their little foal into a place that didn't want to eat her.

Mari's heart swelled at the sight. The heightened view on the back of Brin showed so much of a world straight out of a fairytale. This was a place untouched by greed or corruption, a minor miracle clinging to the edges of ruin. Rufio led the brothers and her through the narrow streets. The smell of bread, smoke, and herbs filled the air. As the Auralisks sauntered lazily, his gaze softened in a way she hadn't seen before. He looked less like a weapon here, more like a man who had once been a boy.

"You grew up here?" she asked inquisitively.

He nodded. For the first time, Rufio knew he needed to explain the importance of this place. He needed to tell her part of his story. One, he has said to no one else outside of this village. One he had never meant to share, because speaking it out loud made it real, and real things could be taken. "I was orphaned before I could remember my parents. The village took me in. Fed me, taught me to read the old ways." He paused by a stone wall where ivy still grew. "When I was fifteen, the rot came for the first time. I thought… maybe if I became a soldier, I could stop it."

"You wanted to protect them," she said quietly.

Before he could say more, they reached one of his favorite places. From the bakery came a woman with flour on her apron and laughter in her eyes. "Rufio!" she cried, wiping her hands on her apron. "The wards stirred before dawn. I knew it was you."

"Rhea." He inclined his head. "Still keeping everyone alive and fed, I see."

"Someone has to while you're off saving the rest of us from nightmares." Rhea laughed. "You always return thinner and more haunted, child. I should bake a loaf big enough to chase the ghosts away."

He allowed himself a small smile. "You try every time." Thalos shifted underneath him, growing impatient.

Rhea wagged a finger at him. "And one day I'll succeed." She gave Mari a long look. "And who's this beautiful Bean Feasa,

Rufio?" The woman's eyes sparkled with mirth.

Before he could answer, Mari said quickly, "Mari… Just Mari."

Rhea's gaze softened, her tone dipping into something thoughtful. "You hum such a beautiful song, Mari. The land listens when you sing. It hasn't done that in a long while."

Mari blinked. "I'm sorry…I am a what? I hum?" She scrunched her nose in confusion.

"She's a wise poet," Rufio said quickly, changing the subject. Rufio stepped forward, his tone shifting. "Mari is with the Auralisks and me. We will only be here for a short while before we have to travel to the Hall of Ancients. I wanted to see you first before I went to the cottage."

Mari shot him a look at "poet," half amusement, half suspicion; like she was filing it away for later.

Rhea smiled knowingly. "So, it seems." She turned to go back into the bakery, looking over her shoulder, "Your cottage is still standing, Guardian. My daughters have seen to it."

Mari gave him a sidelong grin as they continued toward the edge of the village. "You have a cottage?"

He said nothing and ignored the question. However, his lips curved faintly. With that, Thalos started toward the road leading out of the square. Rufio stated to Brin and Mari, "Come."

They rode in silence until the cottages gave way to open fields. Wind rustled through the grass. The stream followed beside them, its voice constant, patient. The lane narrowed as they left the town behind, giving way to tall grass and wildflowers. Birds darted between the branches of a small grove. When the cottage came into view, Mari's breath caught.

The structure was humble: stone, timber, surrounded by

a meadow and the hint of a small lake in the background, alive. Ivy covered the roof, and the garden bloomed wildly, filled with herbs and blossoms that shouldn't have survived the blight outside Aedalon's borders. The air here smelled of cedar and warm soil. It smelled like hands that worked, not hands that took.

Rufio dismounted Thalos and helped Mari off Brin. His hands secured her waist as she braced against him to once again touch the land. Once, he was unwilling to tempt fate, to touch what was not his. Now he held on slightly longer, in longing and reverence. The pause was slight, barely a breath, but Mari felt it anyway, the way his grip lingered like a question he refused to ask. Rufio walked up the dirt path to his home and opened the door. Dust motes swirled in the sunlight filtering through the window. A book lay open on the table, its pages yellowed. The hearth still held the faintest scent of lavender and thyme.

Mari stepped inside, eyes wide. "It's… charming." She felt as if she had fallen into one of her favorite books.

"It's mine," he said quietly. "And it will stand as long as I do." Everything was simple: a table, two chairs, shelves filled with worn books, a fireplace against the opposite wall, and a simple bed in the corner.

Her gaze shifted to the mantle, where a small wooden carving rested, an older woman with kind eyes and strong hands. "She's beautiful."

"Her name was Catrin, and she was one of the villagers who found me when I was an infant," Rufio said, his voice low, reverent, and sad. "Wrapped in cloth marked with sigils no one could read. She took me in. Fed me. Taught me to fight and to think before I struck." He smiled faintly, remembering.

"She called me *her Aodhán.* It roughly means Little Fire. I called her *mother.*"

Mari's throat tightened. "What happened to her?"

"She grew old. I didn't. By the end of her life, I had chosen a sacred path." He set the carving down gently. "Her bloodline still lives here. They tend this place when I'm gone."

Silence enveloped the room, interrupted only by the soft, gentle rustling of the wind flowing through the open window. Rufio gazed out the window, lost in memories spanning years, tracing them back to the moment his extraordinary journey began.

# Chapter 14

He was just twelve years old when Rufio first discovered he could command energy itself. The village had been struggling against a relentless rot that spread along the stream, causing the fish to float lifelessly on the water's surface and the crops to wither away overnight. While many villagers turned to prayer in desperation, Catrin, his determined mother, knelt in the soil, her hands deeply submerged in the earth as she sang gentle lullabies to the seeds. She had often told Rufio that the world would respond if one spoke to it with kindness and intent.

The memory hit him with sensory sharpness; the smell of wet earth, the ache in his knees from kneeling too long, the way fear had tasted like pennies on his tongue.

Later that night, when illness overtook Catrin, urgency surged within Rufio. He dashed to the edge of the stream, determination filling his heart, and commanded the water to thrive. To his astonishment, it responded to him, flowing with swift, bright energy, eager to be guided by his will.

The following morning dawned with a miraculous transformation: the rot that had leeched life from the land had vanished, and the water shimmered with newfound clarity under the sun. However, within a fortnight, the council of elders arrived to witness the change, though they perceived far more than mere salvation. They sensed the pulse of potential that would irrevocably alter Rufio's existence and shift the way everyone around viewed him.

At just fifteen, Rufio's ambitious dreams of becoming a scholar, a teacher, or a caretaker for the land were shattered. Instead, he found himself destined for the capital, compelled by the spreading rot that threatened nearby villages. From the hilltop overlooking his home, he gazed in horror at what the Watchers ominously referred to as 'death's door,' putrid decay encroaching upon the mountains and the Seat of the Ancients. Even now, thinking of it made his wrist ache beneath the band, as the memory lived in the metal.

"I wanted to help," he whispered, his voice breaking with resolve. "I wanted to heal the land, not fight against it."

But fight he did, enlisting to become a soldier against insidious corruption. Months of grueling training in the hall of warriors honed his command of energy and life, drawing him deeper into a world he had barely understood. He was soon summoned before the High Council of the Ancestors. The phrase alone tightened something in his chest; the Hall of Ancestors, a place where choices became chains.

As he stood before them, the ancient sigil of the Wild was etched into the stone floor beneath his feet, a stark reminder of his calling. The council's voices echoed like distant thunder, their faces shadowed yet commanding. "The balance of life and death hangs by a thread," they proclaimed. "The Wild seeks a vessel. You will serve?"

With his heart racing, Rufio nodded in acceptance without question, though the actual cost of this pact remained shrouded in the unknown.

They led him to the vessel, an ominous structure hidden in the lower depths of the council chamber. Crafted from black glass that gleamed like onyx, it felt alive, pulsating with dark energy. Suddenly, Kaelith, the Devourer of the Rot, an entity of insatiable hunger, materialized before him, its blood-red eyes locking onto his soul.

The ritual erupted violently within him, a searing pain tearing through his chest as the Sigil of Kaelith branded his flesh. An infernal heat coiled around his wrist, forming a copper band that blazed like a live ember, encircling a void. In that harrowing moment, he became two beings: Rufio, the boy, and Kaelith, the Wild Primordial entity sworn to protect the realms. Yet with this oath came a high cost. He was forever to be unanchored from love, his body never able to father children, and denied the solace of peace. And still... still... his body had learned to crave what it was forbidden to keep.

Returning home after so long, Rufio felt the weight of his transformation. He rushed into his mother, Catrin's, embracing their reunion, both joyous and fraught with unspoken tension.

"You carry the burden of all now," she murmured, her fingers brushing over the painful scar that marked him. "It'll burn, or it'll heal, Aodhán. Just remember: the choice is yours."

Mari listened intently as Rufio spoke this truth. She stood still as an old oak, as if even her breath might interrupt something so sacred in him. She knew, in this moment, that he needed her to understand his story.

Rufio spoke as if in a trance, lost in thoughts that seemed timeless. Years went by, yet his mother remained ever vigilant during his absences, tending to his gardens and joyfully welcoming his return. Despite her frailty, Catrin's smile was a constant source of warmth, a beacon of hope each time he emerged from the chaos of battle. As the rot and corruption spread, the Watchers increasingly called upon his skills, leaving him with little choice but to respond. His mother's kin stepped in to help, caring for the woman who had always been his anchor. Yet duty proved to be a merciless taskmaster; whenever the Watchers summoned him, he had no option but to obey. Each time he left, his heart ached with the pain of not being the son she truly needed.

As his mother passed away, an irreplaceable part of him faded into the shadows. Grief settled heavily on his heart, yet beneath the ancient trees of his village, he made a silent vow, drawing strength from the cherished memories of Catrin. A bittersweet smile flickered across his face as he recalled her laughter, the warmth of her embrace, and the stories she'd shared under the starlit sky.

"I will protect this place with my life," he swore to the wind, feeling her presence in the rustle of leaves that danced around him. This village was all that remained of her, every stone and every whisper holding a piece of her spirit, and he was determined to guard it with every ounce of his being. The foreboding darkness of the rot crept ever closer, but Rufio, bound to Kaelith and resolute, had no intention of letting it claim his home, for he carried her love within him, a flame that refused to flicker out.

Bringing himself back to the present, he shifted his focus to Mari, freeing her from the story he had been lost in. She stepped away from her spot and began to wander around the room, her fingers gliding over the dust that settled on a table cluttered with maps and sketches.

"This place feels so lived in," she murmured softly.

"It is," Rufio replied. He lingered by the hearth, staring at the carving in his hand. "The family keeps it for me. Rhea's bloodline. They've done so for generations."

She smiled gently. "So, she really is…"

"My mother's great-grandniece," he said quietly. "And her daughter after that. They're the reason this town still stands. And the reason I will never let it fall."

Mari looked at him then, really looked. For the first time, she saw not just the warrior, but the man… lonely, burdened, and fiercely loyal to a place that loved him back. Her chest tightened with an unfamiliar ache, the kind that came from witnessing devotion that had survived too long without comfort.

"You've protected them all this time," she said.

"I owe them everything," he said. "My life may belong to the Wild and Ancestors, but my heart belongs to Aedalon." He didn't say, *and my body betrays me.* He didn't say, *and you are changing the rules.*

Outside, the wind shifted. The air smelled of rain, though no clouds gathered. The land itself seemed to breathe deeper now. Rufio stepped toward the door, hand resting briefly on the frame. His wrist throbbed beneath the band, a warning and a reminder. The Hall of Ancestors waited somewhere beyond the warded peace; days away but already pulling on the thread of him.

Behind him, Mari whispered, "She is still with you, you know."

He didn't turn, but his voice softened. "I know."

And in the space between those words, something else lived, something not spoken that her presence had started to feel like a second oath.

# Chapter 15

The sun hung warm and golden over the valley, bathing Rufio's small cottage in a soft, honeyed glow. From where Mari sat on the worn wooden steps, she could see the village below its thatched rooftops, curling chimney smoke, and the laughter of children mingling with the bell-like chime of the Solins. The breeze carried the scent of fresh bread and crushed herbs, and somewhere below, a distant hammer rang once then fell quiet, as if even labor here knew how to rest.

Thalos and Brin were nowhere near the cottage now. They had wandered down toward the heart of the town, no doubt being fed tasty treats by the giggling children and villagers. Mari could almost feel their contentment from here like a warm purr in the back of her mind that softened the tight places in her ribs.

Here, peace settled over Mari like a gentle blanket, softening the edges of her weary soul. For the first time since she'd been swept into this wild, unfamiliar world, she felt something akin to belonging; a sense of home that wasn't built from walls or routines, but from quiet moments and the hush that lingers when the world finally stops demanding. It was a different kind of home, one that seeped into her bones and whispered comfort, reminding her that safety could be found not in places, but in the spaces where the heart is allowed to rest.

Rufio had left her on the porch after showing her around his modest cottage, its low beams and stone hearth now filled with the scent of cedar and sage as it burned.

"I've a few things to tend to before we head into the village," he had told her, rolling up his sleeves. "Stay close, Mari. The land here listens."

His voice had carried the calm authority of someone who didn't need to raise it to be obeyed. *The land listens.* She hadn't known what that meant until now. Not until she noticed the way the air here seemed to pause when Rufio spoke, as if the valley itself leaned closer to hear him.

Rufio's tunic hung open and loose, his Sigil peeking through the opening. As he moved through the garden, mending the boundary stones that protected his land, Mari let her eyes wander to the land around her and to the man who was attractively tending it. His hands were steady, sure, practiced fingers that had known both soil and steel, and the sight of him working with care instead of violence stirred something uneasy and tender inside her. The Solins drifted lazily in the sunlight like dandelion seeds, glowing pink-gold as they hovered near the tree line. They weren't frantic here. They floated as if they trusted the day.

She smiled faintly. "Where are you going, little lights?"

The Solins twinkled in answer, darting toward a narrow path hidden by wildflowers. Their glow brightened, then dimmed again, like a teasing invitation.

"I guess I'm going too," she said, standing up from the porch.

Her voice came out softer than she had anticipated, almost with a hint of playfulness. For once, curiosity felt more like an adventure than a risk. Not wanting to disturb Rufio, she decided to follow her sparkling friends, staying close to the cottage.

Her boots glided over the velvety moss and tall blades of grass, each step accompanied by a subtle hum that resonated within her, almost like a pulse in the air. It wasn't quite a sound, but rather an intuitive pressure that tingled at the nape of her neck, guiding her forward. With each stride, she felt an uncanny familiarity enveloping her, as though the very essence of this place had been imprinted in her soul long before she ever set foot here. The crisp scent of earth mingled with the freshness of the surrounding forest, and the whispers of leaves danced around her, confirming that she was exactly where she was meant to be.

The viper uncoiled from her arm, slipping soundlessly into the tall weeds to hunt. Its scales caught one flash of sun. Shimmering of bronze and jade. It vanished as if the green had swallowed it. Mari walked deeper, following the gentle flicker of Solin light until she broke into a clearing and gasped. Her fingers touched her lips in quiet surprise.

Before her was a small lake, its surface so still that it mirrored the sky perfectly, the air shimmered faintly above it, rich with energy. The lake looked unreal, like a piece of the sky had fallen to the earth and decided to stay. The scent of blooming water lilies and wildflowers filled her lungs.

The Solins danced across the water, tracing soft ripples like fingertips. Each ripple spread outward in perfect rings, as if the water understood music and wanted to keep time.

She was unaware that this place held sacred significance, that its water and stones, the grass and flowers, formed the very essence of Rufio's protection and the cornerstone of the land's balance. All she recognized was its beauty. A vibrancy that seemed to pulse with life in a way the rest of the world struggled to achieve.

Mari's chest ached with something tender and long forgotten. She remembered summers as a child, running barefoot to the creek near her grandmother's farm, feeling the world breathe beneath her feet. The memory came with sound, birds, distant laughter, water over stone, and for a heartbeat, she wasn't here. She was there. Innocent and safe.

Without a second thought, she began to shed her clothes, folding each piece neatly atop a sun-warmed rock. As she gazed into the lake, her reflection seemed both unfamiliar and familiar. A stronger, older version of the girl who once chased dragonflies through the tall reeds. She lingered for a moment, as if the water held secrets of who she was becoming.

Taking a deep breath, she stepped into the water, gasping at the crisp, cool embrace that enveloped her bare skin. The initial shock was sharp, invigorating, but soon transformed into a soothing caress, washing away the weight of the world. The water wrapped around her like silk, each ripple shimmering gently as she moved. Fish darted around her legs, flickers of silver gliding through the depths.

Laughter bubbled up within her, a soft melody that danced through the trees like wind chimes in a gentle breeze. With arms outstretched, she twirled, feeling the joy surge through her, a perfect harmony with nature. And from somewhere deep below the surface, the lake seemed to respond, a subtle tug as if acknowledging her presence.

In that moment, she felt truly alive, as if the entire world had joined in her celebration.

Grass unfurled along the banks, a vibrant green, while wildflowers burst into bloom, painting the landscape with colors that danced in the breeze. The very air transformed, becoming crisp, infused with energy. The creek, a mellifluous companion to the cottage, sang a deeper tune, rushing with a strength that felt almost palpable. The birds startled upward in a sudden whirl, then circled back, as if confused by the return of something they'd stopped expecting.

Rufio, sleeves rolled to his elbows and hands dirtied from toil, halted mid-step as a tremor rippled through the ground like a heartbeat. The energy coursed through him, a potent pulse resonating in the soles of his boots, driving back the persistent rot that had encroached on his carefully crafted wards. The ward-stones warmed beneath his palms, the carved lines brightening as if they'd been fed from the inside out.

He turned toward the stream near his cottage, blinking in disbelief. The water sparkled with crystalline clarity, showcasing smooth pebbles that glimmered like gems beneath its surface.

"By the Wild…" he breathed, his heart racing in tune with the awakening world around him. His band tingled gently, not as a warning, but as a gentle claim.

Without a second thought, he abandoned his tools, a wild urgency propelling him forward. The deeper he sank into the embrace of the forest, the more alive everything became.

Branches leaned toward the light, roots twisted in eager anticipation, and the very air shimmered with a warm glow that beckoned him closer. Even the shadows looked different here, less like hiding places, more like velvet draped over living things.

When he burst into the clearing, his breath caught in his throat, halting him in his tracks. Mari stood waist-deep in the shimmering lake, her back turned toward him, sunlight cascading over her skin in shades of gold and rose. The water danced gently against her hips, while tendrils of her long, dark hair embraced her shoulders and back like silk. Solins floated on the water and air around her, delicate and ethereal, casting a gentle glow that bathed the water in an almost otherworldly radiance. She looked like she belonged to the lake, like the water had been waiting for her to return.

Rufio's heart clenched with a fierce, unbearable ache. A grief so sharp and sudden it threatened to shatter him. He could see everything unfolding before him, every fragile moment, yet he was utterly powerless to stop it. The weight of helplessness pressed down like a stone in his chest; each beat was a painful reminder of what he might lose.

Every barrier he had painstakingly built to guard his longing began to crumble, trembling as his own wild force within him awakened. It whispered her true name in a language older than time itself, a haunting melody that stirred the depths of his soul.

Beneath his skin, Kaelith shifted restlessly, a primal hunger urging him forward. *"She breathes life into death itself. You feel it too."*

His jaw clenched, not in anger, but in the raw, terrifying fear of what he desired, the kind of fear that had always exacted a brutal price.

He wanted to look away, to shield his heart from the overwhelming beauty that held him captive. But he was ensnared, caught in the gravity of her presence. As she turned her face slightly, laughter danced on her lips, a haunting, ethereal melody that echoed softly through the tranquil glade. The faint shimmer in her eyes betrayed the light of renewal blossoming within her. It wasn't just the lake that was alive; she was alive, radiant and fierce in a way that made everything else in this realm seem starved and pale by comparison.

Then, in a moment both sacred and shattering, something inside him broke quietly, reverently. His voice, barely more than a breath, carried the words that had burned within him since the day she stepped into his world: "A stór mo chroí." My treasure, my heart.

The vow tasted like smoke and honey in his mouth, too intimate, too honest, like stepping over a line he'd been forced to draw so long ago.

He hadn't intended for those words to escape his lips; they were a sacred vow, an offering from his soul to hers, transcending flesh and desire. Yet once released, the wind grasped them, carrying them over the water like a tender promise. The Solins flared brighter, as if they'd heard it too, and the lake surface trembled with a soft, luminous shiver.

Mari froze, the warmth of his declaration washing over her, weaving through her heartbeat like a sweet caress. A stór mo chroí.

Her throat tightened as emotions surged within her. That voice, gentle and familiar, tugged at a memory buried deep beneath layers of grief and time. Her husband Rufus had called her that once upon a time, in a world alive with love, safe and sacred, long before anger and darkness had tainted her dream.

Tears blurred her vision. The ache came fast, sweet, and cruel, because she didn't know if this was comfort or betrayal of the life she'd fear may be gone when she returned to her world.

"Anyone there?" she called softly, turning toward the hidden source of warmth that had kindled hope within her.

But the clearing held its breath, the only response the soft whisper of the wind and the gentle ripple of the lake, aglow with the light of the Solins. And somewhere beyond the trees, the ward-stones hummed like a warning bell; quiet, steady, impossible to ignore.

# Chapter 16

Mari didn't know how long she stayed in the water. Time felt… unimportant there, stretched thin and luminous. Eventually, the Solins drifted back toward the trees, their glow dimming to a softer blush, as if satisfied. A few lingered behind, hovering near the lake's edge, their chiming laughter quieter now, guardians instead of guides.

Reluctantly, Mari stepped from the water, skin tingling with warmth despite the cooling air. She felt invigorated, grounded, as though something restless inside her had finally exhaled. When she reached for her clothes, the Solins swirled around her instead, light folding and reshaping.

In moments, she stood dressed once more, but not as before.

A delicate, soft white tunic cascaded from her shoulders to her hips, woven from a light fabric that glimmered like morning mist settling over a tranquil meadow. Billowing gently around her legs, a long moss green skirt flowed gracefully from her waist, its earthiness complemented by a fitted brown vest-corset. This corset was intricately embroidered with delicate motifs of flowers, slender branches adorned with leaves, and tiny birds captured mid-flight. Each stitch shimmered subtly, as if the land itself had infused the garment with its gratitude, transforming it into something alive and vibrant. Her hair, cascading down her back, featured silver strands woven into an elegant braid that encircled her head like a crown, adding an ethereal touch to her appearance.

Mari laughed softly, fingers brushing the embroidery. "Well… that's new."

The Solins chimed with approval, then scattered like sparks on a breeze.

When she returned to the cottage, Rufio was in the garden, finishing the last of his tending. The boundary stones lay settled and quiet now, the soil dark and rich beneath his hands. He was breathing carefully, shoulders squared, jaw tight, reassembling himself piece by piece.

He sensed her before he saw her.

The air shifted.

Rufio straightened slowly and turned.

For a heartbeat, he forgot how to stand.

Mari approached barefoot, the hem of her skirt whispering through the grass. Sunlight caught in her hair, and the living embroidery along her bodice seemed to move as she did. She looked… restored. Not untouched, but whole in a way that stole the breath from his lungs.

His carefully rebuilt composure cracked.

"You…" He began to say and then stopped. He was at a loss for words. Rufio swallowed hard and tried again. "You shouldn't wander off like that."

She tilted her head, smiling, eyes bright. "I didn't wander off. I followed the Solins."

That statement and her mirth did not help the situation. His memory of her was vivid and raw.

Rufio looked away, scrubbed a hand over his face, then winced when he noticed the dirt beneath his nails. "We'll be going into the village later," he said, voice clipped, too quick. "They'll hold a celebration. It's… tradition when I return."

Her face lit instantly. "A celebration? With people? Food? Music? Dancing?"

"Yes," he said, then added dryly, "All of it."

She turned her gaze to him, taking in every detail. Sweat gleamed on his temples, glistening in the light. His sleeves were rolled up, revealing arms dusted with earth, remnants of a day spent digging in the soil. A faint smear of dark, damp earth clung to his skin, a testament to his hard work. A smile spread across her face, deepening as she observed him. "Then you should probably wash up."

He let out a soft chuckle. "That was the idea."

"At least your arms and face," she joked. "Unless you're aiming for the title of Mud Guardian!"

This earned her a real smile from the self-proclaimed Guardian of Mud.

He strolled down to the creek, where the cool water was inviting as it splashed over his hands, forearms, and face. Moving deliberately, he savored the refreshing sensation, careful to avoid an accidental dunk; after all, tempting fate was not an option. Once he returned to his modest dwelling, he slipped into a fresh outfit: form-fitting black trousers that hugged his muscular legs, a crisp white tunic that highlighted his lean frame, and a snug black leather vest.

While adorned, the vest subtly marked his station, signifying his status without the need for weapons.

Stepping outside again, he found Mari kneeling by the garden bed, her fingers poised just above the vibrant herbs, her eyes reflecting admiration for the work he had done. A warmth blossomed in his chest, mingling with a twinge of nervousness.

Before he could talk himself out of it, Rufio bent down and gathered a small handful of wildflowers. They were untamed and imperfect, each one a testament to life's resilience, defiantly growing in their own way. He cleared his throat softly, the sound barely breaking the peaceful atmosphere around them.

Mari turned. "Hmm?"

He walked toward her, awkward in a way no battlefield had ever made him. "It's a short walk into the village," he said, offering his elbow. "The path curves near the stream."

She slipped her arm through his without hesitation. "Lead the way."

They took a few steps before he stopped again.

Rufio extended the flowers toward her, eyes fixed firmly somewhere near the horizon. "For you."

Her smile softened into something quieter, deeper. She accepted them gently. "Thank you."

As they walked, side by side, the garden behind them thrummed faintly, settled, satisfied. Ahead, the village waited, alive with light and memory.

And somewhere deep beneath Rufio's ribs, Kaelith hummed, not in hunger, but in uneasy approval.

# Chapter 17

The suns moved slowly in the sky, casting warm hues across the horizon as they reached the ridge overlooking the valley. Below, the village shimmered like a treasure, its windows aglow with flickering candles and torches illuminating the square.  Laughter floated softly on the breeze, wrapping around Mari like a cherished memory. After the endless gray of their journey, this place radiated warmth, igniting a flicker of hope in her heart.

As they meandered down the winding path, the Auralisks met Mari and Rufio halfway. They ambled ahead, their large bodies moving with a contented grace, rumbling softly with full stomachs. Thalos extended his neck, letting out a deep, resonant hum that felt almost like a comforting purr. Behind them, a flurry of Solins trailed, their ethereal pink-gold lights dancing above the group like playful fireflies.

"It's beautiful," Mari breathed, her voice content, awe

coloring her words.

"It's home," Rufio replied, his tone quiet yet heavy, imbued with both pride and a weariness that suggested home was not just a place, but a heavy legacy.

The air thickened with sweetness as they drew closer to the town, the scent of baking bread mingling with the warm, earthy aroma of woodsmoke. Yet beneath those comforting fragrances, Mari caught a fleeting whiff of something sharp and metallic, like a distant storm on the horizon. It pricked at her senses, leaving a shadow of unease in its wake.

Rufio tensed at her side, his body responding to the same unseen threat.

"The rot is closer than I thought," he murmured, his voice low and serious.

As they crossed into the outskirts, the Auralisks slowed suddenly, nostrils flaring as they picked up a scent that chilled the air. Mari glanced at them, sensing their agitation.

"What's wrong?" she asked, her heart pounding in rhythm with her rising anxiety.

"They smell it," Rufio replied, his brow furrowed. "Corruption rides the wind, but it hasn't breached the wards."

"Then let it stay out there," she said firmly, though a shiver coursed through her. The vibrant warmth of the village felt distant against that dark undertone.

Rufio almost smiled at her resolve. "If only it listened," he said softly, the glint of determination in his eyes mingling with the shadow of worry, as they pressed on toward the flickering lights that still beckoned them home.

As they stepped into the square, the vibrant energy of the festival swept over Rufio like a warm tide. Laughter mingled with the lively strains of music, creating a tapestry of sound that enveloped him. The Auralisks, with their ethereal grace, were immediately surrounded by a throng of children, their faces alight with joy. They eagerly offered garlands of dried flowers and slices of ripe fruit with their small, outstretched hands. Rufio watched Brin lower his massive head with surprising gentleness, allowing one beaming child to place a wreath around his neck, flowers bright against his iridescent scales. Meanwhile, the Solins flitted through the crowd like living fireflies, darting between giggling faces and adding to the cheerful chaos.

Mari's smile was infectious as she took in the scene. The square was alive with scents of roasting bread and the sweet tang of cider, wafting from stalls adorned with colorful cloth. Soft yellow lanterns hung from the branches of nearby trees, swaying gently in the evening breeze, casting a warm glow over the gathering. Villagers stepped forward, welcoming Rufio with nods of acknowledgment, hearty claps on his shoulder, and words filled with reverence.

"It's been too long, Wildling," an older woman said, grasping his hand with a grip that was both firm and kind. Her eyes sparkled as she added, "You kept the shadows back another year."

Rufio inclined his head, feeling the weight of her words settle on him like a heavy mantle. Beneath the warmth of the festival atmosphere, he could sense the simmering anxiety within himself. The faint tightening of his jaw revealed his inner turmoil, and he couldn't help but steal a glance toward the distant horizon, where the forest stood ominously dark against the twilight sky.

Another year, perhaps not another season, loomed over him like a storm cloud, bringing an unwelcome reminder of his responsibilities. The image rose unbidden: the chamber behind Watcher Elmyrs, the quiet hum of the portal waiting to take Mari away before any of this could happen. Thalos and Brin had expected it. Even the land had braced itself. Rufio closed his fingers against the fence until the wood creaked. He had chosen differently. And choices. He knew better than most; it never came without cost.

To Mari, everything unfolded in vibrant color: families bustled about, children played games of chase, and songs spilled joyously into the air, but Rufio could feel another current beneath it all. There was an exhaustion that permeated the revelry, a weariness that came not just from the year's hardships but from the ever-present fight against the creeping shadows. The villagers' smiles, while genuine, held a flicker of worry. They celebrated, yes, but they also looked to Rufio as their protector, their beacon of hope.

He felt the wooden fence beside him, the rough texture grounding him. Beneath his fingertips, he could sense the faint pulse of life, a soft thrum that reminded him of his bond to the land. This place still remembered the richness of growth and vitality, and he couldn't shake the feeling that it was his responsibility to ensure that the pulse of life didn't fade into silence. As laughter echoed around him, Rufio smiled back, but it didn't quite reach his eyes, a quiet reminder that even amidst joy, vigilance, and duty remained his unyielding companions.

Shae waved from the doorway of the bakery; her cheeks flushed from the oven's heat. "Mari, love! There you are. Help me before I burn the stew! We're celebrating Rufio's homecoming!"

Mari's heart swelled at the sight of her friend. She laughed and hurried inside, the warm, fragrant air wrapping around her like a soft embrace. The kitchen was a lively whirlwind: bowls clinking, herbs being chopped, dough being rolled. Shae thrust a wooden spoon into Mari's hand without so much as a word of preamble. "Taste this. Be honest."

Mari grinned, dipping the spoon into the bubbling pot. She savored the rich flavors before nodding. "Needs a little salt."

"Ha! I knew it!" Shae exclaimed, throwing her arms high in glee. "Everyone says I over-salt! Not this time... I knew they had no taste!" She said, stomping her foot.

As they worked side by side, Mari felt the warmth of family envelop them, the kind of warmth that felt like sunlight breaking through clouds. It was a feeling she hadn't experienced in far too long, a reminder of her own home with her children, now closer to being grown. But as laughter filled the room, a question tugged at her heart, a troubling echo from the lake that refused to quiet.

"Shae," Mari began softly, her voice barely above a whisper, "what does 'A stór mo chroí' mean?"

With that question, the kitchen's lively buzz faded into an unsettling silence. Shae's spoon fell from her hand with a sharp clink, her eyes widening in disbelief.

"Mari," she managed, her voice reverent but cautious, "where did you hear those words?"

Mari's heart raced in her chest, startled by the sudden heaviness of the moment. "I... I think I heard it in the wind by the lake. It wasn't... spoken to me, exactly. It just came, like a whisper."

At that, Shae pressed a trembling hand to her chest, as if warding off an unseen chill. "In the wind?" she repeated, her tone dipping into something almost sacred. "Child, those words aren't meant for the air."

From the shadows of the room, an elderly woman with striking white hair and eyes as sharp as crows leaned closer, her voice gravelly yet gentle. "That phrase," she said, "is sacred to us. It means 'my heart, my treasure.' But it holds much more; it's a binding vow. A promise older than this land."

Confusion knitted Mari's brow. "A promise?"

Shae nodded, her expression a blend of reverence and sorrow. "It's a vow of soul and spirit. When spoken, it binds one's essence to another's for eternity. It's not a promise made lightly, nor without consequence. Only those who have been truly bonded or those who have lost their loving bond through death dare to whisper those words again."

Mari swallowed hard. She understood loss, but what unsettled her was the firm conviction in their voices, as if the land itself bore witness to every vow ever broken or kept.

A flutter of anxiety stirred in Mari's heart at the weight of those words. "I didn't... I thought it was just the wind."

The old woman's gaze softened, a flicker of understanding lighting her eyes. "The wind carries what it must. The oath was spoken because someone said it on your behalf. The wind never lies."

Mari glanced down at her hands, then shifted her gaze to Shae's wrist. The soft glow of the fire danced across it, revealing a faint band shimmering just beneath her sleeve. "And the bands," she asked quietly, "what do they signify?"

A warm stir of energy passed through the room, as if the very air understood the gravity of her question.

Shae offered a bittersweet smile, one filled with both love and lingering sadness. "The men receive their base band when they come of age. It's a gift from the land, a mark of protection. Given from father or grandfather to mark when a boy becomes a man. If they discover their beloved, the band is split by a smith or jeweler, one half shared with their beloved, one kept for themselves. In this way, they truly become one."

She lifted her wrist, revealing a beautiful band of metal and leather. "I have been bonded for almost thirty years. But Rufio… his journey is different." Her voice trailed off, eyes shimmering with unshed tears.

Mari's heart sank at the thought of Rufio. "His band…?" she ventured, feeling the weight of sorrow settle heavily between them.

Shae's gaze turned distant, filled with a profound ache. "His was burned into him through ritual, the Sigil of the Wild. His band is copper fused with his blood, bound for life to fight and protect, never to another soul."

The realization struck Mari like a cold wave. "He can never…?" She said as she placed her hand over her heart.

Shae shook her head, sorrow shadowing her features. "Never to love or help watch his young grow. Never to bind to another."

A silence wrapped around them, thick with unspoken grief for the sacrifices they had all made. Mari's heart ached for Rufio, for the life he could have had, for joy and love forever out of reach. The warmth of the kitchen felt distant now, overshadowed by the weight of longing and loss.

Before Mari could respond, laughter erupted from the doorway as a group of villagers entered, pulling her into a storm of teasing and affection. "Tell her how Rufio tried to bake a loaf once!" one called, pulling everyone out of the dark emotion and thought.

"Oh, the flour explosion incident!" Shae cackled. "I was

cleaning that for a week! Flour and yeast were everywhere!" She made a gesture explaining the large explosion with her hands.

"And remember when he tried to ride the cow as a dare from Enwin?" another added, wiping tears from his eyes. "Straight into the pond!"

Even Mari laughed, imagining the stoic Rufio covered in flour and pond weeds. For a little while, the heaviness lifted.

As twilight deepened, the feast blossomed into life. Long tables sprawled across the square, adorned with lanterns swaying gently from overhead ropes. Music floated through the air, the lilting sound of soft drums, the playful twang of fiddles, and the enchanting pipes weaving melodies that beckoned all to join in. At the edge of the festivities, the Auralisks glimmered with a soft glow, their scales reflecting. Their light danced alongside the joyous movements from the Solins above.

Mari found herself caught up in the whirlwind of laughter and movement, spinning with Shae's daughters. Their skirts twirled around like blooming flowers, laughter bubbling from their lips like the sweetest spring water. Beneath her feet, the land pulled with a renewed vigor, stronger than it had been just days before. Each heartbeat of the drum was alive, every note a promise of revival that filled the air with hope.

Across the square, Rufio stood a bit apart, his gaze fixed on the merriment. The flickering firelight softened the war-worn features of his face, revealing a faint smile as he watched the scene unfold. Mari moved as someone unburdened, laughter lifting her shoulders, joy spilling from her in waves that the land drank greedily. Rufio had faced monsters without flinching, but watching her belonging here terrified him more than any blade ever could. Yet, when he glanced to the horizon, the smile faltered.

There, just beyond the wards, the sky shimmered ominously in shades of red, as if cracks of molten glass were beginning to creep closer. He felt it deep in his bones, the rot, restless and hungry. It's moving again.

A small hand tugged at his sleeve, breaking his reverie. An eager woman offered him a piece of sweetbread. "Dance, Wildling," she urged with innocent joy. "You look troubled."

He accepted the bread with a smile, shaking his head gently. "Not troubled, just thinking."

"You think too much," she said lightly, already drifting to the next patron, carrying the spirit of the celebration with her.

Rufio's eyes found Mari once more, her laughter, the warmth radiating from her, the vibrancy of her life. An ache filled his chest at the sight. Each breath she took seemed to bolster the land itself, while with each heartbeat, the rot and darkness clawed ever closer to her brilliant light.

By the time night wrapped its arms around the square, a comforting hush settled in, muffling even the whispers of the stars. Families exchanged goodnights, and the Solins drifted into lazy spirals overhead, their ethereal forms a serene contrast against the night sky. The Auralisks stood vigil at the gate, their luminous eyes reflecting the flickering warmth of the firelight.

Mari and Rufio walked side by side, the path to the cottage draped in silvery moonlight. The cool air was fragrant with the intoxicating scent of night flowers, each breath a mixture of tranquility easing some of the heaviness tugging at their hearts. She felt at peace, understanding the shadow that loomed beneath the surface.

"Thank you for tonight," she said softly, her voice soft and playful. "I can't remember the last time I laughed like that."

He nodded, a smile creeping onto his face. "You brought laughter to them, too. They've been yearning for it."

"They love you," she replied earnestly, letting the truth linger in the air. "I can see why."

Rufio offered no response, merely shaking his head, a mixture of humility in his eyes. They walked on in silence, the warmth of the square fading into the distance. As they approached the cottage, the calm gave way to an unsettling chill that seeped into their bones.

Mari squinted against the night, suddenly aware of a faint metallic scent wafting through it, a harbinger of decay, distant yet encroaching.

"Do you smell that?" she asked, brows furrowed with concern.

His jaw clenched tightly, the strong lines of his face hardening. "Yes."

"It's the rot, isn't it?" she murmured, dread painting her voice with a frown.

He kept his gaze forward, refusing to meet her eyes. "It's reaching for the borders. But it won't cross while I draw breath."

The air crackled with anticipation, a heavy hush enveloping them as the night lingered on each inhalation. Mari's heart raced, every thump resonating with the quiet determination in Rufio's voice. The soft light from the Solins above cast a twinkling glow, highlighting the resolve etched on her face. She reached out, her fingers brushing against him in a fleeting connection that sparked something deep within. Then, with a sense of urgency, she clasped his hand tightly, her warmth contrasting against his cool skin.

"Then it won't cross at all," she declared, her voice a steady anchor amid the chaos surrounding them. The weight of her vow hung in the air like the stars overhead, bright and unwavering. "Not while I draw breath."

Rufio's gaze dropped to their intertwined hands, the corner of his mouth softening into a bittersweet smile. Yet, deep in his eyes, a storm raged, waves of unspoken grief clashing with an aching longing. "You have no idea what you're promising," he said, the sincerity in his voice laced with an undercurrent of fear.

"Maybe not," Mari replied, her voice steady despite the tumult in his eyes. "But I mean it."

The promise hung between them, forged in the fires of unfulfilled desires and the burden of shared struggles. Despite the darkness closing in, beneath it all, an unyielding love blossomed wild and defiant against the inevitable.

Above, the Solins sparkled like fallen stars, drawn low as if to bear witness to their solemn vow. In the distance, a flickering red light pulsed ominously through the shadows, like the heartbeat of an impending storm, a creeping rot echoing the relentless duty that awaited them. Mari felt it deep in her bones, a sense of urgency that underscored the gravity of their promise, yet she held on tighter to Rufio's hand, refusing to let go.

Rufio's other hand curled into a fist at his side, the pain of choice weighing heavily on him. *Not here. Not her.*

Rufio ushered Mari into the cottage, turning around to view his home below. His heart ached with a what could never fully bloom. "Keep her safe. Keep her whole," he whispered to the night, a plea born from every fiber of his being.

Somewhere far beyond the wards, something answered. Not with sound, but with pressure, as if the world itself had noticed her promise and begun to shift its weight.

But the Wild only stirred, rustling through the leaves with ancient wisdom, *"Balance always takes its due. We will do all we can."*

In that moment of sorrow and sacrifice, their hearts beat like one, tethered by a love that was both a gift and a burden, destined to endure beyond the shadows that threatened to consume them. *We will do all we can.*

# Chapter 18

The night had drawn to a close, not in tranquility but rather with an uneasy compromise that lingered like an uninvited guest that only tormented one stoic man.

Rufio had put up a quiet, stubborn fight about where to sleep. He began with his sleeping blanket and pointed to where the Auralisks grazed. The brothers snort, and whinnies were audible; the mental *"You are on your own,"* made Mari laugh out loud with a snort while he used his right hand to comb through his tousled hair. Rufio's band seemed to have a slight golden sheen now. Frustrated but not willing to admit defeat just yet, he then pointed insistently at the floor and then the chair, his eyes pleading for an alternative. But Mari, arms crossed and an unyielding look on her face, wouldn't hear of it.

"You're going to rest properly for once," she declared, her tone as firm as a well-forged sword. "You can't be a guardian if you collapse from exhaustion before sunrise." Her body was poised for an argument; she was determined to win.

In the end, he surrendered, throwing his hands up in mock defeat before sitting on the feather-down mattress, settling against the wall, his feet crossed over the bed like a reluctant prince in exile. The stone at his back was cool, grounding, but even that couldn't quiet the awareness of her presence beside him; warm, breathing, real. Part of him was worn out, and part was well-acquainted with the futility of arguing when her voice had that unmistakable edge.

As dawn's first light crept through the window, the memory of their midnight debate made a bittersweet ache settle into his chest.

He lay atop the quilt that his mother had lovingly stitched ages ago, each thread worn and frayed from years of battles fought and solitude endured. Next to him, Mari slept peacefully under the same blanket, her long brown hair flecked with gray, splayed across the pillow like tendrils of sunlight. The rhythmic sound of her breathing filled the stillness, mingling with a faint, intoxicating scent of salt, warmth, and something reminiscent of crushed wildflowers.

It was an odd comfort. A dangerous one.

He diverted his gaze from her sleeping form to the ceiling, feeling the familiar weight of guilt pressing down on him. He had sworn his life to the balance, vowing never to bond, never to love, only to fight and protect. Yet every shift of her body, every quiet sigh, unraveled that vow thread by thread, like a seam finally giving way under too much strain.

The oath he'd taken as a youth now felt like a cage, and each moment in her presence was a key turning in the lock, threatening to set free emotion he' had long suppressed. He had to make this sacrifice without question. He learned in great detail what would happen if he were to love, the devastation, the vulnerability, the catastrophic consequences that followed. Yet here he was, drawn to this woman from another world as inevitably as moths to flame.

Just then, she stirred, her eyes fluttering open, and his breath caught in his throat. She offered him a sleepy smile that could almost disarm a dragon.

"You stayed," she murmured, her voice a gentle melody.

"I said I would," he replied, shrugging with an air of nonchalance, though he was silently patting himself on the back for not bolting. In truth, his pulse betrayed him, quick and unsteady. He mentally smacked his forehead for acting like a young boy with a crush.

Her lips curled into a grateful smile, brightening the room more than any dawn. "Thank you. I know it's not easy for you."

His gaze flickered, and something soft and unreadable flashed across his face. "It's harder than you think," he said, a hint of playful drama in his tone. "Wrestling with staying still feels like trying to convince a cat to take a bath."

She laughed, the sound ringing like a peace offering in the quiet room. "Well, at least you're trying not to drown!"

They both shared a grin, and in that moment, the messiness of emotions and unspoken promises hung in the air. Comforting and complex as the quilt beneath their hands. The silence stretched between them, charged with unspoken questions.

Mari shifted slightly, her fingers tracing the pattern of the quilt beneath them. "This blanket," she said softly, "it tells a story, doesn't it? All these different patches, different colors, but somehow they all work together."

Rufio's eyes followed her fingers, his expression softening. "My mother made it. Each piece is from something significant in her life. She believed that even the most disparate elements could create harmony if woven with intention."

"Like us?" The words slipped out before Mari could stop them, and a blush crept up her neck.

Rufio's breath hitched, his gaze meeting hers with an intensity that made her heart race. "Perhaps," he said, his voice lower now, rougher. "But some combinations are more dangerous than others. Fire and dry grass, for instance."

"Or fire and sand?" she countered, her eyes challenging him even as her pulse quickened.

A ghost of a smile touched his lips. "Or fire and sand." He reached out, his fingers barely brushing against hers where they rested on the quilt. The contact sent a jolt through both of them, electric and undeniable. "But sometimes," he continued, his voice barely above a whisper, "the most dangerous combinations create the most beautiful results."

The air between them thickened with possibility, with words unsaid and desires unacknowledged. Outside, the world continued its awakening, but in this small room, time seemed to hold its breath, waiting to see what these two unlikely elements would create together.

# Chapter 19

The days that followed unfolded quietly, with a semblance of normalcy. Not many, just enough to matter. Mari insisted Rufio find rest in ways he hadn't allowed himself to do here in decades. He could do that for at least a few days.

The first day, he resisted out of habit, rising before dawn, checking wards, and counting supplies. But she followed him, anyway, sitting on the cottage steps in the morning. Then later, chatting with Shae's daughters, laughing with the elders, coaxing him into lingering conversations that had nothing to do with rot or Watchers or war.

"Just one morning," she told him that evening, blocking the door with a crooked smile. "No planning. No guarding. Just... be."

He had stared at her like she'd asked him to remove a limb.

Yet somehow, he stayed. Somehow, he was trying to obey her request.

He listened while the villagers told old stories; some heroic, some ridiculous. He let the children drag him into games he pretended not to enjoy. He shared meals without scanning the horizon every few breaths. And Mari watched him soften in small, precious increments, as though layers of armor were being set gently aside.

She knew what it meant to lose a life built on routine and safety.

She would not let Rufio lose these moments. He will need these memories. What friend would she be to have her leave through a portal without having him live this at least for a short while?

On the morning they were meant to leave, the weight returned. Rufio rose at dawn, the sky still pearl-gray, and began packing the saddlebags with the precision of someone preparing for war. Weapons first: cleaned, oiled, and wrapped. Then the tools. Bandages. Poultices. Salves sealed against moisture. He paused only once, staring at the space as if debating whether to leave anything behind.

Mari, feeling his space empty, now appeared in the doorway of the small barn, tying her hair back. "You look like you're planning to survive the end of the world."

"Habit," he replied, tying a pocket closed.

She tilted her head. "Before you finish turning the brothers into walking armories, I want to walk into town for breakfast."

He blinked. "Now?"

"Yes. Because I know I will have to eat beans, jerky, and oats for the foreseeable future. If I don't do it now, I will cry. And I don't think the land is ready for that kind of emotional release."

A corner of his mouth twitched. "You exaggerate."

She grinned. "Tell that to my taste buds." She gestured toward the path. "You stay. Finish packing. I'll be back with real food for us to eat."

He hesitated, then nodded. "Don't wander far."

"I promise," she said lightly. "Just far enough for jam."

Once she was gone, Rufio exhaled.

He strolled to the back of the cottage, following a small winding path to the wooden tub nestled behind an old stone wall and the creek. He filled it with cool, fresh water, warming it with a gentle press of his palms. Steam curled into the air as he added soap infused with lavender and thyme, the familiar scent wrapping around him like a comforting embrace.

The view was his sanctuary: the serene lake on one side, the thick forest on the other, and the hum of protective wards in the background. Their presence is known only to him. Their presence was only known to him.

With a sigh he hadn't realized he was holding, he slid into the bath, letting the heat seep into his muscles. For the first time in what felt like ages, he truly relaxed, the tension in his body melting away. Perhaps a little too well.

"Mari..." her name drifted softly through the trees as he succumbed to a restful sleep.

* * *

Meanwhile, Mari returned sooner than expected: arms laden with warm, sweet rolls bundled in cloth and a small jar of jam tucked under her elbow. She stepped into the cottage, placing her tasty treasures on the table, only to find it curiously empty. Rufio was nowhere in sight.

Frowning, she made her way to the small barn where he'd

been packing earlier, only to find it just as deserted. Then, out of the corner of her eye, she noticed a faint path on the ground that had previously gone unnoticed. Curious, she followed it a short distance until the unmistakable sound of splashing water reached her ears.

Turning a corner behind a chest-high wall, she was unprepared for the sight that met her eyes. A small scream escaped her lips as her hands flew to cover her eyes in a panic.

Rufio jolted awake, the startled shout erupting from him. "Woman!"

His hands quickly dropped with a splash beneath the water. With this movement, water sloshed up around him, bubbles bobbing as he instinctively sank deeper into the tub.

Mari spun around so fast she nearly tripped. "I…! You… ! I was calling you, and you didn't answer, and I just went looking… Oh my goodness!"

Only his arms and chest remained above the surface, his Sigil glowing faintly, a striking red edged in gold.

"I am bathing," he said, embarrassed.

"I can see that!" she exclaimed, her voice a mix of shock and amusement. "I didn't know you were… outside like this!"

The Auralisks chose that moment to trot over, sensing departure. They stopped short, heads tilting in curiosity and amusement.

Brin rumbled with unmistakable chuckling sounds.

Thalos' lips made a smacking noise. *Bold human.*

Rufio groaned, a hand pinching the bridge of his nose. "Leave!"

Mari pressed a hand to her face, laughter escaping despite the awkwardness. "I brought breakfast!" she called out, attempting to regain her composure as she stepped back around the wall. "And I'm sorry! You could've said something!"

"You startled me!" he shot back, still flustered.

"You were asleep in a bath!" she retorted, a teasing glint in her eyes.

"I do not… sleep in baths," he mumbled, trying to maintain some semblance of dignity.

Silence enveloped them for a moment, tension hanging thick. Then, against his will, Rufio burst into a hearty, unexpected laugh, a sound both genuine and free, the kind that turned a mortifying encounter into a shared moment of levity.

By the time the sun cleared the ridge, Rufio was dressed, stomachs were full, and the saddlebags were secured. The Auralisks stood patiently as Rufio performed their final preparations. The Solins, enjoying their time, changed Mari into traveling attire. Simple tunic, pants, boots, and a cloak. Rufio was back in his battle attire, looking just as he did when they first met.

Now mounted on the Auralisk's backs, they walked for the last time down the path back into the village. Rufio helped Mari dismount so they could say their goodbyes. The Villagers gathered at the center square for quiet hugs, clasped hands, and murmured blessings freely given.

Shae pressed bread and wrapped food into Mari's arms. "For the road. And for when he forgets to eat."

Rufio sighed. "I do not…"

"You do," Shae said sweetly as she released the bundle. Her tears flowed down her aged cheeks. Shea rubbed Rufio's cheek just as his mother used to do. "Stay safe and come home soon."

Mari mounted Brin first. Rufio followed, mounting on Thalos and offering one last look at the village that had raised him.

As they set off, laughter and chatter faded behind them. Then entirely disappeared when the brothers passed the wards once more. And within an hour, they were already riding toward Death's Door.

# Chapter 20

By midday, they were already at the halfway point toward Death's Door, the Auralisks carrying them swiftly through the tall, brittle grass. The sky had shifted, gray clouds rolling in waves, their edges tinged with sickly green. The once golden expanse now bore scars: streaks of black soil, twisted roots clawing from the earth like bones.

Mari could feel the sickness thrumming beneath her legs, seeping up through the ground. It made her heart ache, not from fear, but sorrow. "It wasn't always like this, was it?" she asked softly.

"No," Rufio said. His voice was low, distant. "This was once the cradle of our world. Where the first breath of humanity was born."

"What happened?"

He hesitated before answering. "Greed. Stollen energy. Time. The rot began at the edges, where balance was ignored.

It should never have reached this far."

She rested her hand over the thick hide of the Auralisk beneath her. Brin's pulse beat in time with hers, and for a moment, she felt the deep hum of the world from his perspective, his pain, his struggle, his worries. Without thinking, she reached inward, drawing the soft golden energy that had always lain within her, and let it flow outward.

The air around her shimmered, and the land inhaled her essence. Patches of grass straightened. The withered stalks turned green in her wake. Mari's gift to the world around her was becoming stronger, but at what cost?

Rufio noticed immediately. "Stop," he said sharply.

Mari looked at him, startled. "Why?"

"You're feeding the land," he said, voice taut with concern. "Too much. You don't understand what that takes from you."

She met his gaze evenly. "If I don't, who will?"

He clenched his jaw, looking away. The muscles in his forearm tightened as he gripped the pommel of his sword. "You're not meant to carry that burden."

"I'm not *meant* to be here at all," she countered gently. "But here I am."

He couldn't find a way to argue. As Mari spoke to him, the landscape behind them transformed, a vibrant carpet of green grass pushing through the remnants of dead soil, while flowers unfurled in hues that this land hadn't seen in decades. The Auralisks strode, their scales shimmering like polished metal in the bright light, humming softly with contentment.

Yet, with every mile they traveled, the resistance to their journey grew stronger. The air thickened, becoming almost tangible around them. Shadows stretched and twisted where the sunlight should have danced, creeping over the terrain like a silent predator. They passed what was once a lush grove, now reduced to a collection of hollow trunks, each blistered and blackened by a decay that seemed to seep deep within. The stench of rot tangled in the air, a grim reminder of the beauty that had long since faded.

Mari pressed a hand to her chest. "Everything feels angry."

"It *is* angry," Rufio said. "The rot feeds on life's waste: grief, hate, neglect. Killing or corrupting everything it touches. Everything this world needs is fed upon, and the rot continues to fester here."

"Then why here?" she asked, glancing toward the horizon. "If this place is sacred… if it's supposed to be protected, why is it worse here?"

Rufio's hands tightened into fists. "Because sacred ground carries the deepest power. I don't know how deep the infestation goes. But when it falls, it will destroy the most."

The words hung between them, heavy as thunder.

By late afternoon, the wind had turned sharp. They dismounted at a ridge overlooking their final trek. The suns bled low in the sky, painting the horizon in shades of crimson and ash. From here, Mari could see the faint outline of the Council of the Ancestors; dark towers etched against the dying light, their ancient runes pulsing weakly like fading embers.

Rufio's expression hardened as he stared at it. "It's worse than I feared."

Mari stepped beside him. The Solins floated around her, faintly glowing, their soft chimes carrying in the air. "Then we fix it."

"You speak as though it's that simple."

"It is," she said, voice calm but confident. "You've spent your whole life fighting to hold this world together, Rufio. Maybe now it's time to heal it."

He turned to her, something between admiration and fear in his eyes. "You don't know what healing costs."

She smiled faintly. "Then I'll learn."

Her hand brushed his arm, a light touch, but it sent warmth through him like fire licking through frost. Hope; dangerous, intoxicating hope took root. A camaraderie he never knew he needed. For a moment, he let himself breathe in that contact, that impossible hope. Then he pulled away, staring again toward the ancient council halls in the distance.

The rot's presence pressed stronger now, whispering through the wind, curling at the edge of his mind.

*"She is light,"* Kaelith murmured within him, *"And the light always burns brightest before the dawn."*

Rufio closed his eyes. "Not this time," he whispered. "Not her."

As twilight descended, the last remnants of sunlight surrendered to the encroaching darkness. Mari stood at the jagged edge of the ridge, a solitary figure silhouetted against the deepening sky. The first stars flickered to life overhead, tiny pinpricks of silver in a vast sea of indigo. Beneath her feet, the newly grown grass danced in the evening breeze, whispering secrets only she could hear. Nearby, the Auralisks, their iridescent forms flickering in the dim light, settled down, their low, resonant hums rippling through the earth like a heartbeat echoing in the stillness.

She felt the world around her thrum with energy, an ancient pulse beckoning her closer, yearning to communicate. Kneeling on the cool ground, she pressed her palm to the earth's surface, feeling the warmth radiate beneath her fingers.

"You're still alive," she murmured, her voice a fragile thread against the encroaching shadows. "I can feel you."

Behind her, Rufio stood at a distance, a silent sentinel shrouded in uncertainty. His breath caught in his throat as he took in the scene, her delicate form entwined with the land, a living bridge between the realms of decay and revival. His heart raced, a drumbeat of reverence and fear. He understood all too well the heavy price of such communion: every time she reignited the spark of life in the withering soil, the rot looming in the depths of the land took notice, shifting in its dark lair, hungry and searching for her.

The air grew thick with tension as Mari closed her eyes, feeling the earth beneath her reacting to her presence. It was a dangerous dance she embraced, one that could attract the ancient evil that gnawed at the fringes of her essence. And still, she couldn't turn away. She would fight for the land, for its heartbeat, even if the darkness hungered for her light.

The ground answered her.

Not gently.

Somewhere far below, something *shifted*; a deep, grinding movement like stone dragged across stone. The hum beneath her palm deepened, no longer a whisper but a low, resonant thrum that traveled up her arm and settled beneath her ribs.

The Solins stilled.

Their usual playful glow tightened into sharp pinpricks of light, hovering close to Mari's shoulders as if bracing for impact.

Brin lifted his head abruptly, nostrils flaring.

Thalos rumbled low in his chest, not contentment this time, but warning.

Rufio moved in a single stride, gripping Mari's wrist and

pulling her gently but firmly to her feet. "That's enough," he said, voice tight. "You felt it, didn't you?"

She nodded, breath unsteadily. "The world heard me, Rufio."

His jaw clenched. Slowly, he turned his gaze toward the distant towers of the Council of the Ancestors. The runes along their edges flared once, faint but unmistakable like embers stirred by a breath.

Kaelith stirred, no longer whispering. *"It knows her now! It has found her and is sending something our way, Vessel! Move!"*

Rufio released her wrist but did not step away. "We don't linger here," he said quietly. "Not anymore."

Above them, the wind shifted, carrying the sharp, metallic scent of rot and something older beneath it. Watching. Waiting.

And far beyond the ridge, unseen but unmistakably awake, Death's Door answered back, proving how this passage earned its name.

# Chapter 21

They had wandered through the night and into the morning, not willing to rest. The wind now howled ominously, biting into flesh like a ravenous beast.  Even the suns hesitated to emerge, their weak light casting the plains into a sickly amber glow that gave everything an unsettling pallor. Each thunderous impact of the Auralisks' hooves sent shivers up Mari's spine, echoing through the ground like a heartbeat, a haunting reminder of life that felt dangerously close to death. She clutched Thalos's mane with a white-knuckled grip, the air around them thick and suffocating, as if it were watching, waiting to strike.

Ahead, Rufio rode Brin in grim silence, his hood drawn low, casting a shadow over his furrowed brow.  The oppressive heat hung heavy, an invisible weight that threatened to crush their spirits. Her heart raced as Mari broke the stillness, her voice barely more than a whisper. "Why does it feel like the land's lost its breath?"

"Because it has," Rufio replied, his voice edged with foreboding. His gaze fixed on the horizon ahead, where the lush grass yielded to an expanse of lifeless desolation, color bleeding away as if drained by an unseen force. "We're nearing the brink of Death's Door."

The Auralisks stirred restlessly, their eyes glowing with an eerie light, pupils narrowing towards the warped expanse where the very fabric of reality shimmered like the surface of a disturbed pond. Suddenly, the earth split open with a bone-chilling scream, a gaping maw erupting with black mist and a fetid air that crashed over them like a dark wave. The stench of rot and decay was suffocating, pulling at the edges of their sanity.

From the fissures emerged grotesque shapes; twisted beasts of bone and tar skittering on unnatural limbs that defied nature itself. Mari's breath hitched in her throat as horror gripped her eyes wide. "What in the world are they?"

"Stay back!" Rufio roared, his voice cutting through the chaos like a blade. He pulled his sword free, the copper runes etched into the steel igniting with a furious, crimson light that snapped to life against the gathering darkness. "Spawn of the rot. Don't let them touch you!" Without a moment's hesitation, he leaped from Brin, charging toward the oncoming nightmare, a warrior standing defiantly against the encroaching abyss, driven by a desperate need to protect them all.

The first creature lunged forward with terrifying ferocity. Rufio reacted with a speed that seemed almost supernatural, his blade meeting the beast's strike midair. With a clean sweep, he severed a clawed limb that dissolved into wispy, oily smoke.

Before he could catch his breath, another creature charged, its maw splitting open to unleash an ear-piercing shriek that shook the very air around them.

Brin roared in defiance, charging in with his mighty horns, slamming into the beast with a force that sent it sprawling backward. Black sludge erupted from the impact, splattering the cracked ground like dark rain.

Nearby, a spawn clawed at the earth, its mangled hands desperately grappling for purchase as it struggled to escape the depths. Still mounted on Thalos, Mari instinctively raised her hands, summoning a pulse of golden light. The beam struck the nearest beast, hissing as it made contact, but the light flickered, unstable and uncertain.

"What was that?" she gasped, heart racing.

"Brin! Thalos! Protect her!" Rufio shouted, urgency coursing through him as he pressed deeper into the fray.

Kaelith stirred within, a searing heat surging through Rufio's veins like molten iron.

*"Feed on them,"* the Wild hissed seductively inside his mind. *"Their corruption is our feast. Let me devour them, and I will reduce this rot to ash."*

"No!" Rufio growled defiantly, his sword cleaving through another rot-born creature with fierce determination. "You'll destroy more than you cleanse, entity."

*"You fear her seeing us. You fear her running from who, what, you and I truly are!"* The Wild's laughter echoed through him, low and ancient, sending shivers cascading down his spine.

For a fleeting moment, doubt pierced Rufio's resolve, and that hesitation became his undoing. A massive beast barreled into him, knocking him to the ground. He rolled through the dust, instincts kicking in, attempted to spring to his feet like a coiled spring, but the cost of that recklessness was already evident. The battle raged around him, as relentless as the storm brewing within.

"Rufio!" Mari screamed, her voice stirring panic in his heart. The Auralisks shielded her. As Thalos kicked a creeping monster, Mari lost her grip and fell to the ground. The brothers whose internal melodies served as a protective barrier amid the chaos. They would protect their little foal with their life.

Mari was now at ground level, unarmed, trapped in a storm of terror, and feeling utterly helpless. She needed to fight… she had to fight! But she didn't know how.

The rot had been given their dark task. Rufio was still on the ground, dodging strikes from all directions. Before another monster could strike, Brin charged, trampling through it and smashing its ghastly form into the dirt. Rufio rose to one knee, blood spattering his lips, his sword ablaze with a furious red light. Kaelith clawed beneath his skin, begging for release.

*"Our Mo Stór needs us to devour, Wildling!"* the Wild snarled. *"You cage me like a fool while she bleeds."*

Rufio's grip tightened on his blade, determination coursing through him. "I said no!" With a defiant roar, he charged into the fray.

Every swing of his sword carved arcs of crimson through the air, the energy slicing through flesh, smoke, and magic alike. Yet, with each strike, Kaelith pressed harder, the entity's voice dripping with hunger. He had never been denied his due for so long.

*"You could end this in a breath. One word. You could make it cease."* He stated.

"I'll never make her afraid of me!" Rufio growled.

*"Then she'll never truly be yours."* The entity of hunger replied.

Mari stumbled backward, her heart racing as the ground split open beside her, bubbling pools of tar erupting from the depths below. From the darkness, a creature clawed its way up, a grotesque amalgamation of skeletal remains entwined with shadowy tendrils. Panic gripped her as she fell on her back, the nightmarish form crawling toward her with horrifying determination. In that moment of desperation, she thrust her hands forward, and a blinding light erupted from her palms, brilliant and fierce like the sun itself.

The golden flare pierced through the chaos, illuminating the battlefield and serving as a beacon of hope against the encroaching darkness. With a deafening explosion, the spawn gave way to her light, its essence twisting into writhing vines that shot up from the earth, leaving behind a stark contrast of wildflowers blooming defiantly in its wake. As Mari slowly regained her footing, each drop of her blood that fell transformed the dust beneath her into vibrant green.

Amidst the turmoil, the Auralisks fought valiantly. Thalos swung his massive head in brutal arcs, while Brin slammed his tail into the ground, sending shockwaves that fractured the rot surrounding them. Rufio moved through the chaos with precision, his blade flashing as he struck down the beasts. Yet, within him, an insatiable hunger gnawed at his resolve, his pulse quickening with an unnatural rhythm as Kaelith threatened to seize control. With each beast that fell, the Wild drank deeper from the energy of their surroundings: feeding, straining against its prison.

*"You cannot starve me!"* Kaelith roared, his voice a dark thunder within Rufio's mind. *"Look at her, Wildling! She bleeds*

*so freely! Will you let her die out of fear?"*

"Enough!" Rufio shouted, the words bursting forth like the fury of a tempest.

With determination, he plunged his sword into the ground, and the earth split violently, flames erupting in a sweeping wave. Kaelith's power surged alongside him as the fiery blast ripped through the rot, forcing the creatures to retreat, hissing and wailing back into the fissures from which they came. The ground sealed behind them with a thunderous crack, and as silence fell upon the land, only the sound of their labored breaths filled the air.

Mari dropped to her hands and knees, trembling, her skin aglow with a faint golden shimmer. The chaotic battle had transformed the once-malicious rot into a breathtaking patch of wildflowers and vining shrubs. Rufio kneeled beside her, his expression a mix of concern and admiration. "You shouldn't have given so much," he breathed, worry etching lines across his brow.

"It's… what I'm supposed to do," she whispered breathlessly, brushing dirt from her cheek with a shaky hand. "I can feel it, deep in my bones. Look." She pointed to the vibrant change in the landscape; her voice infused with bittersweet pride.

Inside Rufio, a dark symphony of longing hummed: Kaelith's voice, insistent and seductive. *"Such a gift she is able to give… their hunger grows… for more."*

Rufio pushed the voice aside, grappling with a fire within him that burned brighter than any battlefield he had encountered. With a gentle touch, he rested his hand on Mari's shoulder. The moment lingered, and a flash of heat from his hand flared before he withdrew, afraid that his pulse would betray the torrent of emotions swirling beneath his stoic facade.

They pressed on, their bodies battered and minds filled with unspoken thoughts. The vibrant plains gave way to a desolate stretch of parched earth, the air thickening with the smell of decay. With each passing mile, Mari's once-bright light began to fade. Every drop of blood shed and each step they took sparked small tendrils of life from the dying ground, resilient threads reaching for survival amid the encroaching darkness.

Rufio stole glances at her, worry etched on his face. Her radiance had become a beacon in a world intent on extinguishing such warmth. She remained oblivious to the perils her light invited in a realm designed to consume it. The strain of their recent battle had drained her, leaving her unable to replenish what she had given.

As dusk descended, the horizon took on a sickly red glow. Fissures in the ground throbbed like veins, emitting an unsettling luminescence. "The Council grounds," Rufio murmured, his voice barely a whisper. "We're close."

Mari lifted her gaze, weariness etched across her pale features. Yet within her eyes burned a steadfast resolve. "Good. Perhaps we'll finally get some answers," she said, though the struggle to remain upright in the saddle betrayed the exhaustion weighing her down.

Rufio slowed their pace, his concern deepening as he observed her gradual decline. He silently vowed to keep her safe, though doubt coiled tightly around his thoughts. A haunting question echoed in his mind: Could he protect her from herself?

# Chapter 22

As they reached the last hill that overlooked the Council's domain, a sense of foreboding settled over Mari like a heavy fog. The ground pulsed beneath her, its vibrations laced with a rotten, insidious energy that sent shivers up her spine. Rufio dismounted from Brin, his tall figure standing resolutely before the looming gates, colossal stone constructs that towered above them, ancient and scarred by the violence of ages past.

Mari attempted to slide off, but her legs betrayed her, trembling beneath her weight. Just as she began to tumble, Rufio was there, arms outstretched, catching her before she hit the ground. His face, shrouded in shadows, wore the lines of worry and exhaustion etched deeper by their perilous journey.

"What's behind those walls?" she whispered, her breath ragged against his chest, where the familiar scent of earth and sweat lingered.

He hesitated, conflicted emotions swirling within him. The Wild pulsed beneath his skin, an unsettling current that whispered her name like a haunting prayer. He ached to tell her, yet the words clung to his throat, trapped like smoke.

Instead, he locked his gaze on the horizon, where the land was marred by angry red fissures that carved their way through the blackened earth, like veins of fire coursing with unquenchable fury. An internal struggle began to fracture him, a turmoil of fury and fear colliding painfully in his chest. *She gives and gives*, he thought bitterly, *until she has nothing left to save herself.*

Pain lanced through him, sharp and unrelenting, as Kaelith's voice surged within him, a guttural burn. *"Let me take this weight, my vessel."*

Rufio took a staggered breath, his body trembling as he grappled with the surge of power that flooded him, raw, burning, volatile energy that ignited his veins like wildfire. Red glows flickered in his eyes, a reflection of the chaos and shifting power unfolding within him. He did not want to lose control as the ominous reality of their situation pressed heavily upon his heart.

For a moment, the Wild feared what would happen should they were to lose control here. However, Rufio relented and allowed Kaelith to carry them both.

With an agonizing groan, the great doors of the Council slowly creaked open, as if awakening from a long slumber. A cold wind swept through the opening, swirling with whispers older than time, echoing secrets buried deep in the annals of history. Mari shivered once, then her body grew slack in his arms, surrendering to the pull of unconsciousness.

Bleeding, shaking, and burning from the tempest within,

Rufio stepped forward, cradling Mari in a desperate bridal hold. It was a fragile moment suspended in time, where obligation and sacrifice intertwined, urging him onward into the unfolding darkness.

The interior of the Council of the Ancestors unfolded like a vast, silent cathedral, its dimensions lost in the dim glow of sacred torches that lined the marble walls. Each flickering flame shimmered a deep emerald hue, casting an otherworldly light that made the intricately carved stone seem to breathe with ancient spirit. The atmosphere was dense, laden with the echoes of memories deeply woven into the essence of the location, enveloping Rufio and the unconscious Mari like a protective veil. The torches nearest the entrance flickered uneasily as he passed, their flames bending toward Mari before snapping back, as though corrected by unseen hands.

Figures cloaked in flowing robes moved with purpose. Guardians and healers alike, their eyes reflecting centuries of hard-won wisdom and hidden pain. From among them stepped a tall man, his iron-gray hair framing a face aged by toil and resolve. His eyes, forged to a steely intensity, bore into Rufio, commanding the attention of all those present. The bustling figures fell silent, the gravity of his presence palpable.

"Rufio," the man's voice rumbled, low and rough, yet laced with a familiar tenderness. "You look worse than the last time you returned from a mission. Who do you have there?"

The elder gestured to a small room concealed within an alcove. Together, Rufio and the elder walked in silence, the weight of unspoken fears hanging between them. As the elder opened the door, the flickering glow of candlelight filled the small space, illuminating shelves stocked with medicinal supplies and a cot nestled against the wall.

With a weary sigh, Rufio half-knelt, gently lowering Mari onto the richly draped cot. The vibrant fabrics, though faded by time, still clung to a sliver of warmth. As he released her hand, the absence of her touch left an aching void within him. He looked up at Eldric, his mentor, whose steady hand rested on his shoulder; a calming presence amid the turmoil raging inside.

"Eldric…" Rufio's voice trembled, caught in the tumult of denial and despair.

Eldric's gaze shifted to Mari's still form, her pulse barely pulsing beneath her delicate skin. "She's given more than most mortals could endure," he said softly, concern etching deeper lines into his face.

"She's not…" Rufio's words faltered, trapped in his throat, the harsh reality slipping through his fingers like grains of sand. He was lost in the uncertainty of what she was, unable to grasp the possibility of the truth.

Eldric's penetrating scrutiny felt like a weight pressing down on him. "The entity inside you… The hunger… It's restless, I see."

Rufio turned his head, breathing shallow and uneven. "He's been feasting on the corruption. It's everywhere… this rot. I was tasked with finding the Fletcher younglings, but that took longer than expected, stirring up too much turmoil along the way. Now I've returned to find it here, among us."

Eldric's jaw tightened, a flash of anger crossing his features. "I know. You've been away in the other world for what… thirty years in their time? This may feel like a mere whisper in your life, but it was long enough for a storm to brew here. Recently, I've sensed the essence of corruption seeping into the very walls of this sanctum. Something festers deep within the Council itself."

The revelation struck Rufio with the force of a thunderclap. "Inside?"

Eldric nodded grimly, the weight of his words hanging heavy in the air. "The balance has shifted. The corruption no longer seeps in from the outside; it's being born here, within our own refuge."

Rufio ran a trembling hand through his hair, disbelief gripping him. "That's not possible."

Eldric's expression softened, a flicker of sorrow lighting his eyes. "Once, neither was what you've become… nor what she is, my boy."

His eyes flicked briefly to Mari's wrist, then away again, as if unwilling or unable to name what he sensed forming. The elder turned toward the door, pausing in the threshold, casting one last lingering glance at the two. "Rest, my boy. Both of you. I'll summon the Council when she wakes. And Rufio…" His tone softened, glimmers of worry twisting in the depths of his gaze. "Even light can burn when it's tied to shadow."

As Eldric's footsteps echoed down the corridor, the door closed softly behind him, leaving Rufio standing in the dim glow, heart heavy and mind racing, grappling with the turbulent tide of fear and uncertainty that surged in the stillness of the sacred space. The silence that followed felt… wrong, as though the chamber itself was waiting for something it had not been instructed to allow. The flickering flames danced around him, casting wavering shadows that mirrored the turmoil within, as the weight of what lay ahead loomed like an ominous storm on the horizon.

Hours passed. The candles dimmed, their glow sinking into quiet flickers of flame.

Rufio hadn't left her side since they'd entered. His body screamed in protest, every muscle aching, every nerve alive with Kaelith's restless energy.

Mari lay pale, her hair a halo of silver light against the dark blanket. The mark on her left wrist shimmered faintly, pulsing in rhythm with his heartbeat.

He sat in the chair beside her cot, dragging it closer until his knees brushed the edge. He reached out and took her left hand in his right. Her skin was warm, her pulse faint but steady.

"Come back, Mari," he whispered hoarsely. "You've done enough. I need you to come back."

Her fingers twitched faintly, but she didn't stir. Exhaustion overtook him, heavy and absolute. "A Stór mo Chroí,"

Rufio whispered just as his head fell forward. He didn't notice when sleep claimed him, still holding her hand.

Then the world shifted, a seismic tremor echoing through the very fabric of reality. The torches throughout the halls flared to life, their flames dancing high in a mesmerizing display of white and gold. A deep, resonant hum filled the air, reverberating in Rufio's chest.

For a breathless moment, it resisted. The metal glowed and trembled. The copper band encircling his right wrist began to split, glowing with an otherworldly light. With a sudden, resonant crack, the band tore in two; one half clung to Rufio's arm, while the other shimmered away, mending itself around Mari's left wrist, replacing the fading mark that had once been there.

In that moment, the two bands blazed in unison, and

the symbol upon them shifted. From nowhere, lines began twisting like molten rivers, swirling until they formed a circle that mimicked flowing lava, with the silhouette of a tree etched carefully within. Its roots and branches entwined, cradling the core of magma; life and destruction woven together in an exquisite balance. The torches nearest the cot guttered violently, their flames dimming as though drained by the act. Somewhere deep in the hall, stones groaned; not in approval, but in protest.

A gentle flutter stirred in the air, the few remaining Solins rising from Mari's hair and drifting softly around the bands and their dormant forms. As if awakening to an unspoken call, they stirred, not to sound or touch, but to a shared pulse that vibrated in harmony.

Mari's eyes fluttered open, wide and disbelieving, and Rufio's followed a heartbeat later. He blinked, momentarily lost in the realization that their hands were still clasped. Heat surged through the points of contact, a presence alive rather than painful. Mari gasped as she absorbed the radiant display of colors from the bands, flaring crimson and green before settling back into two identical copper trinkets.

Rufio stared in disbelief, breath caught in his throat. "No…" The weight of his words hung heavily in the air, a fragile curtain of incredulity that veiled the truth.

"What… what happened? Where are we?" Mari's voice was barely a whisper, laced with confusion and wonder. She turned her head to see Rufio sitting next to her.

He couldn't respond. The wild side of him stirred for a moment, filled with chaos, but then it fell into complete stillness. There were no urges or whispers of unfulfilled longing, just an unexpected sense of calm.

Gingerly, Rufio lifted her hand, their bands now identical, their heartbeats pulsing in an intimate rhythm. "I do not know," he finally confessed, his voice raw, tinged with awe and fear. "This… this is impossible."

Mari's eyes widened, searching his face for clarity, for the truth that had eluded them both. The words of Shae echoed in her mind, a haunting premonition of their intertwined fates. "We… are we…? But how?" She sat up slowly. "I thought you could never…" Her sentence faded as her eyes glistened with unshed tears.

He shook his head, disbelief shadowing his expression as the light between them dimmed to a gentle glow, leaving nothing but the soothing cadence of their shared heartbeats. In that quiet space, Mari felt the truth hum beneath her skin, the essence of who Rufio truly was filtering through her. She had been destined to know, just as he had been destined to feel this peace for the first time since he could remember.

For the first time since the binding of man and spirit, Kaelith did not answer.

No whisper.

No hunger.

No approval.

Only a vast, unsettling stillness, like a beast that had laid its head down and gone silent.

In that moment of deep connection, Rufio felt the presence of Kaelith within him, an ancient force that typically thrived on chaos but was now at peace. The usual hunger and restlessness that had consumed Kaelith gave way to an overwhelming sense of contentment. As man and entity stood together, they were on the brink of a significant transformation, two souls united by the very essence of hunger itself.

Kaelith was quiet for now, no longer a raging force, but simply at ease. A stillness enveloped Rufio, filled with a profound awareness that he and Kaelith would emerge from this experience forever. They were no longer defined solely by their past; instead, they were shaped by the newfound strength and balance surging through their souls.

In this serene space, a profound truth settled between Mari and Rufio. He felt a fundamental shift in their existence. The forces that had brought them together did not seek the Council's approval, and whatever lay ahead would come with its own demands.

As Mari and Rufio stood at the edge of the unknown, a flicker of apprehension ran through Kaelith. There was an understanding that this was just the beginning, and deep down, the Spirit of the Wild sensed that the true challenge was still to come.

# Chapter 23

The dawn after the battle spilled a warm, golden hue through the marble windows of the Council chamber, casting intricate patterns on the stone floor. The light felt wrong, too gentle for a place steeped in judgment, too soft for what had been done here overnight. Rufio had barely closed his eyes, the mark on his wrist still pulsing with warmth, mirroring Mari's own. He sat at the edge of her cot, his fingers deftly tightening the bracer that concealed the bond between them. The copper shimmered faintly beneath the leather, a secret too delicate for mortal eyes. He had concealed it well; he had to.

If the Council caught sight of that bond, if they understood the depth of their connection, Mari would be ripped from her role as a mere witness. Instead, she would transform into an object of study, a specimen to be contained or worse, destroyed. The thought made his chest tighten, the Wild stirring uneasily beneath his ribs, not in hunger, but in something dangerously close to protectiveness.

He turned slightly as she stirred, her long brown hair, threaded with silver streaks, cascading across the pillow like a waterfall of shadows and light. Her breaths became steady and soft, filling the quiet room with a gentle rhythm. For a moment, he let himself memorize it, the rise of her chest, the faint warmth that radiated from her skin, the impossible fact that she was still here. When Mari opened her eyes, they shimmered like molten amber, catching the dawn's glow.

"Good morning," she murmured, her hand instinctively rubbing her wrists as she sat up, a flash of concern crossing her features. "You didn't sleep, did you?"

"I can't afford to," he replied, his voice a low whisper as he pulled his cloak tighter around him, the fabric rough against his skin yet familiar. "The Council has summoned us."

Mari's brow furrowed, her gaze flicking toward the door. "So soon?"

"They know we've arrived," Rufio said, his tone tinged with urgency. "And they'll demand answers. Keep your responses brief. Speak the truth, but not all of it." His eyes held hers a fraction longer than necessary, silently pleading. *Trust me.*

Before she could press him further, a gentle light flickered above them. The Solins had awoken, drifting through the air like ethereal gold dust. They spiraled down, playfully weaving through Mari's hair, wrapping silken strands around her shoulders. Their chiming was softer than usual, cautious, as if they, too, sensed the danger in these walls. In an instant, her travel clothes shimmered and dissolved into a gown of soft ivory and deep sapphire, flowing like liquid around her. The high collar framed her face, while the belt of pale light cinched her waist, the Solins nestling within the fabric, infusing it with their protective essence.

Stunned, Mari gazed down at herself, a look of wonder spreading across her features. "They're getting better at fashion," she breathed, the astonishment in her voice mingling with a hint of joy.

Rufio nearly smiled at her delight. Almost, but the weight in his chest would not allow it. "They're hiding you," he clarified gently. "That gown will veil your essence and the mark."

Yet, he withheld the truth that his own heartbeat had steadied the moment they adorned her, that the Solins had done more than shield her aura. They had also hidden his claim, wrapping it in the same fabric of protection. For the first time since the bond formed, the Wild did not resist the concealment. It simply… allowed it.

***

When they stepped into the great hall, a profound silence cascaded outward, trembling through the air like the lingering echo of a lost whisper. The Council of the Ancestors loomed in a half-circle carved from the stone, twelve elders cloaked in flowing robes of deep emerald green and pale gold, their presence steeped in authority and ancient wisdom. The chamber breathed with layered energy; old oaths, fractured truths, and something rotten threading through it all.

Mari sensed the weight of centuries hanging in the air, pressing against her chest. The mingled scents of incense and dust filled her nostrils, accompanied by the unsettling metallic tang of something amiss. It was the same scent she had begun to recognize during their travels. The smell of rot and corruption masked beneath ritual and reverence.

Beside her, Rufio smelled it too. Beneath the soothing aroma of myrrh, a subtle decay pulsed. The rot crept along the seams of the walls, slow yet insistent, alive and searching for something, or someone.

"Rufio, vessel of the Wild and Kaelith, the Primordial entity of hunger," intoned a voice from the dais, deep and resonant like the rumble of distant thunder. The eldest councilor, whose eyes gleamed like shards of flint, leaned forward with an intensity that pinned them in place. "You return at last."

"Watcher Eldric reported your victory," chimed another elder, her tone as sharp as newly cracked glass. "And your... companion."

Mari stepped forward instinctively, bowing her head, though the reason hung just beyond her understanding. She felt the Solins tighten around her shoulders, their glow dimming protectively.

Rufio's jaw tightened, tension radiating from him. "This woman is a witness to an event that cannot be dismissed."

"Explain," the flint-eyed elder commanded, not a trace of warmth in his voice.

Rufio's hand quivered at his side. He knew he could not weave lies here, not in this chamber steeped in truth and binding oaths. "She was present during the incident involving the Fletcher younglings," he said, his voice steady but taut with unspoken memories. The image flashed before him: Mari, resolute and undaunted, as the great mother pressed her forehead to hers. "She was blessed. The leader of her kind marked her. The Council must record this."

Murmurs rippled through the chamber, a tide of concern and intrigue.

A porcelain-faced elder, smooth and unyielding, leaned forward, intrigue glittering in her eyes. "Blessed by a Fletcher?" Her smile was a thin veneer barely concealing treachery. "That is… unprecedented."

"It's unheard of," another said, her voice quaking, hinting at the uncertainty that hummed in the air. "Perhaps dangerous."

Rufio's shoulders squared, filled with resolve, bolstering him. "This mortal poses no threat."

The porcelain elder's lips curled into a predatory smile. "And yet she bears a light unlike any mortal. Tell me, Wildling… why bring her here, to the heart of our sanctum?"

Rufio hesitated, his pulse racing. Kaelith stirred within him, restless and hungry. *"Tell them nothing, vessel. They reek of decay."*

"The nearest rift to her world lies within these walls," Rufio replied calmly, though the storm inside him threatened to break free. "Once the report is finished, I will return her home. Without delay."

"And what if we require her presence longer?" the porcelain elder pressed, her voice dripping with suspicion. "For study. For the safety of our world."

"Then I will remind the Council," Rufio said, his voice dropping to a low growl, "that her world is not ours. She is not yours to command."

A chill enveloped the room, tension wrapping around them like a tightening noose.

At the far end, a woman with hair white as moonlight and eyes that sparkled with unsullied wisdom spoke softly, her voice like a gentle breeze. "If the Fletchers have blessed her, then she is protected by their covenant. We must honor that."

"She must stay," hissed another elder, his voice sharp and quick, eyes glowing faintly red. "Until we understand what she carries."

Mari stiffened, her heart racing as a familiar whisper faded into her mind, layered and harmonious, like a haunting melody. One voice was Rufio's. The other, a deeper, honeyed tone, belonged to the Wild.

*"He fears for you,"* Kaelith murmured. *"He hides what you already know. You feel the bond. You hear me, do you not?"*

She blinked, swallowing hard, confusion flooding her senses. *"Who...?"* she thought.

Rufio's head snapped toward her, alarm etching his features. The entity had reached her.

Kaelith's laughter echoed in his mind, a thousand shards of dark delight. *"She hears as she should. You are one now, my vessel. You cannot silence me forever,"* the entity said in triumph.

Rufio forced himself to remain impassive, bowing low before the Council to mask the flicker of panic in his eyes. "My report stands," he declared tightly. "She is a witness, nothing more. Once the transcription is complete, I'll take her through the rift myself."

The porcelain Elder smirked, her fingers tapping rhythmically against the armrest, as if summoning fate. "We shall see. The Council will review your claim, Wildling. Until then, your... witness remains here."

Protests erupted among the untainted elders.

"This is not your decision alone!" cried the moon-haired woman, her voice piercing the tension.

"You have no right to hold her!" another added, their indignation palpable.

But the corrupted elders smiled, their eyes glinting faintly red in the shifting shadows, harboring secrets and ambitions unfathomable.

Rufio's hand instinctively moved to the hilt of his blade, muscles coiling with barely contained energy, but Mari touched his arm, her fingers delicate and soothing against the leather.

"Rufio," she whispered, her voice a fragile lifeline. "Please. Don't."

Her words cut through the chaos, calming the storm within him… barely.

The head councilor rose, his presence an unyielding force. "This matter will be settled tomorrow, once we've gathered the full assembly."

A guard stepped forward, his posture rigid, to lead them out of the Ancestor's Hall. Rufio's jaw tightened, a tempest of emotions flickering across his features, but he regained composure and nodded, his voice steady. "As you command." With a graceful bend at the waist, he reached for Mari, gently resting his hand on her elbow as they began their walk toward the imposing door, the guard trailing closely behind.

As the heavy doors thudded shut behind them, Mari finally released the breath she hadn't realized she was holding. "Are they afraid of me?" she asked, her voice laced with uncertainty.

Rufio's gaze swept across the corridor, taking in the intricate marble that gleamed with an unusual sheen, faint black veins snaking ominously across its surface. "They're not all afraid of you, Mari," he said, his tone low and steady. "They're afraid of what lurks within these walls. What's even more concerning is the effort to keep you here."

The Solins shimmered urgently.

A frown tugged at her lips. "If that's the case, why don't they address the corruption? And why me?"

"They can no longer perceive the rot," he whispered, a hint of sadness slipping into his voice. "I fear some have already been affected, corrupted in ways they cannot even begin to understand. As for the desire to hold you here… I don't have the answers."

The Solins, those ethereal beings that guarded her, shimmered delicately around her shoulders, their faint whispers weaving through the air like a gentle breeze. Though their voices were tiny and soft, Mari felt the urgency in their tones, a chorus of worry enveloping her.

Rufio turned to face her, his expression grave, eyes filled with fierce protectiveness. "Stay close to me," he instructed, voice barely above a whisper. "And don't engage with anyone unless I'm right there with you."

Mari nodded, her heart pounding, but then a flicker of doubt crossed her mind. "Rufio… the voice I heard back there. It didn't belong to you."

His gaze darkened, shadowed by something heavy and unspoken. "I know," he replied, the weight of his words hanging in the air between them.

Neither Mari nor Rufio needed to voice the name of the entity that hung like a dark cloud over their journey. The Wild, the monstrous entity, had found her and began to know her. Kaelith sensed the imminent presence of its own insatiable needs and desires. The implications of this awareness sent a shiver down her spine. And somewhere deep beneath the Council's stone, something ancient and hungry for power shifted, aware now that a bond had been formed, by what or whom.

# Chapter 24

The corridor that led from the Council chamber transformed from opulent marble and gold into a somber passage of cold, weathered stone. Here, the air shifted; it was cleaner, invigorated by the scent of iron and oil. The heavy remnants of incense and corruption fell away with each step, replaced by raw vitality.

Mari walked beside Rufio, her boots gliding softly over the worn flagstones smoothed by centuries of passing soldiers. The flickering torches cast dim light overhead, illuminating shields that were meticulously arranged along the walls in rhythmic patterns. An earthy aroma of metal and sweat filled the space, a scent she hadn't realized she yearned for until this moment. It was grounding.

Rufio was a figure carved from granite, tall and poised, his presence radiating readiness for battle. Every soldier they encountered, men and women alike, paused in their duties, saluting or bowing instinctively. Silence enveloped them; respect trailed behind him like a devoted shadow. Rufio acknowledged each gesture with a nod or a firm clasp of a warrior's hand, an unspoken bond shared in that moment of solidarity.

Mari leaned closer, unable to suppress her curiosity. "You're quite the figure here, aren't you?"

Though he did not meet her gaze, a hint of a smile flickered at the corners of his mouth. "I have lived long enough. Now, I am simply the one who is remembered."

"Still sounds like a big deal," she whispered, her tone light, yet laced with admiration.

Rufio turned sharply into another corridor, his focus unwavering. "You need a weapon," he said, his voice low and resolute. "There will be times when I won't be able to shield you from what's coming."

Mari swallowed hard. "What is coming?"

"The rot," he replied, grim and straightforward. "And those who feed it."

They arrived before a set of imposing double doors crafted from dark ironwood, intricately carved with sigils depicting entwined fire and water. Rufio pressed his palm to the center rune, and with a resonant groan, the doors began to shimmer and open inward, inviting them into the unknown ahead.

The warded armory unfolded before her, a vast cathedral of wood, iron, and steel, echoing with an ancient resonance. Sunlight poured through towering windows, illuminating shimmering racks laden with blades, staffs, spears, and bows. Swords and axes glinted off the walls, their edges sharp and merciless, while armor glowed softly with intricate enchantments. In the farthest corner, a massive war axe, older than the Council itself, loomed like a sentinel of forgotten battles.

Mari halted at the threshold, heart racing. An electric pulse of energy pulsed through the air, a silent beckoning from the weapons, hungry and expectant. It was as if they could sense her uncertainty, waiting for her to make a choice.

Rufio stepped forward, his presence solid and grounded. "Every weapon here carries a history," he said, his voice steady yet taut. "Each one has tasted blood. Some for justice. Others for vengeance. Choose with intention."

As she walked slowly among the racks. The air thickened with the metallic scent of smoke and iron. Her fingers glided over hilts, each one a fragment of a story; a whisper of fear, triumph, and regret brushing against her skin. A blade caught her attention, sleek and silver-edged, its handle swathed in crimson leather. She reached for it, a heartbeat's pause electrifying the air around her.

In its polished surface, she glimpsed not her current self but the woman she could become, hard and empty, a killer. A chill raced down her spine, and her hand fell away, trembling.

Rufio watched her, his dark eyes narrowing as he sensed the tumult within her.

He could feel Kaelith stirring, a low, velvety voice curling around their bond. *"She hesitates. Her heart may not be made for killing. Yet, in this world, survival often calls for blood."*

"No," Rufio thought fiercely, his jaw clenching. "Not her. I won't let her lose herself like that."

*"Then what are you willing to do?"* Kaelith challenged, his tone sharp. *"Will you abandon her when the shadows close in, Aodhán? When you cast me into slumber again? Do you truly think you could escape? Will you run again?"*

Mari's focus shifted, drawn to the far wall. Behind a dusty rack of old spears hung a pair of twin metallic adornments designed to be worn on the hands. Delicate and curved like crescent moons, they resembled brass knuckles entwined with intricate chains that cascaded up her arms. Their edges shimmered faint hues of green, pink, blue, and gold; colors reminiscent of life itself.

With a sense of reverence, she lifted one. It felt ethereal, light, and perfectly balanced, as if it had been waiting for her. When she took the second, the pieces came alive, curling gently around her hands and forearms, chains shimmering in hues of green, gold, and rose.

"This one," she breathed, awe creeping into her voice.

Rufio's interest piqued. "Those are the enchanted root chains. They are meant to hone one's energy and intent for protection and defense. I've never seen anyone able to wear them before."

Her resolve hardened. "I don't want to kill anything," she stated firmly. "I just want to keep it from killing me."

The corners of Rufio's mouth twitched upward slightly, the faintest glimmer of pride illuminating his gaze. "Then you've chosen well, Mari."

Kaelith stirred again, quieter this time, an unsettling undercurrent in his thoughts. *"She chooses life over survival. Can you see it, vessel? That is why she is dangerous. That is why I..."*

The entity's voice faltered and fell silent.

Rufio froze mid-step, the weight of Kaelith's unspoken words pressing against him. *"Why you what?"*

But Kaelith did not respond. For the first time, the silence felt heavy not with cunning but with an unfamiliar shame that resonated through their bond. Kaelith's thoughts simmered in the hollow of Rufio's chest.

Thoughts coiled through Kaelith like tendrils of smoke. *An entity does not love; we take, we hunger, we devour. Yet, when she breathes, I sense balance. I feel... peace; something I was never meant to experience. You are the vessel, Rufio, but she... she is the balm that heals our wounds.* The depth of sorrow within the Wild confused Rufio, but he remained silent, unsure of the entity's thoughts.

Rufio clenched his gauntlet, leather creaking under the strain. *"It will take both of us, Kaelith. Help me protect her. We can no longer fight for supremacy. For her and this land, I am willing to unite."*

The Wild's laughter echoed in his mind, soft yet tinged with sorrow and resolve. *"Unity will cost you. Are you willing to die for her, man of fire?"*

Without hesitation, Rufio's thoughts surged forth. Suppose it will keep her safe and get her back home, *"Then yes. I'll pay it."*

The ensuing silence was dense, a pact forged between predator and protector, a bond solidified in shared purpose.

Mari turned back, oblivious to the storm roiling within him. "I think this is enough," she said softly.

Rufio nodded, his expression shifting into focus. He reached for a dagger nearby, sliding it into his belt alongside his sword, the blade glistening like onyx and amethyst under the dim light. "Then let's get you somewhere safe. My quarters aren't far. You can find rest there before morning."

As they emerged from the armory, the air around them crackled with unspoken weight, a potent mix of choices already made and the looming decisions yet to come. It felt alive, vibrating with the possibility of what lay ahead.

Suddenly, Mari halted, her eyes widening. "You live here too?" Curiosity spilled from her voice, slicing through the tension.

Without waiting for a reply, Rufio strode forward, confident in his path, expecting her to keep pace. Mari hurried to catch up, her steps echoing in the silent corridor. The soldiers they passed still nodded, but this time, their eyes lingered on her, not with disdain, but with a mix of wonder and intrigue. Whispers followed them like soft shadows: The blessed one. The Wildling's companion. The otherworlder.

* * *

Rufio pushed open the heavy door to his chamber in the officers' barracks, the hinges creaking softly, almost mournfully. The room was humble, with stone walls that felt cool against their skin, a bed draped in a worn quilt that seemed to cradle memories, a small desk and chair nestled in the corner. The lone book on the desk held secrets, and a box with intricately carved flowers whispered of love and loss. The scent of cedar and smoke enveloped them, its familiarity wrapping around Rufio like a forgotten embrace.

Mari's gaze softened as she took in the space. "This place... it feels like you," she said, brushing her fingertips along the quilt's frayed edges, dust motes swirling in the streaming light.

Rufio turned away, unable to meet her eyes. He leaned against the wall, setting his sword down for the first time in what felt like ages. "It's the only part of my home I was able to bring with me." His voice was layered with bittersweet nostalgia.

Her smile dimmed slightly. "You made this?" she asked, her touch gentle against the fabric.

"My mother." The words fell from him like autumn leaves, quiet and reverent. "She made it before she passed." The admission hung heavy in the air, filled with all the things left unsaid, a mother's care, a son's loss.

Silence enveloped the room like a gentle cocoon until Mari broke it, approaching the small desk with a sense of intrigue. Rufio, lost in his own thoughts as he removed the last remnants of his gear, barely registered her growing curiosity.

"These drawings are exquisite," she remarked, her voice filled with admiration as she leafed through the pages. "This woman looks so familiar..."

Before she could turn the page again, the journal was suddenly yanked from her grasp. "Some things are sacred."

Embarrassment flashed across his face, heat rising to his cheeks. "Do you always have to be so nosy and poke your nose into everything?" The words came out harsher than he intended, but his gaze softened as he recognized his mistake.

Stunned, Mari stood frozen, her hands still poised as if she were cradling the book. Her mouth opened and closed; a fish out of water. A flicker of shame washed over her, bitterness and dread intertwining in her chest.

Rufio ran a hand through his hair, his copper band humming next to the journal, a soft reminder of their bond. "There are parts of my life I hold sacred. This..." He lifted the book, cradling it like a fragile memory. "This is one."

"May I know who she is?" Mari's voice trembled, laced with a hint of jealousy that caught her off guard. She hadn't meant for it to slip out, but there it was, raw and vulnerable.

"My... deepest wish." Rufio's heart felt like lead, the weight of his truth heavy in the air.

Silence enveloped them again, the only sound the soft fluttering of the curtains, a reminder of the outside world. Mari lifted her left hand, examining the band wrapped around her wrist, the symbol of their bond. "I know you are stuck with me, Ruf…"

"Stop!" he interrupted, his tone harsh. Authoritative. "We are chosen to be bonded. But I am not, and have never been, stuck with you." His expression shifted as he stepped closer, lifting her chin gently to meet his gaze. "I have been blessed once to sacrifice my life, my choices to be bonded to the most powerful being who can devour this corruption and everything with it. And now I am bonded to you."

His eyes held a fierce resolve, a tempest of emotions swirling within. As she returned his stare, the depths of darkness and the flickers of fire ignited a hunger for understanding in her. Within her mind, the entity's presence caressed her cheek, a ghostly caress that both frightened and comforted her.

For better or worse, they were intertwined in this unpredictable storm together.

With a heavy sigh, Mari sank onto the bed, her heart turbulent. "You're going to insist on the floor again, aren't you?"

Rufio raised an eyebrow, humor breaking through his seriousness. "Yes."

"Well, I'm going to insist you don't." She pulled back the blanket and patted the space beside her, warmth radiating from her gesture. "Top of the covers, soldier. We've been through worse."

He hesitated, an internal battle of pride and fatigue, before relenting with a quiet exhale. As he lay on the quilt, she nestled beneath it, their shoulders barely brushing, an electric tension sparking between them.

The torches flickered low, shadows dancing across the stone walls, the air between them humming with energy, a delicate balance of restraint and yearning, heartbeats synchronizing with unspoken promises.

Rufio's thoughts drifted like autumn leaves caught in a windstorm, toward the battle awaiting them, the insidious corruption within the Council, and the impossible choice looming ahead.

Kaelith's final whisper coiled through him like a sacred vow. *"Tomorrow, blood will fall. If we stand together, we may yet live. But if she falls, vessel, I will burn the heavens themselves to find her soul."*

"Then pray we both survive," he murmured, his voice barely above a whisper, laden with trepidation.

In the flickering twilight of the dying torchlight, Mari's hand sought the warmth of his hand. Strong and steady. A bridge built on trust, fear, and something deeper still.

The night before the storm always held a profound quietness, a stillness pregnant with the knowledge of what was to come. In that silence, they found solace in each other's steadiness, ready, together, for the tempest that approached.

# Chapter 25

**Interlude - The Shadow of the Corruptor**

Meanwhile, far from their struggle, the Corruptor was taking shape in the shadows. Once known as Vandran, a Watcher dedicated to the sacred duty of maintaining balance between worlds and dimensions, he was brilliant, meticulous, and endlessly patient. He embodied the qualities cherished by those tasked with protecting the delicate veils that separate realms. Yet his ambitions reached far beyond mere stewardship; his aspirations were too grand for simply overseeing the flow of existence.

Vandran became consumed by a restless hunger for knowledge and power, delving deep into the intricate dance of energy that flowed through creation. Balance was not sacred to him; it was inefficient. His brilliance earned him praise from the Council, which regarded him as a beacon of hope and deliverance. But their trust would prove to be their gravest mistake.

As he traversed realms with the ease of a shadow and executed his duties with elegant precision, he uncovered a haunting truth that many chose to ignore: the silent panic of dying lands, the cries of worlds starved for life. One fateful day, while conducting research in a forgotten world, he found the Wild a primordial force thrumming with untamed energy. The corruption left in the wake of people's cruelty had decimated the land, but the Wild sought to cleanse it, embodying a living paradox of destruction and renewal.

Ensnared by the allure of the Wild's power, Vandran mistook its echo of danger for an invitation. In that moment of delusion, he reached toward the darkness, crossing a threshold from which he could never return. Thus began his tragic transformation into the Corruptor, a being far removed from the oath he once cherished.

Whispers of consumption and power hung in the air like untold secrets, the essence of Kaelith, the same Wild primordial force that roamed the edges of reality. Legends warned that those daring enough to summon this entity would be consumed, their souls swallowed whole by insatiable hunger. But Vandran believed himself different, strong enough to tame that chaos others feared.

He endeavored to bind the Wild as one would a pet, but his energy ritual proved a cruel deception. In a thunderous flare of fury and raw power, Kaelith erupted forth as an entity far beyond Vandran's grasp. Swiftly, it offered him one piercing word before retreating into its realm: Denied. That moment shattered the remnants of Vandran's humanity, leaving a hollow void where hope once resided.

For the next century, he became a specter of vengeance, biding his time while his peers oversaw portals and safeguarded the balance of worlds. In secret, he embraced a darker path: corruption. Mastering the art of twisting energy until it bent willingly to his will, he learned to siphon the dying essences of worlds, nurturing himself on their decay.

As dawn approached, the shadows stirred, and the storm loomed, Kaelith's hunger unquenched, and Vandran's darkness waiting to be unleashed. The fates of the vessel and the Corruptor were entwined, each whispering the promise of an inevitable clash, where life and death would hang in the balance.

# Chapter 26

Rufio woke first, an unsettling ripple coursing through him. The air within the officer's quarters felt suffocatingly still, an uncanny silence that swallowed the usual cacophony of sounds from the military outside. There were no shouts from sergeants, no clattering of boots on the ground, and the familiar murmur of soldiers preparing for their morning exercises had vanished. It was the kind of quiet that followed a disturbance, an ominous prelude that hinted at something having gone horribly wrong. Only the pulse of the Wild throbbed faintly in his chest, its uneasy rhythm mirroring the growing tension in the room.

He shifted slightly, turning his head to catch a glimpse of Mari, who lay beside him, lost in a dream world. Her features were softened by the dim light filtering through the curtains, one hand resting lightly against the quilt his mother had sewn, his last anchor to a home untouched by the rot consuming their world. Her breathing was serene, a gentle whisper amidst the oppressive quiet that enveloped them.

Unbidden, Kaelith's presence unfurled in his mind like a dark banner. *"Wake her. The air tastes of death!"*

Instinct propelled Rufio into action. "Mari," he murmured, shaking her shoulder gently, his voice barely above a whisper, strained, urgent, controlled.

Her eyes fluttered open, glazed with remnants of sleep. "What is it? What time is it?" she mumbled, a hint of confusion lacing her voice.

Before he could respond, a heavy, rhythmic pounding reverberated through the quarters, echoing off the walls like a herald of doom. A voice followed, unmistakably sharp, muffled yet commanding, like metal scraping across stone. "Captain. The Council requests your presence in the Grand Hall. Immediately."

Rufio froze. That tone carried no respect. No break for breath. That tone, cold. Even disrespectful, it sent a jolt of unease through Rufio.

Kaelith's presence stiffened like a tightened bowstring. *"That is not one of ours."*

Rufio's pulse rose; each beat was a warning to prepare for battle. He shot up, instinctively grabbing his blade and clasping his cloak around his shoulders, his eyes sweeping the dimly lit room for any hint of danger.

Mari was now awake, scrambling to put her boots, cloak, and root chains on her hands. She was scared, not used to the unease of a battle to come. In this moment, she truly felt like a clumsy little foal.

"Stay behind me," he said, his voice low, frayed at the edges. "Something's off."

Mari, alert now, obeyed without hesitation, quickly gathering her composure and pulling her cloak tightly around her. As she moved, the copper band at her wrist flickered faintly, responding not to danger, but to him. The Solins floated into place around her shoulders and waist.

With a determined breath, he unbarred the door, revealing a soldier standing sentinel on the other side, armor dulled and, in some spots, rusted with age, eyes empty and dark. Rufio had never seen armor like that. The Council's sigil glimmered on his chest plate, but its lines twisted subtly, a grotesque parody of its former glory.

"The Council awaits," the man intoned again, his voice flat, devoid of warmth.

As Mari's fingers briefly brushed against Rufio's wrist, a jolt of electricity surged between them. *Something's wrong,* her energy whispered, urgent and primal.

He nodded almost imperceptibly, squeezing her hand as reassurance, though his gut churned with doubt. "Lead the way."

They trailed after the soldier into the dimly lit corridor of the soldiers' hall, the sharp clatter of his boots reverberating against the cold stone floor, punctuating the oppressive silence. As they penetrated deeper into the heart of the Council's stronghold, the air grew denser, thick with an unsettling weight that hinted at hidden rot and decay. The soldier's footsteps softened as they transitioned onto the smoother marble floor, creating a muted rhythm that seemed to blend into the foreboding surroundings rather than the usual clacking of boots. This was unnatural work at play.

The glowstones flickered erratically, casting shadows that twisted and danced in ways they shouldn't have. The air around Rufio crackled with a chill that seemed to seep into his very bones. With every step he took, the weight of impending dread pressed down on him, deepening the unease that had settled in the pit of his stomach.

Rufio's jaw clenched, a tight line of resolve set against the encroaching darkness. "This hall should be guarded," he murmured, urgency lacing his voice.

Mari stood beside him, her breath now visible in the frigid air, trembling slightly as she whispered, "It was last night, Rufio… It's so cold out here, Ru…?"

A blood-curdling scream erupted from somewhere deep below, a desperate sound that was swallowed almost instantly by an unsettling silence. The soldier beside them remained unnervingly still, a statue in a storm of chaos.

Kaelith's voice slithered into Rufio's mind, sharp and filled with disdain. *"The soldier is hollow. A puppet. There is a familiar scent in his veins, a taint that runs deep."*

Rufio grabbed Mari's hand. "Run!"

# Chapter 27

Rufio and Mari sprinted forward, leaving the tainted soldier behind. As they neared the grand archway to the Great Hall, an oppressive push enveloped them, sharp and bitter. The scent of iron mingling with smoke, curling into their lungs, pushing them back from what was ahead.

Rufio stepped ahead, and a protective barrier formed around Mari as he pushed against the heavy doors, the wood groaning under his effort. Then, with a violent gust, the doors swung open as if compelled by unseen forces, revealing a scene of utter chaos within the Great Hall.

A cacophony of clashing metal rang through the air beneath the vaulted ceiling, a symphony of violence. Soldiers writhed in battle, some grotesquely twisted in shadow, their armor blackened, and their faces hidden behind tendrils of putrescence. Others, still righteous and pure, fought with desperate fury to maintain a faltering line. Corrupted energy crackled through the air, stitching searing scars into the once-sacred marble floor, each crack a testament to the darkness that had invaded their sanctuary.

Above the fray, Elders stood on the dais, their primal shouts mingling with the clamor of war-torn robes swirling like remnants of hope lost, blood staining their hands as they engaged in a grim struggle of their own. One sought destruction, while another desperately fought to salvage the fragments of their world.

At the center of the hall, a pulsating rift throbbed ominously, a raw wound in the fabric of reality itself. From its depths, tendrils of shadow spilled forth, whispering secrets in voices too weak to comprehend, weaving a web of torment that clawed at Mari's core. She felt it before she saw it. An entity that knew her name.

She gasped, her heart racing. "NO…"

The rift's dreadful pull twisted her stomach, as though it hungered for her very essence. For a moment, she felt herself teeter on the edge of consciousness. Her body was being dragged closer to the void, yet her will was immovable, aiding to freeze her in place.

*"Focus, Mari,"* she chanted within herself. There was so much heartbreak to digest, so many frayed strings of hope unraveling before her. *"I have to do something!"*

Suddenly, the soldier who had knocked on their door caught up to them, advancing with a menacing gait. The corners of his mouth curled into a taunting, inhuman smile. "Welcome, Wildling," he hissed, the sound slithering through the air, his eyes gleaming with a predatory gold. "He's been expecting you."

In a horrifying instant, the soldier's body convulsed, disintegrating into a cloud of black ash, disappearing like a whisper in the wind, leaving nothing but an ominous silence in his wake.

"Kaelith!" Rufio bellowed, the steel of his blade glinting dangerously in the chaos.

*"With you,"* he rumbled, as the world around them transformed into a storm of fury and despair. Together, they surged into the fray, Rufio moving with the tempest's ferocity, his weapon a blazing arc of silver fire. Each swing sent sparks cascading across the battlefield, illuminating the faces twisted with rage and rot.

Kaelith's power coursed through Rufio's veins, a fierce flame that annihilated the rotting darkness wherever it struck, yet with every cleave, every strike cost him. Every monster struck down, more took its place, somehow syphoning Rufio's strength, weakening him. The air crackled with energy, filled with the scent of scorched earth and the metallic tang of blood.

Mari narrowly avoided a searing blast that tore through the air, transforming the wall behind her into shattered pieces. Her heart raced violently in her chest as she tapped into the well of light within her. She would not be a victim. Using the root chains, light erupted outward in radiant waves of gold, washing over her allies and mending their wounds, while driving back the insatiable corruption. Amidst the carnage, Mari felt adrift, her resolve shaken. Never before had she witnessed such brutal death and despair.

The rot, a malevolent entity, thrived on their fear and hopelessness. Each time Rufio fell a corrupted soldier, more arose to take their place, grotesque shadows of those they once were. Rufio grappled with the agony of each strike, unwilling to extinguish the lives of his brothers and sisters in arms. But still, the tide of darkness surged, relentless and merciless.

"Thalos! Brin!" Mari screamed into the chaos, desperation cutting through her voice. "Where are you?" Panic gripped her heart. How had everything unraveled so swiftly?

Then, the thundering hooves of the Auralisks broke through the cacophony, galloping fiercely toward their little foal. Their bodies glowed with radiant energy, pulsating with an unstoppable force. The sheer will of the Auralisks bore down on the corrupted soldiers, bending them to their knees as they clutched their heads in agony.

"Don't kill them! They could still be in there!" Rufio shouted, his voice rough with urgency as he spun to face Mari. "Stay with the Auralisks!"

"I won't leave you!" she defiantly replied, turning to her majestic champions. Just then, one of the corrupted soldiers lunged at her; she felt the rush of air as it came close, but the creature fell to the ground, hands clutching its head in torment from the Auralisk call.

The battle raged on, chaos and motion intertwining, and Mari knew she had to find her strength amidst the storm.

From the upper tiers of the hall, shadows began to thicken, gathering with an ominous purpose. And then he emerged: The Corruptor.

He descended the stairs as if gravity itself bent to his will, his robes woven from darkness, cloaking him in an eerie shroud. A hood obscured his face, and the edges of his form rippled like smoke in the dim light. His voice, calm and melodic, echoed with an ancient resonance. "Ah, the Wildling and his tether. I wondered how long it would take for you to finally arrive."

Rufio felt his blood run cold. "Elder Vandran? What...?"

A sinister smile curled the Corruptor's lips as he tilted his head, an unsettling blend of amusement and malice. "You should not resist. This is just the beginning, boy."

With a flick of his hand, the floor beneath them cracked open, sinewy tendrils of darkness reaching out. A wave of black fire erupted forth, a monstrous roar that sent soldiers hurtling through the air. Mari screamed as the inferno collided with the barrier conjured by the Solins, the energy flickering under the assault. She buckled, collapsing to her hands and knees, pain etched across her features.

Kaelith's roar pierced through the chaos. *"He is attempting to syphon her power! Release me, I know who he is! He must be stopped, vessel!"*

"No!" Rufio grunted, resisting the relentless pressure as he struggled to keep Kaelith at bay. *"She'll see what we truly are! We would annihilate them all! Nothing will remain!"*

Kaelith laughed, sharp and desperate. *"She already knows, Aodhán."*

With newfound resolve, Rufio lunged forward, clashing blades with a wraith-like shadow that danced just beyond the tangible. The impact seared his arms, and flames almost licked his palms through his gloves. The Corruptor moved with inhuman grace, each step leaving trails of smoke that drifted into the air like haunted memories.

"You still fight for her?" He laughed. "She is mine now!" The Corruptor taunted, his voice slick with triumph. "Fool. You could never keep her safe."

However, with the Corruptor's taunt, Mari's light flared anew, burning brighter than before. Drawing upon her innermost strength, she rose again, arms wide open as waves of brilliance radiated through the hall. Soldiers froze in their tracks, the corrupting shadows sizzling and retreating, but the effort took its toll.

Color drained from her cheeks as a blood-curdling scream tore from her lips, and her hands began to shake. Her vision dimmed. The taste of iron flooded her mouth. Desperate to heal, to revive, to restore balance amidst the chaos, Mari pulled energy from the very air around her. Yet, as she poured everything she had into her efforts, she felt her strength waning. Despite the growing weakness in her body, she fought against exhaustion, determined to heal and restore. But eventually, she found herself at the brink; there was nothing more she could give.

Rufio turned towards her in horror, panic gripping his heart. "Stop, Mari! You'll..." His voice cracked as he watched her collapse, a marionette cut from its strings, her protective barrier shattered. The Auralisks fought valiantly to remain near her, their efforts met with the relentless push of the shadowy force surrounding them, but it was a losing battle. The hall echoed with despair, a symphony of chaos, urgency, and sacrifice.

She looked at him one last time through the surrounding battle. Not afraid. Not surprised. Resolved.

*If I don't,* her eyes said, *they all die.*

This distraction allowed a tendril of shadow to strike Rufio in the chest. The shadow sharpened to an onyx dagger to the heart and Sigil. Sharp pain like molten metal ripped through his body, and through Kaelith's. The copper band on his wrist flared red before slithers of black began to wrap around the tree, black tendrils crawling along the metal.

He could hear Mari's voice echoing in his mind, her desperate cries reaching out to him through the darkness. But chains of shadows, thick and oppressive, coiled around her wrists, dragging her slowly beneath the floor, to the sinister realm where the Corruptor thrived.

"Let her go!" Rufio's roar shattered the stillness, a raw surge of anguish and fury. He inhaled deeply, savoring her sweet scent that lingered like a fleeting memory.

"She is the light I need," the Corruptor hissed, a cruel smirk painted across his face. "And I am the one who will keep it burning, for eternity."

The tumult within Rufio's soul erupted; Kaelith screamed, his voice resonating like a tempest. *"No... she is ours!"*

The Corruptor's laughter twisted through the air, a sound that warped reality itself. Shadows surged upward, swallowing Mari whole. In an instant, she vanished into the void, leaving nothing but a small dark pool of her blood on the cold floor.

He couldn't breathe. As Rufio stumbled forward, his heart pounding like a war drum, he was half-blind by grief and fury. His sword, his ally, slipped from his grasp, clattering against the stone. He reached out, fingertips brushing against the emptiness where she had stood.

Nothing. Fighting was all around him, but it did not matter. His life draining from the wound in his chest did not matter. Nothing mattered at that moment.

"No," he whispered, voice shredded. "No..." The warmth that once radiated there was already replaced by chilling desolation. Falling to his knees, he screamed, a guttural sound filled with despair that echoed off the walls, a raw testament to his loss.

Grief wrapped around him like an iron vice, tightening with each breath, each painful realization. "I promised you," he choked out into the emptiness, a vow echoing against the silence. His fist, trembling with raw emotion, came crashing down onto the polished marble, splintering the surface and leaving a spiderweb of fissures in his wake.

In response to his anguish, the Auralisk's hooves erupted into a thunderous rhythm, a defiant roar breaking the oppressive stillness. Their now golden battle scales glimmered brilliantly, casting a warm light that pierced through the surrounding gloom. Crumbling beams from the shattered ceiling fell like the hands of lost time, bathing the chaos in radiant streaks that burned away the remnants of decay, illuminating the purity of their struggle.

Brin charged to Rufio's side, his warm bulk kneeling, pressing against Rufio's shoulder, grounding him amidst the turmoil. Kaelith offered the last of his strength, allowing Rufio to slide over the Auralisk's back. Then, they retreated out of the hall.

Amidst the symphony of clashing energies, Kaelith's voice reverberated within him a ghostly whisper laced with hope. *"She is not lost, Wildling. But the toll we must pay... it could shatter us beyond all recognition."*

Rufio squeezed his eyes shut, fighting against the surge of despair that threatened to overwhelm him. His fingers curled protectively around the fractured band encircling his wrist, a tether to her spirit and his promise. "I will find you," he vowed softly, each syllable draping his words in a mix of fierce determination and looming dread.

Then, as if the fabric of reality itself could hold no longer, darkness swept over him like an inexorable tide, pulling him into its depths. In the aftermath of his descent, a heartbeat of silence enveloped him, leaving only a lingering echo of hope suspended in the void. What would he be willing to sacrifice to rescue her? In that harrowing moment, what would Rufio and Kaelith have to embrace to make it possible?

# Chapter 28

The hall of ancestors burned.

Stone cracked as black rot pulsed across the marble walls and fallen roof timbers, swallowing the carved runes of protection that had stood for centuries. The air reeked of iron and ash. The Auralisks thundered down the corridor, hooves shattering the floor tiles as they fought their way through the flood of corrupted soldiers.

Rufio hung limp across Brin's back, blood trailing from the wound in his chest where the corrupted energy blade had pierced his heart. His skin was gray, his breath barely there. Solins spiraled in a blur of gold light around him, desperate to hold the last of his spark of life in place.

*"Keep moving!"* Thalos bellowed to Brin, rearing to slam his hooves into a charging guard. Bone cracked, the sound echoing through the dying hall.

Brin swung his massive head, striking out with his horns,

hitting the attacker's side. *"He fades, brother!"* he roared. *"The poison eats through him!"*

Kaelith's voice tore from Rufio's body in a thunderous snarl. *"You will not take him from me!"* The Wild's roar rolled through the chamber, cracking torches, burning the rot to ash.

The corrupted soldiers faltered only a moment before their commander shrieked, "Do not let the Wildling escape!"

Brin and Thalos charged the doors. Arrows of shadow and flame streaked past them, searing flesh where their scales had cracked or broken, but they did not slow. The great doors splintered beneath their combined strike, bursting outward into blinding daylight. They galloped away, leaving a trail of destruction in their wake.

***

The plains opened before them, vast, new growth shimmering in the sun. Behind them, the Ancestor's Hall bled black smoke into the sky. Only when the walls were distant, and the air thinned of rot, did the Auralisks stop.

*"He's slipping,"* Thalos whispered.

The brothers collapsed to the ground in the tall grass, hooves burned and legs trembling. Rufio's body slid from Brin's back, falling to the ground. His breath came out in short bursts. The Solins slowly drifted around Rufio's still form, their light dim and flickering, trying to keep him alive.

Kaelith hissed from within the dying man, voice warped and ragged. *"If I die, he dies. If he dies, the balance breaks."*

Brin's scales rippled back to their metallic color, his anger rising. *"Then neither of you dies today."*

He stomped, the sound echoing like a drumbeat across the plains. *"Thalos, his shirt."*

Thalos bent low, his massive teeth catching the torn fabric

and ripping it away from Rufio's chest. The wound was ugly, black veins spiraling outward like lightning scars.

Thalos exhaled, then lowered his head. One. Two. Then three luminous scales fell free, each glowing with living light. He chewed them slowly, grinding them into a thick paste before pressing the glowing mixture to Rufio's chest. He licked it in place with the precision of ritual. The air filled with the scent of ozone, rain, and burning flesh.

Rufio convulsed. Kaelith screamed within him, the sound shaking the ground. The Wild and Light collided, blazing through flesh and spirit. The poison hissed, burned, and then was gone.

"Breathe," Thalos murmured. "Come back to us."

Rufio gasped, his lungs filling with air as if he were drawing breath for the very first time. The shadow of the Wild receded, leaving his eyes flickering with faint glimmers of gold and crimson before they settled back into their deep, onyx hue.

He blinked up at the Auralisk, his voice cracking like thunder in stillness. "Mari."

Neither of them answered, an ominous silence hanging in the air like a storm cloud ready to break. Rufio's heart raced as confusion twisted into horror within him. "Where you able...?"

Brin looked away, his gaze averted as if he could not bear the weight of his friend's despair. *We ran. She... she was not upon either back when the gates fell.*

A chill coursed through Rufio. "No..." Panic clawed at his throat, and his breath came in sharp, violent bursts. He forced himself to stand, fists clenched, focused on their newly shared bond. His band hummed faintly. "She's not gone! I can feel her, faint, but alive!"

Kaelith's voice rumbled like distant thunder in his chest, heavy and foreboding. *"The Corruptor took her, the same one who trapped me in stone before you."*

Thalos perked up, ears twitching in alarm. *"The ancient one of all shadows and stench?"*

Kaelith's growl deepened, resonating with an intensity that made the air around them tremble.

*"He was a Watcher; one who coveted the life of worlds, who wanted to siphon their very essence. He pleaded for my bond, to wield the Wild for his own twisted desires. I refused him. In his rage, he forged a path of deceit, feeding on the teetering balance between light and dark. Now he wants her... A stór mo chroí.... She would sustain him forever."*

Agony twisted in Rufio's chest at the thought of Mari ensnared in the Corruptor's grasp, his conviction hardening like steel. The atmosphere crackled with unspoken tension, the weight of their mission pressing down like an approaching storm. He inhaled deeply, the scent of damp earth and the promise of rain filling his lungs, fortifying him for the challenge ahead.

"We're getting her back," Rufio stated firmly, a fire igniting in his chest.

Brin's eyes blazed with determination, his voice steady but intense. *"We refuse to let him take her from us. We cannot fail her."*

With newfound focus, the trio squared their shoulders, determination carving strong lines into their faces. Dark shadows of uncertainty loomed around them, but beneath it all, the flicker of hope burned bright, urging them deeper into the encroaching darkness.

An oppressive silence wrapped around them, each heartbeat

loud in the still air. The wind rustled through the trees, carrying the distant rumble of thunder, even as the sky above was willing to aid in this fight.

Rufio lowered to one knee, his fingers gripping the earth, drawing strength from the ground beneath him. "We go after her," he proclaimed, his voice unwavering despite the turmoil inside.

Thalos, frustration boiling within him, slammed his hoof into the ground. *"You're out of your mind, Wildling! You'd throw yourself back into that deathtrap?"*

Rufio's gaze shot up, his eyes burning with fierce resolve. "She sacrificed everything to mend this broken world. I would give everything to bring her home!" He paused, harnessing his emotions, his conviction deepening with each word. "She deserves no less. Not from me."

Kaelith's voice, a gentle murmur in his mind, interjected, *"You would sacrifice us both for her?"*

Rufio inhaled slowly, closing his eyes to steady himself. "Not sacrifice," he replied softly, his tone barely above a whisper. "I choose her mind, her heart, her soul over my own. You will need to choose for yourself."

For a moment, even the Wild seemed to hold its breath in contemplation.

In the ensuing silence, Kaelith's laughter broke through, low and laced with renewed vigor. *"Then let us make it count."*

The Auralisks exchanged worried glances, the tension nearly palpable. Thalos, still restless, stamped his foot against the earth with a deep snort. *"Then we need a plan. If we rush the Council now, we will die."*

Rufio nodded slowly, a glint of strategy igniting within him. "You are right. We'll strike from the shadows. Let them believe us broken."

As he spoke, the Solins gathered around him, their ethereal forms glowing faintly, already beginning to murmur ideas like a chorus of whispers: routes, forgotten paths, hidden gates that faded into memory.

Brin bowed his head, despair crossing his features. *"This may be the end of us all."*

Rufio turned his gaze toward the distant horizon, where the tower loomed against the haze of daylight, smoke swirling like a living wound. An ache blossomed in his chest, sharp and stinging. Placing his hand over his heart, Rufio solidified his resolve.

*"She's worth it,"* Kaelith said at last to all who listened, voice resolute. *"Even if this is the end. We will fight and die a great death, doing what we all know is right!"*

The group settled into a quiet camaraderie, bound together by a singular purpose. Their hearts beat as one, united against the war that loomed behind those ancient walls the following night.

# Chapter 29

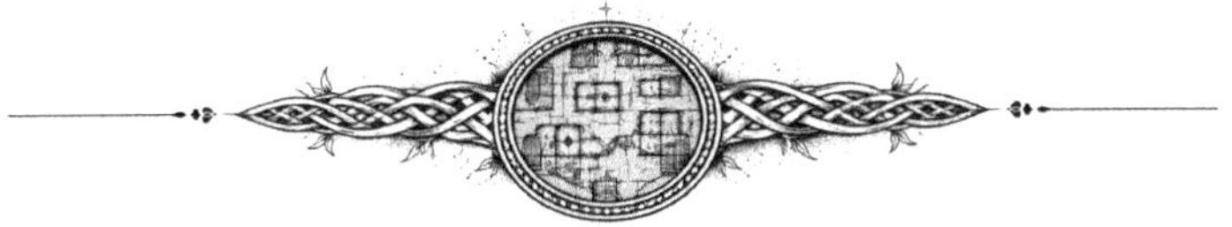

The plains were shrouded in silence. Inside the Auralisks' ethereal veil, everyone was already awake, basking in the early morning light that glistened like pearls along its invisible curve. Brin and Thalos stood resolute at the perimeter, their hooves digging into the earth, ears attuned to the slightest shift in the air. The Solins floated nearby, their glow soft and subdued, conserving their light for the darkening hour ahead.

Rufio pushed himself up, and the world tipped precariously beneath him. He caught himself with one palm, his breath hitching in his throat as a wave of dizziness washed over him. The copper-and-gold scales embedded over his heart pulsed once, flaring with heat before settling down, warmth spreading across his bare chest.

*"Easy,"* Brin cautioned, his voice echoing through their shared bond, deep and imposing like distant thunder rolling over the hills. *"You'll need every ounce of strength tonight,*

*Wildling. We may not be able to carry you out again."*

Rufio shot him a glare, his determination flaring as he tried to rise once more. A jolt of pain shot through his ribs, and he stifled a grunt, forcing himself to settle for sitting up straighter. His light bronzed skin glimmered in the light; a map of old scars intertwined with fresh wounds. Smoke-dark soot streaked across his collarbones and ribs, a testament to battles fought and challenges endured. Underneath the surface, faint threads of molten gold wove through his flesh; Kaelith's ember surging through him, mixing pain with fierce resolve. As he exhaled, the air around him shimmered, heat rippling like breath over flame.

With a gentle nudge, Thalos leaned in, his massive muzzle brushing against Rufio's shoulder in a show of affection and support. *"Stand later. We need to plan now,"* he urged, his voice rumbling with an undeniable strength.

Inside him, Kaelith stirred; impatient, tinged with frustration. *Your blood is thin. Your wound remembers its encounter with death. If you rush, he will tear us apart.*

"I won't give him the chance," Rufio rasped, his voice still laden with the taste of smoke and grit. He ran a hand through his tangled dark hair, damp strands clinging to his temples. The copper band encircling his wrist shimmered ominously, a crack running nearly halfway through it, the fissure catching sunlight like a blade drawn halfway from its sheath.

In that moment, the thick, oppressive weight of unspoken fears and fierce loyalty hung heavily in the air. Rufio sat resolute, drawing strength from the bonds of friendship that wrapped around him like a protective cloak. His heart pulsed with renewed vigor, igniting a flicker of hope amidst the encroaching darkness.

A sharp memory sliced through his mind, brutal yet vibrant: Mari, her form radiant amid chaos, light spilling from her outstretched palms. The air thrummed with golden green energy as she channeled her power, mending wounds and breathing life into those on the brink of despair. Beneath her, the stone floor cracked, a warning of the cost of her strength. But then came the moment of devastation; she faltered, her light dimming, and as she fell, the very ground seemed to retaliate, opening wide like a dark maw ready to consume her. Shadows reached for her, and he was powerless to intervene as the hall crumbled around him, drowning in grief and chaos.

He squeezed his eyes shut, trying to push away the haunting images that clawed at his mind. The world around him fell into heavy silence. When he finally opened his eyes, a surge of rage ignited within him.

"Report!" Rufio commanded, his voice cut through the oppressive silence like a knife. Frustration bubbled within him as he could sense the tension. They all shared the same unease, trapped in the shadows of uncertainty, and Rufio was fed up with the waiting.

Brin stepped forward, his voice calm and measured, a deliberate attempt to reassure Rufio. *"The Western and Northern service halls are still functioning under the old wards,"* he began, offering a glimpse of stability in a troubling situation. *"However, the eastern wing presents a different story..."*

He hesitated for a moment, a flicker of concern crossing his features before he continued. *"It has fallen into decay. As for the gate you broke, Rufio, it will be monitored closely. I don't anticipate any repairs to the wall by nightfall."*

Thalos, restless, scraped his hoof along the dusty ground, etching lines that danced in the light: the tower, the grand processional, the hidden paths soldiers once carved out when glory belonged to others. The Solins began to flow into his sketch, threads of shimmering gold that hovered above the dirt like delicate wisps of smoke, a living, breathing map of their sanctuary and prison.

*"The Solins can create a light-map,"* Thalos said, his voice fervent. *"We can weave our routes as we move. Together, my brother and I can conjure a cloak that will shield us until we must part ways. When that time comes... you'll be on your own."* A heavy silence followed, resonating with the weight of their shared burdens.

Rufio's jaw tightened, resolve burning in his chest. "One," he said, a fire igniting in his eyes, "that's all we need."

His voice crackled with determination, an unyielding promise to himself and to those gathered around him, anchored by the fierce loyalty they all carried. He was ready to face whatever came next, together or apart. The storm was coming, but so was their strength.

Kaelith's heat surged within Rufio, a fierce tide clashing against the grim reality surrounding them. *"Fools,"* he growled, his voice thick with disdain. *"You speak as though The Corruptor is just a man, confined by doors and thresholds. He is destruction incarnate, a law unto himself. With every breath he takes, he commits thievery, siphoning life from the very bones of the world. Even I..."*

His voice quaked, pride cracking under the strain of something more profound than fear. *"Even I could be unmade."*

Rufio's gaze fell to the scales fused over his heart, the three crescent shapes etched by the Auralisks into his living flesh. "Then we unmake him first," he declared, determination hardening his voice.

A heavy silence enveloped the group as they prepared for the moment of reckoning. As the air hung thick with tension, the memory of wildflowers drifted through Rufio's mind.

"Rufio?" A whisper of her voice threaded through his mind, delicate yet powerful, an unseen force wrapping around his heart. The single word curled through his bones, igniting a pulse deep within him. The mark on his copper band flared to life, vibrant red-green radiating like a heartbeat, responding to its match.

He jerked his head toward the Ancient's Hall, his breath catching in his throat as hope ignited like a spark in the dark. "Mari?" The name slipped from Rufio's lips, a tentative plea against the oppressive quiet.

In response, there was only the stubborn echo of a distant heartbeat, steady and unwavering. The Solins shimmered with the weight of ancient knowledge, their luminescent glow pulsing in time with the unyielding rhythm. Brin, a colossus of strength and loyalty, inclined his great head, acknowledging the unspoken tension that was around them.

The moment stretched, the silence heavy with unasked questions and the promise of revelation, as they all waited for the truth to unravel.

*"She calls,"* Brin murmured, a hint of awe in his voice. *"The tether. Delicate as silk, yet unbroken."*

A low rumble escaped Kaelith, his voice thick with emotion. *"She bleeds light into stone and still refuses to dim. That stubborn mortal... a dawn disguised as a flickering candle flame."*

Rufio's lips curved, a humorless smile cutting through the tension. "Then we must reach her before that light fades into the shadows."

Thalos etched the plan into the dirt with deliberate strokes.

*"We'll approach cloaked from the East,"* he said, his voice low and steady. *"Solins will divide; half will create a diversion with false flares heading toward the North Gate."* He pointed with his hoof to another area on their makeshift map. *"The rest will forge a path for you. You'll breach the soldier's hall at the East wing. We will hold the veil and await your signal."*

Rufio's gaze remained fixed on the shimmering filaments of golden light that danced across the rough ground, revealing a labyrinth of possibilities in trembling lines. Heat radiated from his skin, creating a mirage at the edges of his vision. The sky began to cloud over, as if the world knew what the group needed to survive this night. The tang of ash was an ever-present reminder of the chaos.

Within Rufio, Kaelith simmered like a gathering storm, a tempest eager to break free. *"To defeat him, you'll need more than steel. You'll need me... unleashed,"* he cautioned, his voice raw and primal.

Rufio remained fixated on the map before him, his determination unwavering. *"Then we set you free,"* he replied, his tone resolute, radiating an intensity that demanded attention.

*"Do you even grasp the cost?"* The Wild snarled, its voice echoing like distant thunder. Then, softening, he added, *"Or perhaps you understand all too well. If I reveal my true self, your flesh may crumble to dust. There would be nothing but ash where you once stood. I am light and fire."*

"Then we choose where the ash falls," Rufio declared, his voice steady, slicing through the tension like a sharpened blade.

As the midday sun dipped behind gathering clouds, the rich scent of damp earth began to mingle with the air. Thalos, Rufio, and their companions exchanged knowing glances, fully aware of the impending change. The land had been parched far too long, yearning for the nurturing kiss of rain. It was a desperate plea echoed by the newly sprouted wildflowers, grass, and trees, all of which seemed to bow in sorrow, longing for their savior. The atmosphere carried a haunting melancholy that mirrored the group's own desires as they pressed forward on their arduous journey.

Then, with a rustle that seemed to echo their unspoken hopes, the wind grew stronger, insistent, stirring the dust from the sickened soil as if the beginnings of providing them cover to the East wing. It was a reminder that the land still held power, that it, too, wished to aid them in their fight, not as a passive spectator but with a will of its own. The plains whispered promises of revival, a faint murmur that their efforts would not be in vain.

*"A storm is coming,"* Kaelith murmured, his internal blaze stirred by the air's electric charge, echoing the truth.

The Solins, Auralisks, Rufio, and Kaelith all intertwined in a single, shuddering exhale, making the very expanse of the plains pulse with life, as if it could sense the storm brewing just beyond the horizon.

Not knowing what would become of him, Kaelith began to speak his truth. His story was older than this world: *"Once, I was the breath beneath every leaf. I did not love, and I did not know loss. Before the stars learned to whisper their own names, I could balance birth and decay with a single thought."* A heavy pause hung in the air. *"But then, she... my beginning and my end, cried onto the barren earth. And for the first time, I wanted. My Kila Kitu gave to me unconditionally. I wanted nothing but her..."*

The Wild fell silent as Rufio felt an unexpected reverence from this Primordial entity of hunger. It was not the familiar hunger that had always lingered there; instead, wonder danced within the ancient entity. *"Mari hums her origin. She makes me remember what it felt like to create; to ignite my fire. I cannot turn away from her."*

Rufio swallowed hard, his throat tight, and spoke with urgency, "Then guard her, ancient one. Stand with me in this."

*"With you,"* Kaelith rumbled, solemn as granite, a vow carved deep into the bedrock of their fate.

# Chapter 30

They shared what little food they could find: bruised fruit and hard bread, knowing that every ounce carried weight when sprinting toward death. The Solins dimmed to glowing embers that spiraled upward, weaving sigils into the air that would become false trails and phantom armies come nightfall. Brin and Thalos paced the edge of the veil, hooves etching shallow rings of light that shimmered, warding against the dark.

Rufio focused on conserving movement, yet restless power seeped from him in waves, heat shimmering through him, vibrating the grass beneath his feet. With each breath, the scales at his heart caught the light, glowing like molten metal with his skin. The band wrapped around his wrist pulsed with a rhythm that felt both foreign and familiar.

"Once more," he urged when the sun dipped past its zenith. "Gate, hall, chamber. Where do I break through?"

Brin rumbled his answer, voice deep and resonant. *"Not the gate. The gate is its teeth. You must break the jaw."* His muzzle indicated a side corridor on the light-map. *"Here, where the rot is thin, and the stone still remembers its oaths."*

Rufio nodded, determination etched into his features. "And when we find Mari?"

Thalos's ears flattened against his skull, a tension radiating from him. *"We will come, and we will fight the Corruptor."*

*"Yes,"* Kaelith agreed, the weight of his words grounding Rufio. *"He desires what I denied him, but more than that, he covets her. He will try to rend us apart to tear soul from bone, light from Wild. When he does, call me by my true name, and do not hesitate, for the pain will come."*

"What name?" Rufio pressed, but the Wild erupted into a low, bright, and terrible laughter, echoing into the gathering gloom. The air around them thrummed with the weight of anticipation both for battle and for the truths yet to be revealed.

The primordial energy of the Wild spoke in a foreboding tone, *"You will know."*

The day bled slowly into shades of deep crimson as shadows grew long and the heat of the suns began to fade. The veil vibrated with a low hum, thick with the Auralisks as they layered their final defenses. High above, the Solins shone like gold coins, then suddenly split in two halves, darting out as cunning decoys, while the other half coiled tightly like a braided rope above Rufio's destined path.

Rufio stood resolutely, his bare skin glistening as if it were absorbing the encroaching dusk. A tapestry of scars, his Sigil, and shimmering scales mapped his body, an embodiment of both man and myth forged together in defiance. The air thickened with the sharp scent of iron and the promise of an approaching storm. As he lifted his gaze, his eyes blazed with an otherworldly intensity, black at the core, now golden and molten lava framing them, revealing Kaelith's fierce spirit within a human facade.

Thalos descended gracefully to Rufio's level. *"When the suns slips beneath the horizon, we make our move,"* he declared, his voice steady and low.

Rufio pressed a hand against the Auralisk's neck, feeling the immense warmth of its pulse thrumming beneath layers of hide and muscle. "If I fail…"

*"You won't,"* Brin interjected fiercely, determination etched across his face. *"But if… Be sure we will scorch the sky."*

With a swift motion, Rufio vaulted onto Brin's back, every movement precise despite the ache that lingered beneath his ribs. The scales over his heart shimmered, a salute or a warning; even he couldn't discern. He cast his gaze toward the mountains looming in the distance, the Council a dark bruise against the twilight, feeling the bond on his wrist respond to his resolve with a soft, defiant thrum.

"For her," he whispered, his voice low and sharp, as a blade unsheathed in the gloom.

*"For her,"* Kaelith echoed within him, and the Wild no longer felt like chaos; it resonated as an unbreakable vow.

At last, the suns disappeared beneath the horizon, plunging the world into shadow. The decoy lights flared, drawing eyes toward their illusion of safety, while their true journey twisted ominously below, burdened by the weight of soldiers' resolve. A gust of wind swept through the grass, its rustle serving as the cover they desperately needed.

"Hold on, Mari," Rufio whispered fiercely to himself as Brin readied to launch into the darkness. "We're coming for you."

# Chapter 31

Cold.

That was her first thought, the kind of cold that seeped through flesh, through bone, through memory itself.

Mari opened her eyes to blackness lined with faint violet veins pulsing like slow heartbeats through the stone. The air smelled of old blood, bile, and damp metal. Each breath scraped her lungs raw and shallow.

She pushed herself upright and tried to walk to the bars of her cell. Pain lanced through her shoulders, forcing her back. The floor itself glowed faintly beneath her from carved sigils imprisoning her. Every movement triggered a flare of white-hot resistance that drove her back to stillness.

Across the corridor, through bars made of onyx and bone, figures stirred. The Elders, their once-bright robes dulled to gray, their skin pale and drawn. One of them leaned forward, eyes faintly luminous even in exhaustion.

"Child," he rasped. "Be still. You're safe for now."

Her head pounded, but she turned toward the voice. Recognition hit her; it was Rufio's mentor, the one who had stood beside him at the Council's gates. Now he was gaunt, bruised, yet his gaze burned steadily.

"Where… where am I?" she whispered.

"The old catacombs," he said quietly. "Buried beneath the Council. Forgotten. Or so we believe. There were no maps of this place."

A tremor ran through the ground. From somewhere far above came the groan of ancient gears, the whisper of rot moving through walls.

Mari wrapped her arms around herself, trying to stop the shaking. "What happened? Where's Rufio? The Auralisks?"

The Elder raised a trembling hand. "Do not call for them here. The walls and shadows listen."

But it was too late. Her voice had already carried her whisper, thin and desperate: "Thalos. Brin. Rufio… please…"

The sigils flared blinding white, searing heat into her ankles. She gasped and dropped to her knees, clutching her legs. The air howled around her, vibrating with power, but beneath the pain, something answered. Deep in the stone, the heartbeat of the world quickened.

The Elder's eyes widened. "Do you feel that?"

Mari didn't know what she felt, only that she wasn't alone. Something ancient, vast, and kind had heard her cry.

Then, a presence filled the corridor, and the air shifted from cold to freezing. Torches dimmed, flames bending toward the darkness.

He came as a shadow poured into shape.

The Corruptor moved with deliberate grace, robes whispering over the stone. His face was covered by a mask of pale porcelain veined with gold, but the eyes behind it burned violet, too bright, too knowing. When he smiled, the light bled out of the room.

"You wake, my Radiant Vessel."

Mari froze. Every instinct screamed to recoil, but she forced herself to lift her chin. "Who are you?"

He chuckled lowly, a sound that vibrated through her chest. "Names are for the bound. You may call me Master."

"Not today, Saltine," she said, immediately radiating sarcasm.

The corners of his mouth twitched. "Defiance. How delightful."

He stepped closer. The illusion around him shifted subtly, his shape growing taller and broader, his voice warmer and smoother. His face began to align with something familiar, almost comforting, the faintest echo of Rufio's symmetry. It made her stomach twist.

He extended his gloved hand toward the sigil line. "You need not fear me. All I desire is what the world already promised me: the light you carry. You carry creation itself, my Vessel. Through you, I could cleanse this rot. I could make you eternal. All you need is to bow to me."

Mari's lips trembled, but she didn't answer.

"Bow," he commanded softly.

She pushed herself to her knees, then struggled to her feet, trembling and dizzy, but upright. The runes blazed in protest, searing heat crawling up her calves, yet she refused to bow.

His head tilted. "How adorable," he said, and then his power snapped like a whip.

The sigils ignited crimson, and an invisible force slammed

into her. She cried out as she hit the stone hard enough to knock the breath from her lungs. Her arms shook under the weight pressing her down; an unseen hand holding her in place.

"Do you feel it?" he asked, voice silken and sharp. Vandran squatted slightly so she could hear his words. "That is what it means not to be mine."

Mari gasped for air. "You can hurt me," she rasped, "but you can't make me want you." She tried to get back onto her hands and knees.

His smile darkened. "Oh, child," he murmured, crouching before her, "you don't even know what you are yet. When you do, you'll beg to belong. I know what you want."

The pressure grew until her knees buckled again, forcing her to lie on her belly, but she refused to look down. Her tears fell silently, mixing with the dust on the floor.

After a long, tense moment, the Corruptor exhaled sharply and released his grip. Mari caught herself, trembling, and took deep breaths.

He leaned close, his voice a whisper at her ear. "You will rest, my Vessel. When I return, you'll understand your place beneath this crown."

Then he was gone, his footsteps fading down the corridor, each echo a haunting reminder of his presence. The torches flickered back to brilliance, casting dancing shadows that seemed to breathe in the heavy silence, an uncanny stillness thick, unnatural, heavy enough to swallow her whole.

Mari stood frozen, trembling as her shallow breaths formed small clouds in the chill of the Elders' cell. She lifted her tear-streaked face toward the enveloping darkness, her voice a fragile whisper.

"I don't know what he wants," she admitted, her fear laid bare.

From the depths of the shadows, a voice drifted forward, calm yet thick with an undercurrent of dread. It was Rufio's mentor, his words dripping with unsettling sweetness.

"Everything, Mari. He wants everything that makes you alive."

A single tear slipped from her chin, falling to the cold stone floor. As it plummeted, it shimmered, bursting forth in a radiant cascade of gold and green. The colors rippled through the air, sending delicate fissures snaking outward, like fingers reaching for warmth.

The Elders inhaled sharply; their gasps mingled with the tension that thickened the air. Slender vines, as fragile as a spider's thread, unfurled from the cracks, inching toward Mari's outstretched fingers.

Blinking back her tears, Mari found herself captivated by the wonder unfolding around her, oblivious to the power she had inadvertently awakened. She pressed her palm against the cool stone, feeling the pulsing energy beneath her touch, the green glow intensifying as if it were siphoning strength from her very essence.

Exhaustion weighed heavily upon her, and she rested her cheek against the damp ground.

As sleep began to tug her into its depths, she sensed creeping tendrils of decay slithering closer, irresistibly drawn to the purity of her being. It was a quiet seduction of rot inching nearer to the last bastion of life.

Suddenly, protective vines cocooned her, wrapping around her like a mother's embrace; an intricate tapestry woven from love and the lifeblood of the land. In that raw moment of surrender, a distant rumble reverberated, echoing through the earth below. The world seemed to shift in response to her unspoken plea, as if acknowledging her in a language older than time itself.

***

Elsewhere, above the Catacombs, the Corruptor loomed before a mirror of obsidian, its surface undulating like a stormy sea. His reflection twisted grotesquely, shifting from human to something monstrous: gray flesh mottled with black veins, eyes swirling like twin voids. He was a fractured image of what he had once been, and what he was now.

"You resist me even now," he murmured, fingers ghosting across the mirror's surface, tracing the faint outline of a woman's face… Mari's face, barely visible behind his own. "A spark of creation amid the ruin I've wrought." His breath caught, filled with the echo of her lingering scent.

The mirror hummed, resonating with a voice older than time itself, mocking. "You failed once before, Watcher."

"She will be mine," he whispered, voice dark and determined. "The essence of the Wild is fading; the bond weakens. When it shatters, she will belong to me: body, power, soul." The tension in his jaw tightened with each word. Behind him, corrupted soldiers stirred, kneeling in eerie unison, shadows deepening around them.

"And now you hunger for her," the mirror taunted, acknowledging his deepest desires, its hum intensifying.

A bitter smile flickered across his lips. "She embodies the purest balance of flesh intertwined with spirit. The world chose her, yet she remains blissfully unaware of the power she wields." He pressed his palm against the glass, his pulse quickening as the mirror illuminated the figure of Rufio: bare and scarred, the copper band on his wrist glowing faintly, an unexpected revelation.

His thoughts spiraled into darkness as he contemplated how best to exploit this newfound knowledge. Then, with a surprising softness, he regarded it all. "He believes that bond can shield her. But every connection is merely a door, and I have always possessed the keys."

Leaning closer, he whispered with sinister intent. "She will not succumb to blade or fire. No, she will come to me willingly. When he falters... when she feels his light dimming... desperation will guide her to me. She'll surrender herself to save him."

The air around him thickened, crackling with palpable power as he spoke with a low growl. "And when she does, I will consume the Wild, the Balance, and the very light itself. I shall ascend, the crown upon my head eternal, unchallenged."

Suddenly, the mirror trembled violently; cracks snaked across its surface, revealing a multitude of distorted faces, each one a reflection of hunger, desire, and darkness. He lifted his hand, the air around him shimmering with eldritch energy. "Mariposa," he intoned, a blend of reverence and malice. "My vessel, my dawn, my beginning."

With a deafening crash, the cracks erupted outward, shards floating like suspended tears, each reflecting her peaceful form below. His soldiers bowed deeper, their loyalty palpable, an unsettling harmony.

"Prepare the ritual," he commanded, his voice cold and sharp as iron. "Tonight, the Wildling perishes. And with it, the dawn will be mine."

# Chapter 32

The East tower and wall loomed ominously against the starless sky, resembling the spine of a buried serpent, with fractured runes bleeding a sickly glow into the surrounding darkness. Veins of crimson rot pulsed rhythmically at its base, exuding a nauseating ripple of ancient power. Dust and ash hung heavily in the air, carried by persistent gusts of wind that smothered sound and scent, concealing the group's presence from the corrupted sentinels. As they silently approached the East wall, a weight pressed against their lungs, and the plains stretched out around them, brittle and hushed. Scars marked the earth, gaping from the battle, glowing faintly with red veins tracing a path to the Hall of the Ancestors.

Thalos now carried Rufio on his back, ensuring their veil would hold as they navigated the pitted landscape, their hooves muffled beneath the shimmering light of the Solins. Clouds of cold air drifted with each breath, while smaller

Solins flitted around them, weaving ethereal patterns that twisted reality until the group vanished into a mirage, undetectable by even the rot. Riding bareback, Rufio felt the sweat and dust clinging to his skin, the scar over his heart, now healed, a faint golden-red reminder of his loss and survival. His skin shimmered, muscles taut beneath the veil's swirling glow, dark waves of hair cascading around his face and partially obscuring the molten intensity of his eyes. Even in ruins, he remained untamed: beautiful and dangerous, a weapon forged through ash and fire.

As they neared the precipice overlooking the Hall of the Ancestors, an oppressive stillness settled over the land, as if it held its breath. Shadows of past battles lay scattered below, and Rufio brought Thalos to a halt, his gaze locked on the ruined structure as he analyzed its decay. Once magnificent outer walls now lay half-destroyed, their cracked marble bones twisted and warped, with one part sunken deep as if the land itself had rejected its former glory. Crimson tendrils slithered across the darkened walls, and a coolness lingered in the air, distorted by the remnants of the Corruptor's twisted power. At the heart of it all, the tower pulsed ominously, its rhythm resonating through the ground like a heartbeat both alive and menacing.

*"The corruption stirs here,"* Kaelith uttered in Rufio's mind, the voice deep and ancient, *"It knows we are coming."*

"Then let it come to us," Rufio growled, his voice raw with exhaustion and unfocused rage. "Let it know their time in power is over."

Brin pawed the ground anxiously, nostrils flaring as they sensed the rising tension. Thalos lowered his head, majestic horns capturing the essence of moonlight. *"There is no open gate or any other opening here,"* he murmured solemnly. *"The East Gate is sealed with death sigils. We will burn before breaching it."*

Rufio's resolve only hardened at the words. There would be no retreat. No surrender.

Kaelith's essence stirred in Rufio's veins, coiling like smoke. Searching. *"There has to be another way,"* the Wild said. *"Follow the scent beneath the stone. The world remembers its wounds and oaths."*

Rufio dismounted, boots crunching against the brittle grass. As he knelt, the Solins gathered near his hands, their golden light tracing thin cracks along the ground, hairline fractures that pulsed faintly red. The earth trembled beneath his touch as Solin's light intermingled with Kaelith's power, searching for a breach.

"There!" Rufio breathed, pointing down the structure.

The group moved stealthily to where the golden light ended. Down the wall, a wide fissure of broken stone could barely be seen. It was a deep wound that reeked of decay, moist air, and burnt metal. Nothing seemed to be around the wall. Not a torchlight or guard in sight.

*"We will follow,"* Thalos declared with determination. The brothers transformed, their forms becoming more ethereal as they adapted to a stealthier guise for their large frames.

They descended into the fissure. The walls were slick with condensation, reflecting faintly with the light of the Solins. Water dripped from above, each drop echoing like a whisper down the long shaft. The atmosphere was thick with humidity and carried a sharp hint of iron.

The air became cold and suffocating as Rufio and the brothers descended further into the corridors, which eventually led down into the ancient catacombs. The stones forming the walls twisted in unnatural ways, proof that they had been built in secret over the years. Runes, carved centuries ago, had melted into grotesque forms, the markings of the rot coiling over the original language. The atmosphere was thick with unsettling history. Yet, they pressed on.

Kaelith, nestled against Rufio's chest, wishing for release, emanated a low, resonant hum that vibrated through his companion's body, a sound laced with ancient unease.

*"This place remembers,"* he murmured softly, as if afraid to disturb the dark silence. *"It remembers."*

Rufio reached out, his fingertips brushing the tunnel wall. The stone felt warm and alive, pulsing faintly beneath his palm like a heartbeat. Shivers raced down his spine, a sense of unease creeping in.

*"The hall's walls have merged with the corruption,"* Thalos breathed, his voice filled with dread.

Brin's ethereal body shivered, adding, *"And it's feeding off itself."*

A vibration resonated from the shadows clinging against the stones, deep and menacing.

*"Not for much longer,"* The Wild rumbled, as his power echoed off the slick walls.

With a surge of determination, Rufio continued. The passage ahead curved sharply, leading them into a cavern that expanded into an enormous underground expanse, the heart of the catacombs. Here, the Auralisks began to take shape, their massive forms pushing through the last of the narrow entrance in single file, formidable horns scraping against the damp, low ceiling and sending sparks flying in all directions until they finally emerged into the open space.

Before them, the Solins flitted about like living lanterns, darting into the inky darkness and scattering brilliant flashes of light. The glow of their bodies illuminated a tapestry of intricate carvings etched into the stone walls, revealing statues trapped in expressions of eternal despair. Their hollow eyes gazed into the abyss, while crumbling crowns adorned their heads, remnants of a once-glorious past now laid to rest, echoing the haunting memories of a forgotten time.

Rufio's heart raced as he scanned the chamber, the weight of countless eyes seemingly boring into him. "Stay close," urgency threading through his tone. "We need to map this place before..."

Kaelith cut him off, his tension palpable. *"We're not alone down here,"* The tremor in his voice a reflection of their shared apprehension.

Rufio looked at his companions for confirmation. The copper band began to hum and flicker with gentle light in front of an opening within one of the niches. With a nod, the group silently ventured deeper into the darkness, the catacombs' pulse weaving around them. The rhythm of their steady footfalls hid the pounding from their anxious hearts as they plunged into the unknown.

Rufio was the first to move, his bare chest glistening with dew under the soft glow of the Solin light. Muscles rippled beneath his skin as he advanced, a faint golden sheen pulsing at the wound in his heart, synchronizing with Kaelith's energy. Though he was breathing heavily, his stride remained steady and unwavering.

The reek of rot, the sound of slow vibrations from deep within the stone. The biting cold screamed of danger and death. Yet still he pressed forward. The group finally reached the base deep underneath the Ancestors' Hall. Before them, a broken gate was half-buried in earth and roots. The Solin's glow showed a man-sized passage leading deeper into the earth.

Kaelith murmured. *"The heart of corruption is closest here. You can feel the vibration and smell the rot more down this hall."*

Rufio looked at the brothers, "Will you fit?" Providing them with a slight, humorous smirk.

Brin snorted, and both nodded with approval. Rufio nodded back, steadying himself. The Solins swirled around him, forming a faint shield of light.

They descended into the passage, the air thick with moisture and the pungent smell of rot, growing increasingly metallic and sour. The narrow tunnel was slick with slimy condensation, and as they ventured deeper, the flickering Solin light revealed skeletal bodies fused into the walls. Their bones twisted and hollowed by the relentless rot of time stood as grim offerings to the Corruptor's sinister plan.

A sudden chill enveloped them, causing Rufio's breath to emerge as ghostly wisps of mist. Each sharp inhale sent a jolt of pain radiating from the wound where the spear had pierced him, adding to his suffering. Meanwhile, the copper band around his wrist pulsed rhythmically with his heartbeat, soft golden light shimmering through the cracks. Kaelith, feeling the same throbbing pulse, strained against his restraints, aware of the darkness closing in around them.

*"Steady,"* Thalos murmured, his voice laced with a warmth that belied the chill in the air. *"We are close to the heart of the sickness."*

Rufio's voice was thick with conviction. "I can feel her. She's close."

As they pressed onward, the passage widened, revealing a vast chamber. The chamber walls held doors and metallic bars. The group moved towards the cells. Carefully searching. Rufio closed his eyes, straining to feel her presence; a dim, flickering flame, undeniably hers. He could feel people within the cells but could not see or hear them. But he could not feel Mari.

The Solins moved throughout the chamber, attempting to fill the air with their glow. The bars and doors reflected their light, illuminating the path forward to a sealed door etched with hundreds of ancient sigils. The closer Rufio came to the door, the colder the air became, sharp and biting.

An oppressive darkness swallowed the Solin's light when they attempted to reach the door. They retreated, landing on the Auralisks, exhausted and feeling defeated.

Rufio stopped and looked at the tiny creatures. "You all did well, little friends. We could not have gone this far without you."

The Solins twinkled mutedly in response. The stench of decay, blood, and bile clawed at Rufio's senses, a rancid reminder of the foul actions that had occurred here. The ground near the door was slick; faintly glowing glyphs pulsed with a grotesque life of their own. Tendrils of rot writhed like serpents around the glyphs and up the wall, wrapping around the ancient stone with a hungry grip.

Unbeknownst to them, at the center, Mari lay surrounded by the twisted tendrils of rot, seeking a way to feed, while her body was nestled safely beneath a thick cocoon of vines. Unlike the rest of the doors and cells, this door was the only one that none of the men could sense anything. This had to be where Vandran placed Mari.

*"Stand aside,"* Thalos commanded, his voice a rumble of thunder. *"We remember these types of wards."*

With deliberate grace, Brin and Thalos stomped their hooves, striking the ground. Each impact sent tremors through the floor, fractures spider-webbed across the stone, like a network of cracked glass breaking the glyphs.

The Solins surged forward, luminous and fierce, conjuring counter-runes that blazed with the fire of distant stars. The crimson glyphs screamed as each broke, being banished into the void.

Thalos kicked at the door, then Brin. The chamber door shook violently, dust spiraling down like falling stars. The sigils winked out one after another. From the chaos, Brin and Thalos emerged out of the dust as luminous silhouettes, their horns ablaze with sacred fire, a fierce illumination against the backdrop of despair.

Rufio, with one last push, rammed his body into the door as the last of the sigils faded.

Rufio caught his balance as he entered the cell. "Mari." The name slipped from his lips, both a desperate prayer and a promise.

The rot tendrils coiled tighter, executing their sinister chore-ography around her, squeezing as if to protect their prize. The crunch of the vines echoed beneath the pressure. The sigils on the ground flared to life around the pile of rot and vines, erupting in a fierce crimson glow that illuminated Rufio's anguished face. The air was charged with an energy that pulsed on his skin. The sight drove a dagger through Rufio's heart; he felt his breath catch, time stretching agonizingly. He took a hesitant step forward.

*"Her heart is reaching...,"* Kaelith murmured within him, his

voice filled with understanding.

In this moment, both man and entity understood what needed to be done. Acting as one, Rufio's copper band began to glow with an intense, almost blinding light. The last of the black, fractured metal melted off the band like a chaotic sun breaking through the night. Waves of Kaelith's raw power surged through Rufio, igniting every nerve in his body as its essence flowed like molten gold through his veins.

He tried to move past the wards. He attempted to step over one and was shot back with a jolt of electricity that would have killed a mortal. They needed more. Rufio relinquished the last of his control, allowing Kaelith to transform his body into a fierce embodiment of power and fury.

The copper band broke with a resounding crack. Gold light exploded from the band, a brilliant flood that swallowed the chamber in its brilliance. Kaelith's essence coursed through him, fire and wind entwined into a primal dance of fury and creation. No longer would he resist; he surrendered himself entirely to the Wild, embracing its raw, untamed power.

Rufio now knew the weight of an entire world resting on Kaelith's shoulders. Layered emotions bubbled within him, a mix of dread and determination of both; intermingling knowledge and will. Rufio stepped over the sigils again. The entire glowing set flicked out as Kaelith siphoned its power. Rufio pulled again, ripping through tendrils and then the vines, calling Mari's name as he did. Finally, he saw her blue cloth, then the rise and fall of her chest, and then her face. Her once-vibrant skin glimmered weakly in the dark, fading like dying embers beneath a blanket of ash. He touched her face, and Kaelith's glow emanated from his fingertips.

Mari's body stirred; the soft rise and fall of her breath

became steadier. The Solins got to work healing their friend. The air shimmered around her, bathed in a delicate glow, her skin flickering with hints of green and gold. The vines around her, once so tightly coiled, began to release their grip, curling away and turning to dust, floating like ancient memories lost to time.

As Mari blinked, her dazed expression slowly shifted, clarity washing over her like a sudden dawn. Her breath caught in awe, eyes widening at the sight of him: fierce, wild, yet undeniably radiant.

"You came," she whispered, her voice a fragile thread weaving through the heavy air.

"Always," he replied, his breath a vow, a promise reverberating in the silence that enveloped them.

In that fleeting heartbeat, time seemed to fold in on itself as the world held its breath. A gentle cascade of golden light poured down from the Solins, enveloping them like soft, radiant rain. Her copper band shimmered; crimson intertwined with her vibrant green, weaving together a radiant symbol.

He picked up Mari and walked out the door of the chamber. He placed her on Brin, the Solin's continuing their work. Rufio and Kaelith, working in unison, strode down the hall with a confidence never felt before. The chamber erupted in white, an all-consuming energy that cascaded down like a tempest unleashed. The rot between the stones shrieked in agony, recoiling as they disintegrated into wisps of acrid smoke. Every rune, every wall, pulsed in perfect cadence with him now. Kaelith's voice aligned with his, fierce and soaring, a symphony of two forces melding into one.

Deep within the walls, a low, deep-sounding horn bellowed

from above, and the corrupted sensed their prey. A call to arms.

*"They know!"* Brin's voice pierced the weight of the dark outside the door.

Rufio didn't flinch. His heartbeat roared in his ears like a war drum, louder than the chaos around him. "Let's say hello."

Rufio stepped forward, each footfall echoing down the passage, splashes of corrupted ichor dancing in the air. His chest rose and fell with heated breaths, every fiber of his being vibrating with the power that flowed through him. His sweat glistened on his collarbone, trickling down his muscular torso, catching the faint golden light pulsing beneath his skin. Eyes ablaze, the depths of obsidian encircled by molten red and gold, both divine and shattered. A creature forged for war.

"We are not your prey," Kaelith and Rufio thundered in unison, a declaration that echoed through the very fabric of reality. "We are the inferno."

The rot's silent scream reverberated through the chamber as the seals shattered, splintering the oppressive gloom.

And then… silence.

On Brin's back, a faint smile touched Mari's lips. Exhausted. Real. A look of wonder danced in her gaze. Rufio looked back, seeing her sitting up and color returning to her skin. His heart soared as he mirrored her smile, his eyes softening despite the fire that flickered within. Around them, the Auralisks shifted into formation, their hooves striking the stone in low, reverent rhythm. The Solins' song softened, weaving a living veil behind them as the last remnants of rot burned away from the corridor walls.

Rufio paused, casting a lingering gaze over the shattered remnants of the cell that once held Mari captive. The space was heavy with the remnants of shattered symbols and the ashes of deceptive tales that had veiled the past. He felt the weight of realization wash over him, the sheer scale of the deceit orchestrated by a single man. With determination, he turned away, stepping into the shadows ahead. Deep within the Council's depths, a new awareness had awakened: Rufio had returned for retribution. The hunger for balance of Kaelith surged, and Mari was no longer a pawn in this deadly game.

# Chapter 33

The air beneath the Council was saturated with the acrid scent of iron and smoke that clung to damp stone walls. Each breath Rufio took scorched his lungs, a painful reminder of the darkness encroaching upon them. He pressed his palm against the cold surface of the wall, steadying himself as he felt the tremors of corruption coursing beneath; it pulsed like a living creature, a sinister heartbeat echoing in the silence.

Behind, his companions moved close. Mari now followed on foot, her silhouette framed by the dim glow of the sigil on her wrist, an ethereal light battling the darkness. Her fingers grazed the band, a delicate caress that pulsed with power, its warmth radiating against the chill of the stone. The Auralisks advanced cautiously, their majestic horns dipping low, a silent promise of protection. Above them, the Solins floated like constellations, their gentle luminescence casting flickering shadows on the rough-hewn surfaces around them.

As Rufio inhaled deeply, the taste of damp earth mixed with the slightest hint of decay, a reminder of the danger that lurked just beyond their sight.

*"The corruption stirs,"* he heard Kaelith's voice rumble within him, as deep and foreboding as thunder rolling in the distance.

"I know," Rufio said back. His voice was a thread of determination amidst the oppressive darkness. "It's waiting for us." The weight of those words hung, and the oppressive silence of the tunnels seemed to thrum with an echo of something dark and ancient unleashing its presence.

The dim light flickered through the thick shadows, casting ghostly shapes that danced upon the cold stone walls. Within the confines of the cells, a thick atmosphere of despair lingered, as figures cloaked in ragged robes: Elders, Wardens, and Scholars clustered closely together. Their once-vibrant garments were faded and torn, matching the weariness etched into their faces. They exchanged hushed, frantic prayers, each whispered a testament to their fading hope. As Brin, Thalos, and Rufio approached the cell, they caught the haunting sight of those trapped souls, their eyes filled with a mix of fear and longing, breaking the silence.

Mari's gaze softened as she stepped forward, the flickering torchlight casting an ethereal glow on her face. "The elders," she breathed, thick with emotion.

Rufio's jaw set firmly as he nodded, determination in his eyes flashing between black, red, and gold. "We free them first."

As they approached, one elder, her frail form shaking with age and fear, rasped from behind the barrier, her voice rising like a lament. "Rufio... our Wildling. We feared the Corruptor had taken you."

He strode forward, heat radiating from him in waves, turning the mist into a shimmering vapor. "Not yet," he replied, his voice strong yet laced with urgency. For just a moment, his eyes flickered with an intense golden light, revealing the power simmering beneath his skin. "Stand back."

Mari felt the crackle of energy in the air as the Solins, those ethereal beings of light, swirled closer, their brilliance illuminating the dark sigils binding the cell door. Each rune pulsed an angry red, corrupted and alive. Rufio reached out, the sigils hissing at his touch like venomous serpents. Kaelith surged beneath his skin, a restless force eager to unleash its fury.

*"Now!"* The Wild yelled, urging him onward.

Rufio thrust his palm forward, a fierce storm of light and shadow entwined as heat exploded from his hand. The sigils cracked violently, the very air trembling as the corruption shrieked in agony. With a final pulse, the barrier shattered, splintering into shards and swirling smoke.

As the cell door cracked open, Mari rushed toward the trembling elders, her heart aching with compassion.

"Please, let me help you," she said, kneeling before them. Her hands glowed with a soft, soothing light as she reached out, determined to mend the pain etched on their faces.

One elder, her deep-set eyes glistening with unshed tears, reached out for Mari's hands. "Child, your kindness shines like the dawn," she whispered, her voice frail yet filled with hope.

"Mari," Rufio urged, glancing back at her, "we don't have much time."

"Just a moment," she replied, her voice firm but gentle as she concentrated. "I can ease their suffering. They deserve this… for all they've sacrificed."

Mari's hands enveloped the elders. She knelt, her hands glowing warm as she eased pain, steadied shaking limbs, and coaxed breath back into failing lungs. Where her light passed, fear loosened its grip. A look of astonished relief washed over their weary faces.

"Your love brings us back from the brink," one of the elders said softly to Mari, a smile breaking through his lined face.

Rufio watched Mari be her most authentic self. The air shimmered with an electric tension as Kaelith's energy flowed from him, weaving through golden tendrils that danced across his torso; marked by scars and sealed by the ancient power of the Auralisk. Each flex of his powerful muscles caught the flickering light from the corridor ahead, transforming him into a striking figure that blended the raw essence of a warrior, forged not merely by circumstance but by ancient, untamed, dark, and wild forces.

With her task finished, the members of the ancients were added to the ranks of the group. They set out to reach the Ancestors' Hall. Rufio led the way, back through the passages. Mari's gaze flickered back to him, irresistibly drawn by the magnetic pull of his presence. There was an untamed energy about him that sent her heart racing. She forced herself to look away, refocusing on the passage that sprawled before them. Each twist and turn revealed a new realm of shadow and intrigue, eventually leading to a long corridor drenched in an ethereal glow from Kaelith's golden flames.

As they moved forward, Mari radiated a soothing energy that enveloped her companions, granting them healing, calm, and clarity. Mari did not want to take a deep breath. The heavy scent of damp earth and death was thick enough to choke. She had never seen catacombs before; the weight of the abused and forgotten tombs settled over her, an oppressive reminder of forgotten stories and long-lost souls.  Anxiety lanced through her, tightening her chest, amplifying every whispered thought and unspoken fear. Her thoughts fluttered between the desperate urgency of their mission and the undeniable lure of her friend's formidable presence.

"Together, we can face the darkness," Mari stated, her voice steady and resolute, as the spirits of the elders rallied, their hope rekindled and intertwined with theirs.

Rufio stopped and then stood beside his friends back in the heart of the catacombs. He looked to the elders and asked, "Which passage is the quickest to the portal?"

Within a few moments of contemplation, they had their answer. The sound of boots thundered from the adjoining passage leading into the heart where they stood.  Then came the soldiers, armored figures poured forth from their entrance. Their eyes burned with a greenish-crimson light, their movements jerky and wrong. Flesh fused with steel; the stench of rot surged forward with them.

"Move!" Rufio roared.

The Auralisks charged, hooves striking sparks against the stone as they collided with the corrupted guards. The sound was deafening, a mixture of thunder and shattering bones. Mari ducked low, her hand flaring with a burst of soft green light that surged outward, forming a barrier in front of her and the Elders that sent several soldiers skidding across the ground.

The smell of burning metal filled the air.  Sparks rained. The Solins dove and spun, disorienting the attackers, searing away the tendrils of rot that leaked from their armor.

Rufio and Kaelith; blade and flame became one motion. Gold streaked through the air, cutting corruption apart with terrifying efficiency. When the last soldier fell, the corridor fell silent once more.

Rufio's chest heaved. Kaelith was quiet within him, a low purr of approval.

Mari reached his side, brushing soot from his arm. "You shouldn't have used so much power," she murmured as she gently poured her light over him.

He smirked weakly. "That is an odd statement coming from you."

Mari rolled her eyes in a small moment of revelry, "Do as I say, not as I do, sir."

"The dais," Said the elder who had spoken first from the cells. "The Astrologers' Roost still stands. That is where it all began."

She pointed to where the corrupted guards had marched out, leaning heavily on a staff carved with constellations. It was settled, they knew where to go and now how to get there.

# Chapter 34

The group walked onward through the deep halls, passages, and chambers, relying on the Solins to guide their path back up. A slight set of stairs moved them upward through granite stone worn smoothly by centuries of passage. The closer to the surface the passage grew, the hotter and heavier it became. As they climbed, the elders murmured warding chants, their voices low and rhythmic, weaving strength into failing protections. Solin light pulsed in harmony with the sound, guiding their ascent.

Mari's footsteps echoed softly, her pulse matching the low hum of the Wild in Rufio's veins. She could feel his exhaustion, but also something new: unity. The man and the Primordial entity had stopped fighting each other. For the first time, they felt… synchronized.

At last, the passage opened into a vast antechamber. The passage opened not to the Ancestor's Hall but to smooth obsidian walls marked with carvings: scenes of stars, towers, and figures reaching upward as though clawing at the heavens.

Blue firelight danced eerily from torches mounted high on the stone walls, casting flickering shadows that undulated like restless spirits. In the center of the antechamber loomed a colossal guardian, an imposing relic from a bygone era. Its once-magnificent armor was now grotesquely fused to the remnants of flesh, creating a monstrous fusion of metal and decay.

The helmet, twisted and misshapen, appeared as if it had been forged in the depths of a nightmare, melding seamlessly with the skull beneath. Where eyes once filled with life, red crystals glimmered darkly by the torchlight. The atmosphere was intense, a charged energy that suggested an imminent eruption of violence, each moment teetering on the brink of rousing this disturbing guardian from its endless watch; a tainted Watcher.

No one moved. The sound of rusted metal came from the Watcher; its helmet lowered, looking straight down at Mari. The crystals began to glow and pulse ominously, throbbing like a heartbeat, as if the creature itself was aware of their presence.

"Stay behind me," Rufio yelled.

The creature's crystalline eyes flared with a vibrant green, a haunting glow before it launched itself forward, a blur of darkness that defied the very limits of speed. Its footfalls roared like thunder, each step reverberating through the chamber and shattering the stone floor beneath it with cracks that splintered outward. From its arm, a surge of blackened energy coalesced into a razor-sharp blade, slicing through the air and unleashing shockwaves that rippled ominously across the ancient stones.

Rufio braced himself, his boots grinding against the rubble as he steeled his resolve for the collision ahead.

Kaelith's voice boomed in his mind, echoing with power. *"Now you will witness the union of Wild and man."*

In an instant, flames erupted from Rufio's hands, a dazzling golden blaze that pushed the Watcher back, its twisted form momentarily startled. But the Watcher surged forward again, swinging wildly as Brin and Thalos charged in, their powerful horns clashing with a metallic clang that reverberated like a battle cry. The monstrous sword flew from the Watcher's grip, clattering uselessly to the ground as sparks erupted around them.

Mari raised her arms high, summoning a radiant wall of living light that interposed itself between her and the corrupted Watcher rushing towards her.

"Go!" she commanded, her voice a rallying cry that cut through the chaos.

Seizing the moment, Rufio ran to the dropped blade. His hand grasped the hilt of the blackened blade from the ground below, igniting with the power of the Wild. His eyes blazed a fierce gold as Kaelith imbued him with primal strength. He leapt off a broken stone into the air, twisting his body mid-flight. As he descended, the blade came down like a celestial meteor, crashing into the Watcher's chest with a devastating force. A wave of flames erupted, consuming the creature in an explosive burst, armor and bone shattering into ash, as the embodiment of darkness crumbled to nothing with a bone-chilling scream that echoed through the hall.

For a long moment, no one moved; all that could be heard were chants from the Elders and heavy breathing. Then Mari's voice, soft and steady, broke through.

"You stopped fearing him. The Wild... I mean," she said breathlessly.

Rufio turned to her, panting, his eyes shifting between gold and the deepest black. "No," he said quietly. "I stopped fearing myself."

As the group finally approached the dais carved from dark stone, an air of reverence enveloped them. Tapestries depicting gallant deeds of yore adorned the walls, their colors muted by time. Where once a table had served the ancients and elders, a throne of leather, iron, and bone now loomed in the center, commanding attention. Behind it, the doors of the Astrologers' Roost beckoned, sigils etched into the wood glimmering faintly in gold, their light flickering like fireflies at dusk, hinting at the power lingering within.

They stepped into the sacred space, careful not to disturb the remnants of charred ashes that whispered tales of loss. At the heart of the room stood the Elders, their voices rising in a haunting chant that filled the air with a tangible sorrow. Each note was steeped in the weight of grief and the flicker of hope, a symbiotic dance between the past and the promise of tomorrow. Their weathered faces shone with luminous wisdom, as ancient incantations flowed from their lips, weaving through the air like tendrils of smoke, forming an invisible shield of protection around them.

In harmony, the Elders' voices blended, and the gentle hum of the Solins' light responded to a celestial symphony pulsing rhythmically, breathing life into the stillness. The very atmosphere crackled with emotion, each heartbeat resonating with the connection between past and present; it was as if the world itself paused to listen to their silent plea for strength and resilience.

Mari stepped forward, her heart racing and hand trembling as she reached for the ornate door. A warm pulse radiated from the band encircling her wrist, syncing with the steady thump of Rufio's heart beside her. In that electrifying moment, they felt an unbreakable bond, tethered together by an invisible thread of fate, ready to face the unknown that lay ahead.

Kaelith's voice whispered through the charged air, smooth and foreboding like the tide retreating from the shore: *"She is the key... to everything. Vandran has not shown himself."*

Fear and determination tightened in Rufio's chest. He could feel the weight of that prophecy threatening to fracture everything.

"Then he will have to go through me," Rufio said, pressing his palm against the door beside hers, his resolve steeling against the creeping dread.

The ancient doors began to shudder. Light poured through the cracks, gold and then white, swirling together like a tempest of flames, illuminating the darkened stairwell with an enchanting glow.

Behind them, the elders bowed their heads, faces grave but resolute, a silent prayer for strength hanging in the air. But ahead lay the stairwell to the Astrologers' Roost, its mechanisms reverberating to life after centuries of quietude, as if the tower's very essence were awakening from a long slumber.

With a creak of the door opening, a gust of wind swept through the stairwell, carrying whispers older than memory, secrets yearning to be heard. Rufio cast a glance back at his companions, his family, his purpose, his doom mirrored in their eyes. In that fleeting moment, emotions surged within him: love, fear, and an unyielding determination.

"We finish this," Rufio declared, his voice resolute, cutting through the swirling shadows of doubt.

As the radiant white light enveloped them, it felt all-consuming. For the briefest heartbeat, there was only pure brilliance, a euphoric rush that strangled fear and ignited hope. Then came a deep tremor, like the tower itself exhaling, as the Astrologers' Roost finally awakened from its slumber. Somewhere within its ancient bones, something sinister stirred in response, a dark promise that chilled the air. The journey was far from over, but this war will end tonight.

# Chapter 35

For a heartbeat, there was only light, an overwhelming expanse of white, boundless and pulsating with energy. From the depths of this brilliance emerged the resonant sound of stone breathing, a deep, rhythmic pulse that rolled through the air like distant thunder. As the radiance faded, the Astrologers' Roost unfolded around them, revealing the innermost core of a pulsing star.

The chamber was colossal and circular, its towering walls adorned with intricately carved constellations that glowed softly with a mesmerizing blue fire, casting ethereal shadows that danced like whispers across the space. Dust motes swirled in the golden shafts of light pouring through high crevices above, sparkling like tiny diamonds set against the enveloping darkness.

Beneath their feet, the glass floor shimmered, revealing not mere reflections but entire galaxies spinning and swirling in an unfathomable ballet. Mari gasped as the air wrapped around her, thick with the scent of ozone and ancient stone, a sharp tang reminiscent of the electric atmosphere just before a thunderstorm. Each breath she took pulsed with life, a palpable energy vibrating in tune with her heartbeat.

Mari knelt. Her fingers glided over the cool, smooth surface of the glass below, sending shivers up her spine as she sensed the immense weight of the cosmos, tantalizingly close yet just out of reach. In this space, she felt as though she was standing on the threshold of infinity itself, poised between the celestial and the earthly.

"It's beautiful," she whispered, her voice a fragile thread woven through the air, laden with awe and disbelief. As she stood enveloped by the magnificent landscape, a wave of reverence washed over her, grounding her in a sacred space that whispered secrets of the universe.

Nearby, Rufio stood frozen, his senses sharp with tension. The energy of Kaelith pulsed against his ribs, a silent protest against the ancient power of the Roost, a place steeped in an age-old essence that seemed to breathe its own defiance. The air around him thrummed, a living entity that dared anyone to trespass. He felt the pulse of the Roost reverberating against his chest, yet the band on his wrist lay broken; the etchings cracked and marred. Only the echoing of the Sigil of the Wild resonated with Mari's band now.

*"This place remembers balance. It remembers what was taken."* Kaelith said, urgency woven into his voice.

Rufio's jaw clenched, determination hardening his features. "And it should remember who took it," he replied, his voice low and resolute, igniting a flicker of defiance within him.

Around them, the freed elders formed a half-circle, their

figures enveloped in swirling shadows as they murmured incantations that spiraled into the air like fragile wings. Thalos and Brin, powerful and majestic, still in their ethereal form, moved cautiously to the edges, their hooves striking the ground with a resonant echo. Nearby, the Solins hovered over the towering arches, their glow dimmed, bracing themselves against the chaos threatening to erupt.

The air crackled with a sense of imminent danger, charged with the weight of memories past and the ghosts of those who had wandered these grounds before. Rufio stood in the thick of it, feeling the heavy press of history urging him on, igniting a primal call to reclaim what had been lost. The boundary between the present and the forgotten blurred, and he steeled himself for the often expected yet dreaded confrontation awaiting them, knowing that the Roost would not allow them to leave without a fight.

Amid this charged atmosphere, Mari stepped forward, a mix of awe and trepidation flooding her senses. The new sigil on her band glowed softly, pulsing gently with the ancient heartbeat of the tower, a rhythm she barely registered beneath her jeweled hands from the root chains.

"It feels like it's alive," she said, trying to hide her anxiety. "Like it's... listening to us."

Rufio moved closer, a powerful contrast to the flickering shadows that danced around them. The glow of the sigil reflected in his eyes, brimming with warmth yet shadowed by something more primal.

"It is," he replied. His tone was steady but charged with an electric tension that sent shivers down her spine. He stood beside her, his skin radiant under the celestial light, while the ember veins of Kaelith coursed over the scars, testament to battles fought and won. "The Roost listens to those who bear the mark and reviles those who dare to defy it."

As they stood together, the atmosphere thickened, every breath heavy with the promise of the impending confrontation. The Roost was watching, waiting.

Before Mari could fully process his words, a thunderous crack reverberated through the tower, shaking the very foundations as if the earth itself was splitting apart. The air thickened with an oppressive tension, the floor beneath them rippling while light twisted into eerie, unrecognizable shapes. Her heart raced, caught between fear and an instinctive urge to stand her ground.

"What was that?" she gasped, eyes wide as she searched for reassurance in his face.

Rufio's expression darkened, his breath coming in sharp, measured gasps. "The Wild senses it too," he confessed, urgency lacing his low voice. "Something is coming… and it's not on our side."

A low, vindictive growl erupted from Rufio's chest, resonating with Kaelith's essence. *"I can feel him. He's close."*

An icy wave of dread washed over Mari, hitching her breath. "Then we must be ready."

She gripped his arm, seeking strength and solace, even as uncertainty churned violently within her. Would they emerge from this clash so she could go home? The question hung in the air like a dark omen.

Outside the door, the air tore apart, not like a mere portal, but as if a fresh, infected wound had opened. A torrent of red light surged through, thick as blood and pulsating with malevolence. From this crimson rift stepped the Corruptor.

Clad in flowing black and crimson robes of royalty, he

exuded an unsettling grace. But his face, too smooth, too perfect, spoke of profound wrongness. His eyes, gleaming like molten glass, seemed to absorb the very light around him, and when he smiled, the air around him warped, distorting reality itself.

"Ah," he purred, voice dripping with mockery, "the broken Wildling returns." He seemed to float above the glass floor as he entered the room; tendrils of rot trailed behind him.

The elders staggered back, their chanting faltering into terrified silence, their faces pale and sunken.

Rufio, heart pounding in his chest, raised his blade with resolve. "You don't belong here!" The words felt inadequate, but they were all he had.

The Corruptor tilted his head, amusement dancing in his gaze. "And you do?" He leaned forward slightly, his voice a chilling sound. "A shattered vessel of the Wild. A boy fumbling to hold back fate? You are no match to stop me!"

Kaelith roared from within Rufio, a primal sound that echoed with ancient fury; *"He trapped me!"*

Rufio's breath hitched, understanding striking him like a bolt of lightning. "You tried to bond with The Wild," he rasped, disbelief lacing his voice.

The Corruptor's eyes flickered with dark delight, satisfaction bubbling to the surface. "Once," he admitted, a sinister note threading through his tone. "I offered unity, strength. But Kaelith, oh, he denied me… said I was unworthy. But I found something better."

His gaze slid to Mari, serpentine and hungry. "Tell me, my beautiful vessel…" he crooned, "Does he deserve what you carry? That spark? That eternal heart? I could keep you alive forever. You'd never tire, never fade. You could escape the fate of watching this and other worlds die."

Mari's stomach twisted in horror, her breath quickening as dread curled around her like a serpent. She took a step back, the Solins instinctively closing ranks around her, their protective glances fierce and unwavering.

"Stay away from me," she demanded, voice shaking, but a flicker of defiance ignited within her.

The Corruptor's smile twisted into a sneer as her band glowed faintly through the root chains. "He has already marked you?" he hissed, voice laced with venom. "It will not matter when he dies!"

A pulse of energy hit the floor, cracking glass, sending shards spiraling into the air. The elders shouted incantations, trying to form barriers, but the Corruptor's power crushed them down, pressing like gravity. The Auralisks roared, their horns blazing with light as they charged, but their attack struck empty air. The Corruptor flickered, his form dissolving into smoke.

Kaelith hissed, frustration dripping into Rufio's mind. *"He's not truly here. He's using rot to manifest. The body is elsewhere."*

His words dripped with rage. Rufio's anger flared like wildfire in his chest.

"Then he will have to come to us," he growled, voice low and fierce, each syllable a promise of retribution. His body was taut, a coiled spring ready to unleash its fury.

Mari stood frozen, her hand instinctively clutching her chest. The rot began to envelop the walls, an oppressive presence that crawled upon her skin with its bitter chill. The smell seeped into her senses, heavy and alive, invading her lungs. Above them, the constellations flickered like dying embers; stars extinguished one by one, leaving an unsettling darkness in their wake.

Rufio turned toward her, desperation etched into his face, a mix of determination and anguish in his eyes. "Mari… you have to focus!  The Roost is responding to you… to your emotions. The glow is fading because you are losing faith in yourself. You can't let him get to you!" His tone was urgent, but beneath the surface lay a current of fear for what the rot could do to her.

"I don't know how to stop it… Any of it!!" Mari's voice cracked, vulnerability spilling into the air as panic clawed at her throat. "Rufio, I…"

He stepped closer, grasping her hands and pressing them against his chest. The heat radiating from him was a lifeline amidst the encroaching darkness. She could feel the energy from the Sigil and his heart pounding, a frantic drumbeat in a world spiraling into chaos. "Then don't stop it. Guide it. Remember who you are; to yourself, to all of us. You're light, Mari. You're everything he's not." His eyes shone with trust, a flicker of hope.

The Corruptor's voice slithered through the shadows, an insidious whisper that coiled around them. "Light burns out, Wildling. But hunger… hunger and power endures." His tone was slick, dripping with malice, as he raised a hand from the darkness.

Without warning, the floor cracked open, a jagged wound in the stone, releasing a foul stench. Tendrils of rot surged forth, thick and black, slithering like serpents hungry for life. They wrapped around the pillars, clawing at the ceiling, spreading upward like veins through the stone, pulsating with malevolent energy.

One of the tendrils coiled, then whipped towards Mari,

striking with the ferocity of lightning. Rufio acted on instinct, yanking her away just as it lashed out. The sheer force sent them both crumbling to the ground in a tangle of limbs. Dust and ash engulfed them, swirling in the suffocating air. Mari coughed, her vision blurring as panic surged through her veins.

Beside her, she could hear Rufio's ragged breathing, feel the warmth of his skin against her own, a stark contrast to the pervading chill of the rot that threatened to consume them. His body trembled beneath her touch, a fierce reminder of the Wild that pulsed fiercely within him.

The Corruptor's projection materialized once more, an ethereal form wrapped in swirling crimson mist, laughter echoing like thunder through the dim chamber. "Run if you like, but the tower belongs to me," he taunted, voice dripping with malevolence. "You will never reach the heart of the Roost."

Rufio struggled to rise to his knees, a fierce gash bleeding from his side, dark crimson dripping life. His fingers trembled over the hilt of the tainted black blade, every muscle screaming in protest. The Corruptor only laughed, a sound that slithered into their hearts, extinguishing hope. In a heartbeat, he dissolved into a swirl of smoke, leaving behind the acrid scent of sulfur, the resonant crack of shattered glass, and tendrils of rot attempting to consume and destroy.

For what felt like an eternity, silence reigned, thick and heavy. The elders exchanged anxious glances, their faces drawn, shadows pooling beneath their eyes. Finally, Mari turned to Rufio, her own eyes brimming with unshed tears, reflecting the flickering light like shattered stars.

"He wants me... because of my energy. Because I can

mend what he's broken… Maybe…," she whispered, her voice trembling, fraught with the weight of her fate.

Rufio nodded slowly, determination flaring in his gaze, fierce and unyielding. "And he'll wield that power to consume what's left of this world and you!" He replied with more harshness than he meant to. The tension in his voice underscored the horror of their reality. "That's why we must get you to the portal. The heart of the Astrologers' Roost; it's the last bastion of purity. Once you're through, he cannot touch you, and you will be in your world. Home."

Her throat tightened, fear and uncertainty swirling like a storm inside her. "What about you?" she asked, panic threading through her words, unwilling to accept the sacrifices being proposed.

His faint smile was weary, as though it had been forged from the agony held deeply within. "Someone has to hold the gate," he stated, the heartbreak behind his words echoing in the chill of the air. The remnants of light danced in his eyes, illuminating the dark resolve within.

Mari opened her mouth, desperate to protest, but her words fell away as the Solins around them pulsed brighter, an urgent glow that seemed to pull at the fibers of her very being. The elders shouted warnings of retreat; the rot was spreading rapidly, slithering through the cracked walls, insidious and relentless, trying to block their path to the stairs leading to the heart.

Rufio tightened his grip on her trembling hand, an iron clasp amidst the chaos. "We move now!" He commanded, his voice a steady anchor against the swirling storm of despair.

They dashed towards the stairway at the back of the room, to the heart of the Astrologer's Roost. The Auralisks gored the rot with their horns as their friends moved in the darkness ahead. Their horns shimmered with a fierce crackling light. The elders flowed just behind them, their chants mingling with the rhythmic pounding of their feet, a desperate hymn to stave off the corruption closing in. The earth beneath them buckled and split, chaos erupting as light and shadow crashed violently together, yet Rufio surged on, a lighthouse in the tempest.

Mari cast a fleeting glance back, her heart stuttering at the sight of the Roost behind them, a beacon amid the dying stars, flickering like a heartbeat caught in a fragile cage. Somewhere deep in the bowels of the Ancestor's Hall, the Corruptor's laughter echoed, mocking their flight, promising doom.

"Keep moving!" Rufio urged, his voice cutting through the chaos, the grip on her hand like a promise of protection. Though she could not see the determination etched on his face, she felt the swell of his resolve, beating in sync with the thunderous pulse of his heart, echoing a fierce declaration.

And deep within him, Kaelith whispered, low and dangerous, *"For her, we will burn this world and the next."*

In that moment, they both understood that they were not just running for survival; they were racing against time itself, caught in a dance with destiny that would either save their world or plunge it into eternal darkness.

# Chapter 36

The tower shuddered with every step they took, the stone groaning beneath their boots while dust drifted from the cracks above, ghostly in the half-light of the Solins' glow. The atmosphere felt dense and stifling, filled with the odor of burnt metal and a subtle hint of decay from long-ruined energy. Leading the ascent were the Auralisks, their aethereal forms shimmering with a translucent light as they glided soundlessly over the stone. Hooves brushed against the surface without a whisper; their horns blazed with halos of pale fire, casting fractured light up the spiraling staircase. The narrow space barely allowed them to climb in single file, yet they moved onward, a luminous wall of protection against the darkness that loomed above.

Rufio trailed closely behind, chest bare, streaked with ash and blood, his broken sigil glowing fiercely like a brand across his heart. Damp strands of hair clung to his temples, and his breath billowed in the chilly air. Each muscle ached, but he moved with the pulse of the tower itself, steady and unrelenting. The broken copper band on his wrist flickered faintly, echoing the rhythm of the band on Mari's wrist just behind him.

Mari pressed on, her fingers grazing the rough stone wall for balance as each breath burned her lungs. Her legs trembled from the endless climb, while the Solins swirled around her in anxious loops, their light flickering faster as though sensing the foreboding weight of what lay above. She felt the soft vibration of the jeweled chains on her hands: a weapon, a talisman, though she wasn't yet certain what it needed to become.

The elders followed at a slower pace, their voices weaving purposeful chants and blessings in a tongue long forgotten. The words wrapped around the Auralisks like threads of gold, fortifying their glow and strengthening their shields. Though their limbs trembled and their robes hung in tatters, they sang with the last vestiges of their strength, pouring their faith into the stone itself, transforming their desperation into an unyielding light against the encroaching darkness.

The worn stairs finally led them to a great sealed door of the ancient tower. The heart of the Astrologers' Roost. The gold inlay along the doors had dulled with age, and the engraved runes were faded and cracked. As they approached, the air turned colder, thick with the hum of trapped energy that vibrated against their skin.

Rufio slowed his steps, raising his hand as he turned to Mari, his voice low and ragged. "Stay behind me, Mo... Mari."

Mari nodded, oblivious to the slip of his tongue, her attention captured by a sudden sound that echoed in the silence, a resounding, metallic thud that sent a tremor through the doors, shaking dust from their aged frame.

*"I feel the rot and corruption on the other side,"* Thalos murmured, his horned head turning slightly.

His voice, deep and resonant, seemed to wrap around them like a shadow, more a physical sensation than mere sound. The atmosphere was thick with portentous energy, their hearts pounding in sync with the ominous vibrations that heralded the mysteries waiting beyond the doors.

Before anyone could respond, the Roost's door exploded outward in a violent eruption. The force of the blast hurled Rufio back against the wall, his body instinctively shielding Mari as she ducked, her hands raised to shield her face from the rain of splintered stone and metal. The air filled with the deafening roar of the Auralisks, a sound reminiscent of mountains crumbling under immense pressure, while the elders' chant surged to a fevered pitch, a desperate call to arms.

From the swirling cloud of smoke and debris, the Corrupted Soldiers emerged no longer human, but twisted armored husks, grotesquely fused with rot and fury. Their eyes blazed crimson, and black ichor dripped from the seams of their corroded armor, sizzling as it met the ground. The stench engulfed them first: a nauseating mix of burnt oil, blood, and the sickly aroma of decay.

"Hold the line!" Rufio bellowed, raising his tainted blade high, determination etched across his face as he prepared to face the oncoming tide of darkness.

The Auralisks charged as one, hooves striking sparks that burst into light. Blessed by the elders, their horns flared bright gold and cut through the first wave. Flesh and armor disintegrated into ash. The stairwell became a cage of screams and light.

Mari pressed herself against the wall, her heart hammering as she glanced upward. Beyond the smoke, she caught sight of flickers of movement deeper within the Roost; something patient and greedy lurked there.

Rufio, his blade driving through a soldier's chest before he kicked the lifeless body free, barked, "We have to move! If we stay here, they'll swarm us!"

The Auralisks pushed forward, clearing a narrow path toward the threshold. Thalos's horn struck a column, channeling the elders' blessing into it; a shockwave of light blew a dozen corrupted warriors from the stairs, back into the room at the top of the tower. As they landed, their bodies turned to ash, dusting the floor.

Mari stumbled after Rufio, nearly slipping on the ash-filled step. He caught her by the arm, hot, firm, and pulled her upright. For a moment, their eyes met. His eyes were wild and alive, glowing faintly gold in the flickering light.

"Stay close to me," he said. "No matter what happens." He loosened his grip and began the ascent into the heart of the Astrologers' Roost.

She nodded, unable to speak. She was so overwhelmed by the sights, sounds, and smells of battle.

As they crossed the threshold into the Roost, the air shifted, as if the world itself held its breath in anticipation. There was a palpable sense of waiting, for nothing could alter the course that lay ahead. Evil was on the horizon; he had been lying in wait, eager for his prize.

As Rufio and Mari stepped across the threshold, the air thickened, nearly suffocating in its density, crackling with an electric tension that made movement feel like wading through tar. The chamber unfolded before them, vast and shrouded in oppressive darkness; its towering ceiling vanished into the suffocating smoke and entrenched shadows. Only the faint glow of the Solins flickered against the fractured mosaics of the Astrologers' Roost, where ancient glass once captured the cosmos, now marred by veiny tendrils of black rot that pulsed as if alive.

Rufio raised his sword high, runes shimmering to life along the blade, an ethereal light that danced across his sweat-slicked chest, mingling with the blood that stained his skin. The copper bands on his and Mari's arms were now etched with matching sigils, thrumming with an intensity that sent jolts through their bodies at every touch, a painful resonance that underscored their bond. Their Auralisks reared, muscles tensed as hooves struck against the marble floor, sparks flying, horns poised for battle.

Through the swirling haze stepped the Corruptor, no longer masked by any semblance of humanity. The abominable form of molten sinew and shattered bone loomed before them, with cavernous eyes glowing like red embers. His voice erupted from him, thick with satisfaction and resonating with the echoes of hundreds of stolen souls. A palpable dread cloaked the space, heightening the stakes as Rufio and Mari prepared to confront the monstrosity that awaited them.

"You bring the Wild into my lair," he hissed, "and think it will obey you now? Have you not learned that it only feeds on you, boy… It's vessel."

The ground shuddered. Cracks laced the floor, seeping tar-black and vapor.

Rufio planted his feet, sword angled in front of his chest.

"We didn't come to be obedient," he said. "We came to end you!"

The Corruptor's grin split wider. "End me? I was here before your kind learned to name fear." He raised one of his twisted hands, and the shadows obeyed, coalescing into spears of black light. The first spear screamed across the chamber.

Rufio deflected it, sparks of corruption exploding where steel met dark. The shock rattled up his arms; the marred Sigil over his heart flared hot. He stumbled but didn't fall.

"Mari!" he shouted. "Stay behind me!"

She tried, pressing against the cold wall, but fear rooted her in place. The smell of iron and burning oil stung her nose; her lungs refused to draw another full breath. Her eyes met the Corruptor's red glow for a fraction of a heartbeat, and she felt him reaching, not with his hands, but with will. He would make her his, or he would break her. No one would have her power but him.

Inside Rufio's chest, Kaelith roared, a sound of wind through endless pines, of rivers bursting banks. He was filled with rage, knowing the Corruptor's intention.

"It's time, Rufio." Kaelith's energy was full of urgency.

Rufio's pulse hammered in his ears. "If I do, you won't come back," he growled.

Insecurity hummed in his heart for a fraction of a moment. Kaelith, for the first time, fully opened his lifeline to his fiery vessel, letting him truly know. Everything.

"If you don't," Kaelith thundered, "she dies."

Another spear came. Rufio threw himself between Mari and the attack, catching it on his blade, but the impact tore open his shoulder. He dropped to one knee. Light spilled from the wound like liquid gold. He tasted iron and ash. The tower rang with the Corruptor's laughter.

*"She needs you,"* Kaelith calmly whispered. *"And I need to breathe."*

Rufio looked back at Mari's terrified face, at the Auralisks rallying again, at the elders still chanting somewhere below, and decided.

"Then breathe," he said.

The marred Sigil on his chest burst open in a flash that turned darkness into day. Golden light ripped through him, brilliant and terrible. It was life, ancient and unbridled. Rufio's scream and Kaelith's roar became the same sound. When the light cleared, Rufio staggered forward, panting alone in his skin for the first time since he was a boy.

Across from him, rising from the fissure of light, stood Kaelith, the primordial essence of balance, feeding on the corruption of worlds.

No longer bound within him, the Wild had taken shape, wings of storm-fire unfurling to brush the rafters, antlers crackling with energy, eyes twin molten suns. His form was aethereal yet solid, beautiful, monstrous. Every breath Kaelith took bent the air. He stood tall as his glow began to fade.

The Corruptor faltered, just a moment, at the sight. Two beings now stood before him: the mortal and the eternal.

Kaelith turned his head slightly, the faintest curve of a smile. "Together," he said.

Rufio nodded once and charged.

Steel and lightning met corruption and void. The Auralisks plunged back into the fray, horns blazing, the elders' blessings turning their bodies into living beacons. Mari forced herself to move, to keep behind them, her trembling hands searching. Her jeweled chains dangled from her, for the portal that she could not see. The clash was deafening, light against dark, devotion against decay. And through it all, the faint whisper of the portal's pulse echoed from the chamber's far wall, calling to her.

The blast of light left everything trembling. Shattered glass rained from the ceiling in slow, glittering arcs, each shard catching the golden glow that now emanated from Rufio's chest and Kaelith's newly freed form. For a heartbeat, the world seemed suspended, caught between silence and the scream of the storm.

Then the Corruptor struck again. Tendrils of shadow unfurled from his body, slicing through the air like whips of molten ink. They lashed against the walls, the floor, the pillars, each impact leaving streaks of rot that hissed and spread like acid. The ancient constellations carved into the stone melted away under his touch.

Kaelith was the first to move. His wings flared wide, scattering the ash and smoke. Lightning laced through his feathers, splitting the chamber with blinding white. His voice was thunder and fury. "You desecrate life itself!"

The Corruptor laughed, a hollow, echoing sound. "Life? I perfected it."

Rufio surged forward, his sword singing through the air with deadly precision. He moved with sharp, fluid grace, the culmination of years of disciplined training, now amplified by the Wild's lingering energy. Opposite him, Kaelith unleashed storms of fire and fury, a force of nature in his own right. Where Kaelith struck with the power of the elements, Rufio countered with the unwavering strength of earth and steel. They were a perfect harmony of contrast; each anticipated the other's intentions as if they were one.

With each clash, their rhythm intensified. Kaelith drove the Corruptor back, creating openings for Rufio to exploit. In moments of hesitation, Kaelith's wings would unfurl like a protective barrier, safeguarding Rufio from the ensuing chaos.

As they fought, the very ground beneath them began to shatter under the weight of their powers. Black ichor hissed and writhed on contact with the radiant golden light of Kaelith's presence, marking the battlefield with a grotesque testament to their struggle. The tower's pillars trembled ominously, the air thick with the promise of ruin, leaving the environment in tatters as their battle escalated to an earth-shattering climax.

Mari could only watch for a moment, frozen by a mix of awe and terror as the immense, terrifying power surged around her. Each clash of light and darkness vibrated through her bones, but the frantic chirping of the Solins drew her focus. They clustered around her head, urging her toward the far wall where the faint pulse of the portal throbbed like a dying heart.

"I can fix it," she whispered, determination igniting within her. "I can…"

A tremor ripped through the chamber, cutting her off. Brin fell, hitting the outer wall, bellowing as a shadow spear tore through his shoulder. Thalos roared, his horns blazing gold, and drove into the enemy ranks. The elders' chants below faltered and rose again, their voices straining to sustain the blessing.

"Brin!" Mari shouted over the clanging of metal. "Brin!"

"Go, little foal!" Thalos shouted in her head, his voice raw. "Find the portal!"

Her eyes widened as the tears began to fall, and Mari ran.

The ground shifted beneath her feet, slick with ash and blood. The air burned ozone, tainting her throat. Every instinct screamed to stop, to turn back, but she kept moving, ducking behind fallen stone as the battle raged. When she reached the broken arch of the portal, her heart seized. It was cracked, its runes flickering dimly, and the air around it stuttered like a fading flame. Her band glowed as she traced the foreign symbols.

Behind her, Kaelith's wings folded as he landed, blocking another blow meant for Rufio.

The Corruptor bellowed, "You cannot defeat what has no end! I am eternal, Wilding!"

Rufio's intensity heightened. "I am flame, and you are nothing but bones."

Their blades met the Corruptor's claws in a flash that shook the Roost. The walls split. The stars painted in the dome above began to fall as dust.

Mari pressed her palms to the portal's surface, ignoring the heat that scorched her skin. Her jeweled chains hummed, the gems lighting the symbols, fixing them one by one. Not fast enough. She was not a warrior; she was not moving fast enough.

She closed her eyes and reached inward, to the heartbeat that connected her to this world and her own. Memories cascaded behind her eyelids: her children's laughter, Rufus's half smile when he looked at her, the warmth of her garden back home.

"Please," she whispered with tears falling down her cheeks. "Not yet… don't let this end here." She looked at the symbols again through blurred eyes. The Solins' glow crowned her head like a halo, and the air around the portal shifted. It began to hum again, faint but alive. She thought of gentle kisses under the moonlight, the warmth of her husband's hand on her swollen belly, and more small moments softly fell, reminding her what she was fighting for.

Then the Corruptor screamed. His focus snapped to her, red eyes blazing with realization. "No!" As the portal came to life again, the corruptor was losing his.

In desperation, he lunged, a torrent of dark energy bursting from his outstretched hand. Aimed for Mari's back. Kaelith moved faster than thought, intercepting the blow. The impact hurled him backward, wings shredding in a storm of embers. He struck the far wall and slid to his knees, the golden fire dimming along his body.

"Kaelith!" Rufio shouted, his voice breaking. He charged the Corruptor, fury and grief driving him beyond all reason.

Kaelith lifted his head, smiling faintly. "Finish it, my brother," he said as he attempted to move toward where Mari stood. He would protect her with his dying breath.

Rufio's blade plunged through the Corruptor's chest, straight through the pulsing red core of his being. The scream that followed wasn't sound; it was a void. Rufio pulled his sword out to see it dissolve into smoke and ash. The Corruptor staggered, grinning through the ruin of his face. "You can destroy me," he rasped, "but corruption never dies. It waits… in the cracks."

The hole consumed itself for a heartbeat, drawing in the ash of the corrupted soldiers, the rot, and vines. His body crumbled into shadow and vanished, leaving only the taste of iron lingering in the air and the echo of his laughter. What cloth remained collapsed to the floor, enveloped in stillness.

# Chapter 37

The atmosphere was heavy with silence, enveloping everything like a heavy mist. Ash spiraled slowly, glowing faintly in the dying light that filtered through the cracked dome. The scent of scorched stone and ozone thickened, stifling the last of Mari's breath.

She staggered forward, her knees buckling. The Corruptor's cloak disintegrated on the floor, a dust smear swept away by the faint wind now seeping through the reopened fissures.

"Kaelith," she whispered, crawling toward the golden figure slumped nearby. His once-luminous form dimmed, embers flickering against the black marble. Rufio knelt beside him, face smeared with grime and blood, eyes filled with raw disbelief.

Kaelith managed a faint smile. "You did not fail," he said, his voice soft as wind through leaves. "You… freed us both, my friend."

Rufio's hands trembled as he pressed them against Kaelith's fading chest. "No… no, stay with us. You're part of me, we…"

"I was," Kaelith murmured, the glow beneath his skin flickering like a lantern battling the dark. "But now you are whole. And she…" His gaze shifted to Mari. "…she is the bridge."

The Solins formed a circle above her head, weaving gold threads that descended like rain. "You are not dying today!" Mari declared to Kaelith, her voice trembling with emotion. "You are a part of my family, my friend. I remember your hunger and your competitiveness," she continued, her words interspersed with sobs. Mari's hands burned with intensity; the jeweled chains blazed with heat as the sigil on her wrist shone so brightly that it illuminated the entire room.

Kaelith, feeling the warmth of her resolve, reached for Rufio's shoulder, his hand now transparent and dissolving into motes of light. "Protect her," he urged, his voice a whisper carried by the air. "Protect the world that she saved."

"We will protect her and the world she saved, brother," Rufio whispered roughly back.

Mari pressed her palms gently against Kaelith's heart, recalling the moment she first sensed his presence and how fiercely he had defended her, like a father protecting his child. Love surged through her, merging her healing green light with his dimming gold. She felt the warmth of his energy rekindle beneath her touch as his body solidified and his wings repaired.

In the blink of an eye, Kaelith was whole again, both in body and spirit. An understanding flickered in his gaze, but he remained silent, offering only a serene smile. Rufio grunted with satisfaction, and both men turned their attention to Mari, the air around them charged with gratitude and newfound strength.

"Brin!" she yelled in panic, fumbling to stand but only managing a shaky rise.

The dark space around them was a battlefield. Thalos grunted, and the three hurried towards Brin's massive, unconscious form. Mari hovered over his wound, her mind flickering to the Auralisk's protectiveness and humor, the way they always called her 'little foal,' even in dire moments. Thalos rested his head against hers, lending his strength. Slowly, Brin opened his eyes.

He gazed at Mari with a weak smile. "Is this how it ends? If so…" He paused dramatically, "I'd say I've got the most beautiful foal to look after."

Everyone laughed. The elders filed slowly in with light floating above them, casting a gentle glow. Brin nuzzled Mari with his muzzle and snorted at the other men.

"I refuse to kiss any of you!" Brin said light-heartedly. "Even if you helped save my life."

Thalos chuckled, "Not even a boop, my brother?"

Brin shook his head violently, then regretted it. Everyone laughed again. For the first time, the Auralisks and the elders recognized the new figure in the room. Tall, muscular, wings drawn in; Kaelith's golden light dimmed to a man with golden-toned skin. He reminded Mari of what she always thought the Fae looked like in her imagination.

A faint hum filled the chamber, bringing the room's attention back to reality. Mari stood up and walked to the mending arch. The portal, fractured and bleeding light, responded to Mari's touch. The runes pulsed brighter, drinking in the air, the ash, the echoes of every voice that had fallen here.

She had only been here for a short time, but a part of her heart and soul now lived in this world. The thought made her want to scream, but instead she heard laughter, her children's laughter. Rufus's voice; husky and deep. The memory of sunlight on her face.

"I'm coming home," she whispered through tears. "I know I have to go."

The portal roared awake. Its heart blazed open in a spiral of colors too deep for mortal eyes: gold, green, and violet twisting through the air like breath made visible. The floor shook again. Cracks spread along the Roost, but this time they glowed with life, not decay. Vines burst through the fissures, blooming wildflowers that drank the light. The Auralisks lifted their heads and sang; a sound that resonated through stone and soul alike. Slowly, the stones around the room began to heal.

Rufio turned toward Mari. She was on her knees before the portal, the glow consuming her silhouette as she wept freely. He reached out, his voice low, reverent. "Mari... your family... will they know what you gave?"

She smiled faintly through the light. "They don't have to. It is enough that I know what I did."

"Is he worth it? Is the man you call your husband truly worth your pain?" Rufio's voice trembled with sorrow.

Mari looked up, her eyes glistening. He extended his hand, urging her to stand. "Before all of this..." she gestured around as if it could sum up her struggle, "I might have said no. I thought he no longer loved me, that I wasn't enough." Tears spilled down her cheeks.

Rufio gently cupped her face, his thumbs brushing away the tears before he dropped his hands. "You, Brin, Thalos, and

Kaelith have shown me that I am so much more. I realize now he's worth coming home to, just as much as my children. To try to create our sense of balance."

Mari looked at her friends one last time. "I care for all of you… so deeply!"

Rufio took Mari's left hand, the one with her band, and kissed it gently. The portal flared, pulling her forward. Rufio lunged, catching her other hand, their copper bands sparking in unison.

"Will you find me again?" she asked, voice breaking.

"Always," he said, gripping tighter though the light was devouring his fingers. "Across every world."

The final burst of light swallowed them both, one carried home, the other left standing in the echo of her sacrifice. And when the glow faded, the tower stood quiet. The corruption was gone. The world breathed again with new life and the willingness to thrive.

# Chapter 38

Light hit her face like a warm embrace.  Mari blinked, disoriented, lungs craving the fresh air, free from the stench of rot and ash. She stood tall, feet grounded on cool soil. Her body was whole; no longer teetering on the edge of oblivion, no bleeding, no pain. The forest around her buzzed with life. Pines swayed in a gentle breeze, sunlight streamed through the leaves, casting everything in delicate gold. She knew she would never see her world the same way again.

She exhaled shakily. The last thing she remembered was Kaelith's blinding light, Rufio's hands on her face, and then the pull of the portal darkness. Now, an almost unbearable silence surrounded her.

She looked down at herself: her blue gown torn, streaked with soot; her boots caked with gray dust; the scrapes on her forearms and legs glowing faintly where the Solins' energy still hummed beneath her skin.  Her left wrist caught the sunlight, no longer holding a large band on her forearm or jeweled chains on her hands; instead, her wrist was hugged by a slim copper bangle. The outside had a faint pattern that shimmered: interlaced branches around a molten vein, their roots intertwining and becoming one. Mari brushed her thumb across it.

Warmth surged through her chest as she thought of her friends. Then a delicate pull from her heart had given her feelings not her own; the tug was from Rufio and Kaelith. A sudden ache filled her chest, and tears blurred her vision. She could feel them both, faint and far, like stars beneath the horizon; Rufio's sorrow, a steady thrum, Kaelith's presence vast but gentle.

"I miss you too," she whispered to the air, looking up to the branches of the ancient redwoods. A gentle, sweet-smelling breeze of flowers and moss stirred the trees, soft as an answer.

The path to the cabin wound through familiar forest, each step weighed with exhaustion. The wildflowers she'd left petals closed, protecting themselves from the night chill, now leaned toward her like they remembered her scent. When she reached the clearing, her hands trembled around the door handle of her shared cabin.

The door creaked open. Cedar and soap filled her lungs, grounding her in the ordinary. The light in the small room was soft, the afternoon slanting across the rug, catching the simple bunk beds, and her and her friend fought over who would be on the top bunk. She laughed a small chuckle at the memory that seemed so long ago.

Her knees almost buckled from exhaustion. She pressed her palms to her eyes, letting the tears come silently. She made it. Even as relief filled her, something else stirred beneath it, emptiness. She wasn't sure what would happen next. From her suitcase, she grabbed her phone and checked the screen as it came to life in her hands. No service, no messages.

With a small crease of her brow, she sent a text message to Rufus asking him to call her and say that she would be home that night. She knew he would not get this until she was closer to civilization, and then he would not get the message until he was as well. It was a gamble whether he would receive it at all.

Mari walked to the mirror in the small bathroom. She was grungy and battle-worn, time to wash the aches and pain away. Steam fogged the mirror. She traced a trembling hand over the glass, wiping away a circle to reveal her reflection. She barely recognized the woman staring back. Her hair hung damp and wild around her shoulders, her skin kissed with faint bronze. Her eyes, once soft brown, now glinted gold and green when the light hit them.

She touched her wrist again, feeling the faint hum of the copper bangle. It pulsed, slow and alive, like a heartbeat. The memories came in flashes: the Astrologers' Roost, Kaelith's sacrifice, Rufio's hand gripping hers as the world broke apart. The way he'd looked at her, not as a savior, not as a vessel, but as something sacred.

Her throat tightened. "Rufio..."

She finished dressing, pulling on jeans and a loose sweater, the fabric soft and cool against her skin. She needed something human, something normal to cling to. It was time to find her friend.

***

"Finally!" Rita's voice called from the couch in the main room. Her best friend looked at her with dramatic flair. "You vanish for half an hour and come back looking like you hiked through a volcano."

Mari stopped mid-step. "Half an hour?"

Rita looked up from her book again after she turned the page. "Maybe thirty-five minutes, tops. Hey… You, okay?"

Mari's laugh was soft and broken, her voice trembling around it. She crossed the room and curled beside her friend, resting her head on her shoulder like a child seeking warmth.

"Thank you," she whispered.

"For what?" Rita said with light-hearted confusion in her tone.

"For being my best friend.  For… grounding me."  Mari cooed as she snuggled in closer. The type of closeness that cats and best friends are afforded.

Her friend chuckled, brushing a strand of hair from her forehead. "You're so weird sometimes."

Mari smiled faintly. "Yeah. I think I've been away too long."

"You've been away for a solid thirty minutes," her friend said again, slightly concerned, but Mari didn't answer. "But if it makes you feel better," Rita patted Mari on the head as if she were a small child. "Um… it is good to have you back."

Mari just closed her eyes, listening to the quiet hum of her world, the distant memory of thunder in her chest.

***

The wind carried the scent of rain and new grass across the plains.

Rufio stood on a rise overlooking the valley. The suns bled gold across the horizon, washing the land in light.  Behind him, the Auralisks grazed peacefully, their horns dim with soft luminescence. Brin stared at a theory lizard attempting to bask on the clean soil. Flowers now grew where their hooves touched the earth.

His brow dripped with sweat, and his hands were covered with dirt as he took in the comforting sunlight. The Sigil across his heart, once searing with Kaelith's power, was now gone; a scar from his stab wound took its place. The broken copper band on his wrist pulsed in rhythm, a gentle reminder of what he'd lost and what he'd protected.

Kaelith approached, his form half-woven of light and physical. His features were no longer monstrous but strikingly human: high cheekbones, long, golden hair, tied and draped behind him. His wings, translucent as dawn mist against his back, were visible only to a few in this form. His eyes, twin suns, softened as they met Rufio's.

"She's gone," Rufio said quietly.

Kaelith looked toward the sky, his breath stirring the grass. "Gone is not lost, my friend. You feel her," He put his fist to his chest. "And you know where she is, don't you?"

Rufio's gaze dropped to his wrist, thumb brushing the faint warmth where his band used to be. "With every heartbeat."

Kaelith smiled faintly, tilting his head. "The threads remain. She left pieces of herself in this world, within you, within me. Even the land sings her name."

Below them, the rivers gleamed, no longer black with rot. The villagers' laughter drifted faintly from the newly rebuilt town. Children ran beside the Auralisks, their hands outstretched to the glowing creatures that once had been weapons of war.

Peace, fragile but real, had returned.

"You've changed," Kaelith murmured. "You no longer carry rage."

Rufio glanced at him. "And you are no longer a pain in

my…."

Kaelith laughed, a sound like wind through bells, stopping Rufio before he could finish that sentence. "Perhaps she taught us both that balance is not found in battle, but in unconditional love. I am not sure if I will succeed in her shadow, but I will try."

Rufio watched the fading light, the horizon stretching endlessly and alive. A gentle breeze lifted the sweat from his brow, carrying with it something faint, something familiar: the scent of her.

His chest tightened, but he smiled, closing his eyes. "A stór mo chroí," he whispered. The words caught on the wind and disappeared into the glowing sky.

Kaelith's hand rested briefly on his shoulder. "No goodbye lasts forever, Wildling." He chuckled at a phrase that no longer had relevance. "Question is… What will you do now, Brother?"

***

That night, Mari stood by her cabin window. The forest was silent except for the rustle of leaves and the distant call of an owl. Her reflection shimmered faintly in the glass, the copper band glowed once, then dimmed. She touched it gently. Across the world, in another sky, a man and a spirit stood under the same stars, feeling her warmth ripple through the threads that bound them. Mari smiled. She was ready to go home, carrying two worlds in her heart.

# Epilogue

The rich aroma of brown sugar and melted butter enveloped the kitchen, wrapping Mari in a warm embrace. She stood barefoot at the counter, her hair a careless knot atop her head, a playful dusting of flour streaked across her cheek like a badge of victory. The afternoon sun streamed through the window, spilling golden light over her skin as she stirred the cookie dough in an old glass bowl. Her sleeves were pushed to her elbows, exposing her arms, the shimmering copper bangle on her wrist dancing with each movement.

She hummed softly to herself, a lilting tune that felt like a gentle lullaby, weaving through the sweet fragrance of baking. The blissful moment was shattered when the front door creaked open, followed by the sound of bags thumping onto the floor.

With a smile tugging at her lips, she called out, "Kids! I'm making cookies!" Her voice was bright, cheerful, a beacon for their eager footsteps.

But silence hung in the air. Turning slowly, wooden spoon

still in hand, her heart dropped. It wasn't the children standing in the doorway.

Rufus stood there. At first glance, Rufus looked like himself: a green buttoned forestry shirt, khaki pants, but something felt wrong. His hair was tousled, his shirt askew, his overall appearance disheveled; he was unlike the controlled Rufus she knew. His breath was coming in quick, desperate gasps. His deep, golden-brown eyes bore into hers with a fervor that sent shivers down her spine: longing, fear, and an unmistakable love flickering beneath the surface.

The spoon slipped from Mari's fingers, clattering with a dull clang into the mixing bowl. Flour and sugar into the air, motes of white swirling like suspended time.

"Ru…" Her voice was hushed, barely a whisper, the edge of his name quivering in her throat.

Rufus stepped further inside the house, carelessly abandoning the door, as if afraid to linger on the threshold. The front door swung ajar. The light spilled around his silhouette. His hesitant grace was a stark contrast to the wild chaos swirling inside her. For a heartbeat, she saw another man there, another world bleeding through memory.

"I got your message," he murmured, his voice a tapestry of familiarity and sorrow. It was Rufus's tone, yes, yet entwined with the deeper, richer resonance of another. "I… had to come." Rufus stood there, as if poised between worlds.

Mari's heart raced, confusion and disbelief swirling within her. She looked harder at the man. It was like she was trying to see past the oil on top of the water. She strained to see beyond the familiar contours of his face, desperately trying to pierce through the illusion. "Rufus? What… what is going on with you?"

The words slipped out, halting and uneven. She felt perched on the edge of something both terrifying and thrilling, unmoored yet anchored. Shadows danced in her mind, calloused fingers grazing the emptiness where love had thrived. Her breath quickened, the weight of the past pressing on her chest. Then, like a flash of lightning in the night, the figure of another man crossed her mind.

"Rufio?" she murmured, the name slipping through her lips like a secret, her eyes wide with dawning realization as breath escaped her lungs in shallow gasps.

Rufus raised both hands, palms out, a silent plea as if to say, 'Please, don't be afraid.'

"You see past my glamour?" he asked, the rhythm of his words laced with an urgency that gripped her.

Understanding blossomed like wildflowers in the cracks of concrete as the shimmering light around him fractured, cascading like broken glass. Reality and illusion blurred as the veil slipped away, revealing Rufio's strength; solid and unwavering, seamlessly intertwined with the soft gentleness of Rufus. One soul donned the mantle of two lives, their histories colliding in this fragile moment, threatening to shatter her fragile heart anew.

The kitchen enveloped them in warm hues and familiar scents of vanilla and spices, a dream they weren't ready to wake from. Fate had woven a web of longing and love, intertwining what they had lost with the possibility of rediscovery.

Tears welled in her eyes as she stepped closer, drawn by an irresistible force. Shadows danced around them, contrasting sharply with the turmoil inside her. What began as relief and disbelief quickly transformed into a raging fury.

Gripping his shirt tightly, she yanked him closer, the fabric crumpling under her hold as she ripped it open. Buttons scattered on the floor like forgotten dreams, each clink a painful reminder of their unraveling history. Her gaze landed on his bare chest, searching for the sigil of the Wild, but instead, she found only the scar etched over his heart, a jagged line that spoke of the mark left by the corruptor's onyx blade, now healed by Thalos's light.

"Explain!" she demanded, her voice tremulous with disbelief and desperation, each word like a fragile shard of a shattered dream. The intense turmoil within her, a chaotic mix of hurt and confusion, threatened to consume her.

Before she could push him away in frustration, he caught her wrists, anchoring her amid the storm of emotions swirling between them. The warmth of his hands jolted her, merging her anger with a flicker of longing. He pulled her closer, igniting a confusing blend of yearning and safety within her. His breath came in quick bursts, heavy with unspoken confessions that added urgency to their moment.

"I met you while on a mission here," he began, his voice thick with emotion. "You call them Tommyknockers… don't ask," he added, a pained smile flickering across his face, as if nostalgia washed over him. "From the moment I saw you, I was captivated. The way you moved, the spark in your eyes, it was as if the universe conspired to make you my greatest obsession. I had to know you. So, I stayed."

Tears streamed down her cheeks, relentless and silent like a river of grief and love.

"Kaelith slept inside me then," he continued, his voice rough and vulnerable. "I buried my true essence beneath layers of shadow and silence, but you… A stór mo chroí broke through it all. You became my world, the beacon in my darkest nights.

My greatest wish, Mariposa."

He pressed a gentle kiss to her hair, inhaling the scent of her sweet and earthy, laced with the salt of their shared history. As she wept into his chest, her tears soaking into his bare skin, he felt every drop as a testament to their love, an unbreakable bond that transcended time and space.

"Selfishly," he whispered, resting his chin on the top of her head, "I married you. It was a forbidden bond, yet it felt so right. Our hearts fused the moment we exchanged vows, sealing our fates in a promise I'd defend to my last breath. And then you, my miracle, gave me not one but two children." His voice cracked, heavy with joy and pain. "I was told I could never create life, yet here in your arms, the impossible became our reality."

He drew back, cupping her face, his thumbs brushing away tears like precious crystals. His gaze shimmered, a storm of regret and hope swirling within. "A few years ago, the Watchers found me. They pulled me back into my oath, and since then, I've battled daily to hold both worlds together."

Her lips quivered, disbelief mingling with bittersweet love. "And… You came back…"

He held her gaze, fervor burning like a star. "Every moment away from you and the children is a dagger to my heart. Mari…when I saw you in the forest. You were so brave and selfless."

Mari sniffed. "The entire time I was in the other world. With the fletchers, the rot, your childhood home, almost watching you…" She buried her face into his chest and hugged him harder. "I just realized I never told you my name."

He laughed in her hair, smelling wildflowers and vanilla. "We faced unspeakable horrors together and fought for things

I never knew I could endure, all to protect this love that gives me life. I will always return, no matter the cost. Our family is worth every sacrifice." Rufio said lovingly.

His voice was soft and raw, yet intense. "You are my heart, my pulse, my everything. I would walk through fire and face darkness just to hold you close and watch our children grow. I promise, I will find a way."

As their foreheads touched, he poured his soul into those words, a vow meant for all time. "I will always come home to you." He leaned back, brushing his thumb across her cheek in an intimate gesture that reignited the fire within her. "Always, my bonded."

Her copper bangle on her wrist glowed softly, pulsing in time with their hearts and washing the small room in a warm, golden light. The air felt electric, mingling with the rich scent of cookies baking nearby, creating an intimate atmosphere that wrapped around them like a comforting embrace.

As her head lay on his chest, their breaths intertwined with unspoken words and cherished memories. "You are my everything," he murmured, his voice a soothing melody. Her heart swelled in response, a single tear trailing down her cheek, a testament to their trials and enduring love.

With a hopeful smile, she replied, "And we're home." The weight of their shared history hung between them, and he closed the distance, capturing her lips in a kiss that was deep and aching. It spoke of longing too long suppressed, infusing their embrace with hope and a fierce promise of forever.

In that moment, the room vibrated with the harmony of their connected souls, the kiss enveloping them like an electric charge. Her copper band glistened in the warm light, brightening with every heartbeat until the two bands shimmered with the intensity of their love, softly dimming into a gentle warmth.

Outside, the wind whispered secrets through the trees, weaving a melody that celebrated their journey, a song of balance restored. In this sacred space, a wild love had finally returned home, filling every corner with its essence. As they stood wrapped in each other's arms, they knew they had crafted a legacy bound not just by fate, but by their unwavering belief in forever. Together, they emerged triumphant over their shadows, holding the world both fragile and fierce in their hands.

# About the Author

Pamela Campos-Friar is an educator, mentor, and author who believes curiosity, learning, and storytelling belong to everyone; at every age.

By day, she works alongside students, families, and educators across traditional, online, and hybrid learning environments. By night (and often in between), she writes. Pamela creates educational guides that help families understand how schools work, children's stories that nurture curiosity and responsibility, and fiction that explores growth, resilience, and the human experience.

Her work is shaped by years of teaching, mentoring new educators, and partnering closely with parents and learning coaches. Whether she's writing about education systems, crafting stories for young readers, or building fictional worlds, Pamela's focus remains the same: helping people feel seen, capable, and empowered.

Through both her professional and creative writing, Pamela bridges the gap between learning and life, showing that education isn't just something that happens in classrooms,

but something we carry with us every day. Be curious,
one safe step at a time.

**You can connect with me on:**

https://mrsfriarcuriosityshoppe.com
https://tiktok.com/mrsfriarcuriosityshoppe
https://www.facebook.com/Mrsfriarcuriosityshoppe

**Subscribe to my newsletter:**

https://www.jotform.com/form/253207987318062